Misbehaved

CHARLEIGH ROSE

Misbehaved

Chapter One

Remi

Let me start off by saying I don't hate my life. To someone from the outside, it might look like a *bad* life, but I don't care. I know the truth. I have a roof over my head. I'm frying juicy steaks in the kitchen. My dad, Dan, isn't abusive or in prison, which basically puts me at a huge advantage in comparison to the rest of the kids in my neighborhood. I have Ryan, who looks out for me, and, for the most part—albeit in an unconventional, fucked-up way—I feel loved.

Mostly.

But feeling loved doesn't mean that I'm happy with my circumstances. It doesn't mean I'm content with the street I live on that manages to taint every man, woman, and child that is unlucky enough to land here. It doesn't mean that I won't try to run away.

I live in Las Vegas, the city that sucks out your soul and spits out whatever's left of you. Your job is to pick up the pieces and find out who you are.

I'm about to. Planning to. *Soon.*

I flip the steak, and the searing pan hisses in delight. Take two steps to my right. Stir the boiling pasta. *Al dente*, just like Ryan likes it. Walk over to the sink. Wash my hands. Look out the window, the screen is hole-ridden and the frame rusty and eaten by the scorching heat and age. Then I smile. I see Ryan kneeling on our yellow overgrown grass, in front of the cracked, bruised asphalt of the road, working on his Harley. As if he senses me, he lifts his gaze to mine.

Stern. Severe. A little on the psycho side. But, he's my family nonetheless.

Ryan is not my biological brother. My mom, Mary, died in a car accident when I was two. I don't remember her, and although I'm sad that I never got to know her, it's my dad I truly hurt for. All I have left of Mary Julia Stringer is an old, beat-up camera from the nineties, and I hold on to it like it's my lifeline.

I used to use my high school's dark room to develop the film myself, but now, I'll have to figure something else out. I'm autodidactic. Self-taught, if you will. That doesn't come without a price, because I'm probably no good, but taking photos is what I love. Dad says Mom always had a camera in her hand. Funny how those things can be passed down without even knowing her or having her influence. It makes me feel connected to her.

A few years after she passed, my dad took another stab at dating. Enter Darla and ten-year-old Ryan. I knew Darla was bad for Pops, even at the tender age of five. She smelled like smoke and cheap perfume and always went out of her way to make me feel like a burden. But Pops seemed happy—at first, anyway—and I got Ryan. So, it wasn't all bad. Over the next five years, however, things deteriorated, along with their relationship. Darla started skipping out on us for days at a time, and even flaunted other men in front of my dad. After more than a few knock-down, drag-out fights, Darla had finally bailed for good. When my dad found Ryan, who was only fifteen, packing his things up, he told him to unpack his shit and go set the table for dinner, and that was that. Darla was out, and Ryan was staying. When I asked my dad why she left, his response was something along the lines of, "Darla's a whore. Don't be like Darla."

Duly noted, Dad.

The night Darla left was the first night I snuck into Ryan's room. It was innocent, of course. I wanted to comfort him, even though he showed no signs of being particularly saddened by his mom's absence. At first, he stiffened when he felt the bed dip under my weight. But my intuition had been right, because that night, Ryan held me and cried himself to sleep while I rubbed his arm and sniffled quietly. He never cried again, and we never spoke about it, but he still sleeps with me on occasion. Except now, it's Ryan who sneaks into my room.

And it's not innocent. Not anymore.

The years passed, as they always do, while Ryan still lives at home, neither my dad nor I want to see him leave. Maybe it's because Dad is rarely at home. He makes the Las Vegas-Los Angeles route twice a week, and occasionally takes longer trips that have him on the road for weeks at a time, which leaves him very little time for actual parenting. Since sleeping by myself in this rundown house, in this horrific neighborhood is pretty much a death wish, I'm happy to have Ryan by my side. With his tall frame, bulging tattooed muscles, uniform of wifebeater and don't-fuck-with-me expression plastered to his face, you'd have to be stupid to break into our house.

And it's not the only reason I am happy to have him around. We need each other. It's always been us against the world. Not that the world was particularly against us. It just didn't care.

I start making the sauce for the pasta. Tomato. Basil. Olive oil. A shit-ton of garlic. I read the recipe somewhere on the internet after Ryan and I saw it on some cooking show that aired on one of the few channels we have.

Maybe it will make him crack a goddamn smile for once. He's always been a bit of a ticking time bomb. The homemade, highly unpredictable type. But lately, I feel like he's seconds away from exploding.

Tick, tick, tick.

For the rest of the meal prep, I'm on autopilot. I chop, stir, drain, flip, arrange everything on the plates, take out two bottles of Bud Light from the fridge, and set the table. Then I proceed to kick the whiny door and bang my fist against the screen a few times to draw his attention.

"Dinner's ready," I yell.

"Two secs." I hear the clink of heavy tools dropping onto the concrete near the yellow grass he is kneeling on. His bike's been fucked for two weeks now, and he can't take it to the shop because he spent his last few bucks on bailing out his best friend, Reed. Not that having a broken-down bike has slowed him down any. The guy is never home anymore.

"Steak's getting cold. Get your ass inside or I'm eating without you," I mutter and slam the screen door with a bang.

I wait for him, slouched on my chair in front of our plates, scrolling my thumb along the touch-screen of my phone—one of the three things that my dad makes sure we always budget for: the rent, the food, and my phone. Most kids would be pissed to have an older model, but I'm just happy this thing has internet capabilities. Ryan saunters in and collapses on the chair opposite me, not bothering to wash his dirtied, greasy hands.

I chance a glance at him. Ryan looks like a man. He's looked that way for a long time now. His arms are ripped—not in the gym rat way, just in the way of a guy who does manual labor—and his body is big, wide, and commanding. Long, dirty blond hair that almost touches his shoulders, brown eyes, cut bone structure—the only good thing he inherited from his deadbeat real dad. Every time we hang outside the house together—which, admittedly, is not often these days—girls I went to school with throw themselves at him. He's screwed half of them, I know, even though they're underage. If I'm being honest, it seems to be half the charm about this guy. Other than the fact that he is inked from head-to-toe. It's that slightly unstable, dangerous vibe he gives off. Every girl wants to be good until a bad boy whisks her off her feet and corrupts her.

And every girl hated the one who stood in their way. That'd be me. At least in their mind. Sure, Ryan would fuck them, but that's all they ever got. He always stood a little too close to me, stared a little too long. They noticed. And they were ruthless. So, I was deemed the brother fucker. I didn't really care. Ryan didn't help matters by forbidding the entire male population of Riverdale to stay far away from me. He was out of high school before I even began, but he's somewhat of a legend around here. No one in their right mind would willingly cross him.

"How's the steak?" I ask, keeping my eyes on my own piece of meat as I slice it carefully.

"Juicy." He laughs, his mouth full. From my peripheral, I see a trail of bloody liquid traveling from the corner of his lip to his chin, but he doesn't make any move to wipe it. He takes another bite, his eyes honing in on me. "So, when are you going to turn eighteen?"

"You're my brother," I grind out. "Shouldn't you at least pretend to know this kind of crap?"

"I'm a shit brother," he retorts, his voice as dry as his steak is juicy. "And when asked a question, you fucking answer. It's really that simple, Rem."

That's the part where I should probably mention—he calls me Rem. My name is Remington, and my friends call me Remi, but Ryan, much to my dismay, has been calling me Rem since day one.

"August sixteenth," I groan. Ryan moves his eyes up and down my body as much as he can with the barrier that's the table between us.

"What's two more weeks?" he mumbles as he rubs his lower lip with his thumb, and it's glistening with the olive oil from the pasta and the juice of the steak.

"Until what?" I ask, playing dumb. He knows I'm not dumb. In fact, he resents the fact that I want more out of life than my high school diploma. But his comments have become increasingly inappropriate over the past few months, and even though it's flattering, sometimes alarm bells go off in my head.

"Until your big brother can show you just how much he loves you." Ryan chuckles sinisterly. I let loose a nervous smile. I know Ryan wants to get me into bed, but more than that, he wants to own me. Own my thoughts, my actions, my body. He *thinks* he already does. In his twisted mind, he calls it love. Why wouldn't he? It's not like Ryan has ever seen a good example of it. Hell, neither have I. In his mind, he protects me, takes care of me, and he *needs* me. In a way, I need him, too. But, I just can't ever see us happening. This—what we're doing right this moment—is what the rest of my life would look like. Me cooking dinner, wishing I were anywhere else, and Ryan being perfectly content to work on his bike and get tanked with his shitty friends every night. *No, thank you.*

It's not like the attraction is not there. I had a major crush on him when I was younger. I thought he hung the moon and the stars, making everything brighter in my dull universe, and I think I did the same for him. But if he were the one, it wouldn't feel so freaking wrong every time his throbbing dick "accidentally" presses against my ass at night.

Getting up from my seat, I take our plates to the sink and saunter back with a new beer, cracking it open in front of him. When I do, he snakes one arm around my waist and grabs me in one swift movement so that I'm straddling him on his lap. I can feel the seam of his zipper grinding into my crotch. Not gonna lie—it feels nice.

"Hey," he breathes into my mouth, always a whisper from a kiss, but never there. Where he wants to be.

"Hi." I swallow visibly.

"So." His hand travels into my inner thigh, and I feel

something stiffen underneath me. I take a deep breath. The room is dark and dingy and small, cluttered with our old furniture, *with our pasts*. It's not exactly romantic, but I can't deny the heady feeling coursing through me.

"You a virgin, Rem?" he whispers into my lips again, and this time it could qualify as a kiss. A part of me wants it to. The other part begs me not to go over that invisible, fragile line that I'm straddling just now. "You saved yourself for me? Kept this untouched?" His fingers hover over my groin, barely touching.

"No." The word comes out more like a groan. Never mind the fact that I've only done it twice. I don't need to tell him who it was. He knows. Zach Williamson. Eleventh grade. The only guy I dated for more than two months before I got bored. We actually made it through a whole semester before I dumped his ass. I didn't care that I'd given him my virginity. I wasn't waiting for "the one". To be honest, I've never really thought that one person putting their body part into another person was that big of a deal. It's probably a good thing I didn't have high hopes, because both times were pretty anticlimactic.

There's something in Ryan's already-hooded expression that becomes even darker and more severe, and for a minute, my heart beats faster for the wrong reason. Not because I'm excited, but because I'm unnerved. I wait, studying his expression carefully, before his hard stare turns into a half-assed, placid smile.

"Good," he says and squeezes my butt a little too hard, indicating that he doesn't think it's good at all. "I don't think you could handle me without a little practice, anyway."

Then his lips are not hovering anymore—they're kissing—not slowly either. He doesn't ask for permission. He is not tentative or unsure. His tongue invades my mouth in an instant, and it catches me off-guard. As I suck in some air, he takes the opportunity to deepen our kiss. I place both hands on his cheeks to ease him away, and he throws my hands off.

Possessive. Hungry. Angry.

"You taste like heaven, little sister," he hisses into my mouth. Nothing about this feels right. People know us as brother and sister. The fact that we're not blood-related is only somewhat consoling. Hell, even the kiss doesn't feel right. Like we're doing it all wrong. I feel him squeezing my ass harder, digging his dirty fingernails into my flesh, and wince.

"I've been waiting so long for this." His words not only pierce—they penetrate me—along with his fingers that are now dragging themselves slowly, roughly toward my sex. I breathe out harshly.

"Ryan," I drop my forehead to his, "you're hurting me."

"I know." His tongue continues attacking my mouth, his hands even more aggressive on me than before.

Panic. It trickles into me slowly. I know Ryan. Know him well. He is not a bad guy—definitely not a good guy, but not a rapist either—and he knows damn well my dad would kill him if he ever seriously wronged me.

"You're starting school tomorrow," he says, licking his way down to my chin and neck. I let him, and even though I don't want this, I can't help my body's reaction to his touch. It's humming, singing, asking for more. And why not give in to feeling good with someone I know and trust with my life? Still, something holds me back.

"How you gonna get all the way to Henderson every day?"

"Take the bus," I answer flatly. I'm not giving up on this opportunity. My dad somehow came up with my tuition to one of the best high schools in Nevada. Private. Top-notch. Said he's been saving for years, and only just now—my senior year—saved enough to send me. Not that I'm complaining. I think Dad secretly feels guilty about being gone so often. That, and he's heard what the kids at school say about me. That I'm a whore. A brother fucker.

After my best friend, Ella, moved away, they got worse. I was a lone ranger. An easy target. The boys were all afraid to interact with me—pussies—but the girls? Girls are vicious and sneaky. Like the boys, they're also afraid of Ryan, but they did shit on the down low. Stashing shit—literal shit—in my locker. Stealing my clothes when I was in the shower after P.E. Stuff that couldn't be directly traced back to them, even though we all knew who did it. And while I honestly never really cared what other people thought of me, I was being offered a golden ticket out of this shithole town, and I'm not giving it up. Especially not for something as miniscule as transportation.

"The buses don't run that early, baby girl." Ryan laughs, and why did I think he was that attractive in the first place? His smile is too big, his teeth too pointy, like a wolf's, and the scent of his sweat is too sour.

"Nice try. I checked, Ryan. They're twenty-four hours."

"You can walk, my ass." He pulls his head back, laughing. "You're not taking the bus alone. I'm giving you a ride back and forth, got it?"

I hate depending on anyone for anything. I may not have a car, but I've worked since the day I turned fourteen. My dad signed a waiver, much to Ryan's dismay, and I got a job at the Dairy Queen around the corner—where

I reluctantly quit once I found out I wouldn't have time to work when school started. When I need to be somewhere, I walk or ride my bike. Like I said, I despise being dependent on anyone, but if there's one thing I hate more, it's mornings. Specifically, early mornings. And to get to school on time, I'd have to wake up at an ungodly hour.

I want to say no.

I should say no.

But as his rock-hard erection grinds into me violently, I say something else entirely.

"Fine."

Chapter Two

Remi

Most kids hate school uniforms. I've never been like most kids.

Besides the fact that I won't have to put any effort into my daily outfit, it's actually kind of hot—in a naughty, low-budget porn sort of way. Plaid navy blue skirt that ends just above the knees, pressed, white-buttoned shirt with an ironed collar, matching blue blazer, and black knee-high socks. I'm missing the Oxfords that are supposed to be on my feet, but Ryan already shelled out over two hundred dollars for this uniform, and I couldn't ask him to spring for shoes, too. He'd want something in return even if he did have the money, and my dad won't be home for another week at least. So I'm rocking my beat-up, trusty Chuck T's. All I need is fucking piggy tails and an anal bead necklace to make it onto one of those cards littering the strip.

I walk up the most intimidating set of stairs I've ever seen in my life, while unbraiding my hair and letting it hang freely down my back. Ryan miraculously got his bike fixed in time to bring me to school this morning, and riding on the back of a motorcycle means a fuck load of tangles.

I yank my earbuds out of my ears and pause the Halsey song on my phone as I make my way through the air-conditioned halls of West Point. Everything about West Point is different than Riverdale. Riverdale was full of graffitied tables, old, crappy vending machines, and borderline dilapidated buildings. But, the biggest difference is that West Point is all indoors. At Riverdale, and most schools in Nevada, each class was in a separate building. Forget about even trying to find a lunch table inside—everyone tries to escape the oven that is Las Vegas by eating in the cafeteria. I'd only been lucky enough once. At least I won't have that problem here.

I ignore the curious and catty eyes and focus on the slip of yellow paper with my locker number and combination in my hand. *88A.* I'm completely out of my element, and I feel naked. Exposed. Like they can all see right through me, like they *know* that I don't belong here. I force myself to keep my head high. West Point is the complete opposite of Riverdale, but high school is high school, and these vultures can smell weakness a mile away.

I locate 88A, and of course, it's the top locker. I flip my long, brown hair off my shoulder and stand on my tippy toes to work the lock. I half expect them to be electronic based on everything else in this high-tech school. Finally, it pops open and I check my schedule to see which books

I can stuff inside for now, because my backpack is heavy as hell. I cram my old school checkered Vans backpack inside, only taking my textbook for my second class, Speech and Debate, my binder, and a pencil.

Homeroom is basically an hour of taking attendance, daily announcements, and social hour, from what I gather. I hang back, observing the different cliques, and I'm pleasantly surprised when I seem to go unnoticed.

My second hour classroom is empty when I arrive, and I have my pick of any seat in the house. I pause in the doorway, taking in the shiny, new desks free of crude carvings, and I bet they don't even have gum stuck underneath. Somehow, this feels like Crossing the Rubicon. There's no going back now. And I can either hide out in the back or take a seat up front and take what I came here for by the balls. *Own this fucking preppy school, Remi*, a voice in me commands. A smirk tugs at my lips as I take a seat front and center, directly in front of the teacher's desk. And I hope he or she isn't a spitter.

Students start pouring in, and I busy myself with studying my schedule. AP English Language and Composition, AP Statistics, French, and, of course, Introduction to Speech and Debate. I'm in way over my head, but the dread doesn't come close to the excitement that rolls through me. I hear everyone settle in their seats around me—my hair falling like a curtain shielding me from their view—but I can still feel their stares and hear their whispers.

All of a sudden, the chatter stops and a deep, imposing voice assaults my ears. Goose bumps prick my arms, and I'm not sure where it's coming from, because I've never responded to a voice like this in my entire life.

"Class," the low voice says. Really? That's his

introduction? No 'Hello, how was your summer'? I assumed the teachers here were all about buttering up their students and rich parents. Guess Teach here didn't get the memo.

"Most of you know each other, but we have a couple of new faces this year. Let's get this out of the way, because there's a lot of work ahead of us. Miss LaFirst?" His tone is clipped and abrupt, and *why can't I look up?* Jesus Christ, what is going on, and how do I make it stop?

"Yes?" a hesitant, feminine voice chirps.

"Care to tell us a little about yourself?" I can practically hear his eyes rolling.

"I, uh, just transferred from Asher."

"Riveting," he drawls, his footsteps getting closer. "Anything to add?"

"No." Her voice is small. Fuck him. I'm already over his condescending ass.

"Good. Mister..." he trails off, I assume to check the name on his attendance sheet. "Stringer?"

And it's my turn to roll my eyes—the correction is on the tip of my tongue—but when I sweep my hair out of my face and get a look at him, the words die on my tongue.

The word *handsome* does not do him justice, and for the first time in my life, I am rendered speechless.

His jaw and cheekbones look like they've been carved in stone, quiff haircut, and his narrowed eyes—a fascinating mixture of gray and blue—are scanning me intently. Luscious lips, the bottom lip so much fuller than the top one, and strong, straight nose fill in his carved face. His slightly wavy, thick, black hair is pushed back off his face in a way that makes him look more like a man than any guy I've ever seen before.

Like a young Clint Eastwood, I inwardly muse.

He can't be the teacher. He just can't. How the hell are we supposed to concentrate?

Irrational anger fills my gut, twisting around a hot ball of lust that's growing bigger south of my naval. I have to look at this face all year long and pretend to not be affected? But as I throw my silent tantrum, I realize that he is still waiting for an answer.

"Remington Stringer?" he questions again, his patience hanging by a thread. He's directly in front of me now, looking right past me. He has one hip propped on his desk, and he is wearing a crisp, white dress shirt—the sleeves rolled to his elbows—elegant, dark denim jeans, and shiny brown shoes. I have to crane my neck to see his face, he's so close. If nothing else, it snaps me out of my physical reaction to his proximity.

"Here," I manage to croak out, and I hate how weak it sounds. His eyes dart to me, and he lifts one disbelieving brow.

"You don't look like a Remington." The smirk on his face is enough for me to snap out of my trance.

"And you don't look like a teacher, but here we are." I hit him with the same sarcasm he so generously serves to everyone else. My eyes grow wide, my classmates snicker, his jaw hardens, and all I want is to reach out and grab those words and stuff them back into my mouth.

What the fuck is wrong with me?

He looks me up and down, and I don't know if it's disgust or annoyance coloring his gorgeous face. Whatever it is, it tells me that I've already landed a spot on his shit list, which is the last place I need to be right now. God, how do I go from sitting at the front row so I don't miss a word he says to slinging insults? I really am a piece of work.

"I apologize that I don't meet your standards," he mocks. "While we're on the subject of standards, West Point has a strict dress code. Sneakers are not acceptable footwear." He sends a pointed look toward my shoes.

Awesome.

And just like that, things go from bad to worse.

"Headmaster Charles' office, Miss Stringer." He tilts his head to the door, his face still perfectly composed, devoid of any emotion. His level of self-control is something I have yet to encounter. "Chop-chop."

"Please, I can't..." I clear my throat, hating myself for breaking, and loathing myself even more for my stupid slip of the tongue. *Can't afford shoes. Can't go home. Can't fuck this up.* But I also can't say any of that out loud.

"You can't...?" He crosses his arms over his chest expectantly.

He doesn't know me or my life. To him, I'm just another preppy, rich kid with an aversion to authority.

"Never mind," I grind out through gritted teeth.

I gather my shit and hit up Headmaster Charles' office—good thing I remember how to get there. I had orientation last week, but this school is huge—and plead my case. His secretary informs me that he's in a meeting, so I wait on one of the oversized leather couches against the wall. After about half an hour, his door opens and a blond boy with dimples for days makes his exit. He looks around my age, maybe younger, but who knows. His eyes don't have the hardened look about them like I'm sure mine do.

"Miss, uh," Headmaster Charles snaps his fingers, as if my name is on the tip of his tongue.

"Stringer," I offer, a polite smile plastered on my face.

"Remington Stringer."

"Ah, yes, Miss Stringer. What can I do for you?" He motions for me to enter, and I take a seat in front of his desk. His luxurious office does nothing to make me feel like I belong here. He has a fucking tea set and little bronze sculptures on his desk and massive bookshelves that put my local library to shame. The deep brown walls are riddled with decorative frames that boast of his achievements. I bite back the urge to make a joke about rich mahogany and leather bound books, because for some reason, I don't take him as an *Anchorman* fan.

"As you know, I'm new here," I begin.

"Yes, I'm aware," he hedges, steepling his fingers.

"I was sent to the office because I don't have proper shoes. I don't have an endless amount of money, or any, really, at my disposal. I'm lucky to even be here. The uniform alone was enough to break my bank, but I made it happen. I don't know when I'll be able to afford a new pair."

I decide to get straight to the point because I know I don't have the luxury to be tentative and overly polite. I think the man in front of me respects that, or at the very least not appalled by that, because Headmaster Charles' eyebrows knit together as he steals a glance at said shoes, silently assessing the situation.

"This school and getting into a good college are the most important things in the world to me, sir. And while I promise to get some shiny new Oxfords as soon as I can, I'd hate to think that West Point was the kind of place to kick someone out because they didn't have the means to buy your fancy shoes. And frankly, I'm not here to put on a fashion show. I'm here to learn."

Are my shoes really that offensive? Or did Mr. D-bag simply want to teach me a lesson? I want to strangle him. Just thinking about his smug face makes my heart lose its usual tempo and go crazy in my chest.

"Enough with the theatrics, Miss Stringer." He waves me off. "Get proper shoes when you can and return to classes in the meantime. What's your second period? I'll let your teacher know."

Well, that was easy. Almost too easy.

"Speech and Debate."

"Ah. Mr. James. I should've suspected."

Mr. James? I didn't even catch his name before getting kicked out. New record.

My face must show my confusion, because he elaborates.

"He's stern, if not a little cranky. But he's an invaluable source of knowledge. As you have probably experienced yourself, he is not the type of person you'd like to debate *with*. All the same, learn to get by in his class, and you'll do just fine at West Point, Miss Stringer."

"Thank you, sir," I say as I get up from the seat in front of him and turn for the door.

"And Miss Stringer?" Headmaster Charles calls out. I pause at the door and look back.

"Your transcripts were impeccable. West Point can open a lot of doors for you. Don't waste it."

"Yes, sir." I gulp, feeling somehow scolded and complimented at the same time.

"That'll be all," he dismisses me and returns his attention to the stack of papers at his desk.

Good riddance, I think. *And now for the hard part— softening Mr. James' cold, cold heart.*

⌐⟶

The rest of the day is a blur. When I get back to Mr. James'
class, he doesn't even give me a second glance. Thank you,
Baby Jesus. I attend my classes, take notes, and generally
lay low, which is exactly what I aimed for when I first got
here. I'm kind of relieved to see my second period was a
glitch, because, while I appreciate the opportunity to attend this out-of-this-world posh high school, what I really
need is a scholarship to a good university. I have no idea
what I want to study. I have no clue where I want to be
when I grow up. I just know it needs to be out of Nevada.
Something that allows me to be completely independent,
which means I'm already behind. These kids have had their
paths handpicked since diapers—some even before—I'm
sure, and I'm just over here hoping I get into college, any
college, far away from here.

Lunch is an affair with a *The Great Gatsby* flare at West
Point High. The cafeteria looks more like a glitzy airport
with floor-to-ceiling windows overlooking Nevadan hills,
red-bricked walls, and new and shiny tables that look more
like diner booths, only from deep oak. This place is free of
the slightly annoying yet very depressing scent of cheap,
oily, mass-made junk food. The combination of the swanky
space and spotless, ironed uniform makes it feel like I'm
walking in a parallel universe.

I don't like it and I don't feel like taking a place near
any of the people I've met during my periods, so I grab
a tray, get myself some fresh medley vegetables and sau-
téed chicken breast—wanting to yell at the lunch lady 'IT'S
JUST FREAKING CHICKEN, WHY DON'T YOU CALL

IT THAT?'—and take a seat at the far end of the room.

Sitting on the headrest with my feet on the bench, I stare at my lunch and try to calculate my next social move. The general idea is to stay away from trouble and not get into shit that could get me expelled. That means I can play nice with everyone, but I don't necessarily have to make friends. I simply need to make sure I don't make any enemies either.

Still staring at my untouched lunch, I feel something hit the side of my thigh and lift my head up. It's the blond kid who got out of Headmaster Charles' office, and he just smacked me with his binder. I quirk one eyebrow in question. He kind of looks like everybody else here. Rich and clean and cocky as hell. Now that he is close to me, I can see that his eyes are royal blue and that he has really full lips—too full, maybe—and hair that would make any respectable boy band envious.

"Can I help you?" I ask, not able to completely tamp down my attitude.

"I don't know." He tilts his head to the side. "Can you?"

It's the tilt of his voice that gives it away. Gay. So gay. I'm talking Cam form *Modern Family* gay. And I can't really explain it, but suddenly, I feel a lot less guarded.

"Depends on what you're looking for." I offer a smile that's also an olive branch. I think he takes it.

"I'm looking for good company and bad influence."

"Then I'm your girl."

"Glad to hear." He tosses himself theatrically onto the seat opposite me and sighs. "Because everyone here looks like a total bore and I'm losing my mind." His eyes roll, and we both burst into laughter when we look down at the tray he just put on the table, because it's full of kale salad with apples and other bullshit.

"Christian." He points at himself.

"Remington." I stub a finger to my chest. "But my friends call me Remi."

"Then I guess that's what I'll call you, too."

Christian tells me that he is another one of the few new students, and he is also a senior, so that practically makes us related somehow. Maybe not the best analogy, because my stepbrother makes a habit out of sticking his tongue down my throat and trying to get into my pants, but I digress. Christian just came back from studying at a Swiss boarding school with a really long, really French name. He was supposed to finish his studies there and go to Oxford University. However, his grandfather, the dude who holds the purse strings in his family, is dying, so his parents decided to move him back here so the whole family could spend some more time with their beloved patriarch. Christian says he doesn't really mind either way, because he tries to have fun no matter where he is, and I actually believe him.

The conversation is easy and so is forgetting how this day has started. Maybe that's why I'm so shocked by the end of it. After lunch—in which Christian and I exchanged phone numbers and promised each other to meet after the last bell rings—I attend my last two classes. The block schedule is yet another thing I need to get used to. We have four classes per day here. Two before lunch and two after. When Christian and I finally meet in the hallway, we make our way to the main entrance of the red-bricked building.

We're laughing and talking about Britney Spears' crotch tattoo when I hear the low rumble of a Harley. I freeze instantly, because the sound is so aggressive and out of place in comparison to the chirping of the birds, the little fountain in front of the entrance, and the low hushes of well-behaved students, and that throws me back to my reality.

Leather boots.

Tattoos galore.

The scent of possessiveness, poverty, and despair in the air.

Yes, they all have a smell. They smell like Ryan.

"Yo, Rem! Look at your fine ass in that uniform." Ry laughs like it's the first time he's seen me like this, pulling out his helmet and checking me out without even hiding it. I immediately turn scarlet red. He's supposed to be my brother. *Supposed* being the operative word. I can see Christian staring at me from my peripheral, wondering what the hell is going on. My hold on the straps of my backpack tightens, and I force a smile. Funny how aware I am of our inappropriate dynamic now that I'm at West Point.

"That's my *stepbrother*," I say, putting emphasis on the word *step*. I don't think pseudo-incest will earn me any brownie points in this school. Even cool-as-a-cucumber Christian will frown upon that. "He's my ride."

Christian just nods, and the movement is faint, just like his wary expression. I know that look. I've seen it before, so I look away. Pity.

Don't you fucking pity me.

"See you tomorrow?" Christian asks. And my gaze drifts back to him because looking away was a huge mistake. Now I know for a fact that everybody around us is looking back and forth from Ryan to me, trying to fill in the blanks.

"Sure will." I give him a fist bump—and damn, if the prospect of a new friendship doesn't cheer me up a little—and take a brave step toward my stepbrother. Then another and another. I descend the massive stairs leading to the fountain overlooking the high school's entrance, and when I'm close enough to Ryan, he pulls me in for a hug. An incredibly awkward, greedy hug. I don't have biological siblings, but I'm not sure our groins are supposed to touch.

Ryan lets me go after long seconds, and with each passing one, I realize that I'll never fit in here. And it's not just my worn-out shoes. When he releases me, his nostrils are flared, his jaw clenched, and he's staring straight at Christian. I bring my hand up to cup Ryan's jaw, brushing my thumb along his stubble, quieting his storm in the way only I seem to be able to. Panic swirls in my gut. I know what he's thinking, and I need to distract and defuse. Ryan has always been overprotective, but over the last few months, he has crossed defensive territory and is now squarely lying in batshit-crazy zone.

"Missed you today," I murmur, holding my breath. I wait for his reaction and sigh with relief as his eyes soften at my touch.

"Guess what?" Ryan smirks, and I know Christian is forgotten. For now, anyway. Ryan is gorgeous, there's no denying that, but instead of swooning over that smirk, I'm jaded to it.

"What?" I ask, still standing too close to him and too close to his bike and too close to the situation I'm desperate to get out of.

"Got you a present."

"You did?" I raise an eyebrow, skeptic. He nods,

turns around, and pulls out a brand new, shiny red Shoei helmet. My heart drops. He can't afford this.

"Check it out," he says. I grab it. It's heavy as hell, but I'm not complaining. It's much better than the German style one I wore on the way to school that looked like an old school military helmet. But I also know that Ryan is broke as hell, so the fact that he has money worries me. There is no way he came by it honestly.

"Ryan?" I don't need to ask the actual question. Just the fact that I'm looking at the helmet like it's a bomb and not a gift spells it out for me.

Ryan clears his throat. "What? Been picking up extra shifts at the garage lately," he says. He could be telling the truth. He has been gone a lot lately, but the look in his eyes tells me he's hiding something.

I have so many things I want to say to him, but the only thing that comes out is "okay". Because I know he is volatile, and I don't usually mind—I can take care of myself—but I don't want a scene. Not here.

"Get on the fucking bike, baby. I don't got all day."

I hop on, eager to get out of here. Ryan has always been my safe place. My comfort zone. But right now, it feels like two worlds are colliding, and I'm desperate to keep them firmly separate.

He snakes his hand backwards and gives my thigh a squeeze before he starts his Harley and revs it up, leaving a cloud of dust and smoke behind us.

Through the veil of filth, I chance one last glance at West Point High for the day.

I see Christian on the stairway, watching us with a concerned expression, his backpack still slung casually on one shoulder.

A group of snobbish girls look at us from their place, sitting on the steps with their lattes clutched tight.

And Mr. James standing there—hands in his pockets—looking even more pissed off than he was earlier.

Chapter Three

Pierce

*W*here the hell did she come from?
   Not from here, that's for sure.

   I've been teaching privileged kids long enough to know the odd one out when I see one. Not to mention, I *was* one. When I walk into class and see her in the first row, I ignore her completely, just like I do with the rest—high school girls tend to be a little overzealous—it's best not to encourage them. I don't notice the way her wide, innocent eyes take me in. I don't notice her crimson pout. And I definitely don't notice the way her body fills out her uniform unlike any other girl her age. To me, she is just another student. At least that's what I tell myself.

   She doesn't look like the rest of them.

   That's my second thought, and it's somewhere so deep in

the back of my head, I'm not sure I have the necessary access to wipe it from my mind. I've taught Speech and Debate at this school for four years now, and I know all these students. I don't mean the names or the faces. *The type.* The ones who think they are only as good as their worst grade. The ones who will scheme and plot and betray if it means being the best, even at someone else's expense. That's what Headmaster Charles gives me. The best. We give them the tools and discipline they need to succeed in whatever careers their mommy and daddy have chosen for them, and they go on to be perfect, little carbon copies of their parents.

With her dirty white Converse and chipped black nail polish, I know she's different. Either way, I was caught off-guard when she called me out in the middle of class and I was forced to respond quickly.

I told her to get her stuff and leave, and *almost* regretted it, because I'm not sure what her story is. She's either rebelling against her parents or a scholarship student. Those are the only two options at this school. My guess is she's a little bit of both. I know the type, because I *was* the type. I fought and resisted my parents every step of the way growing up. I wasn't fit for life as a robot. I liked music and art and drinking. A lot of good that did me. I'm still the black sheep, but somehow, I ended up teaching in the same world I rebelled so hard against, only I was in California. Imagine that.

I scrub my hand down my face and close the laptop screen I've been staring blankly at for the last ten minutes.

Why the fuck am I even giving her a second thought?

I leave my belongings and decide to grab a pack of smokes and a Cherry Coke from across the street before I come back to finish putting together the rest of the syllabus for the year. See? Rebel. These should've been ready to pass out on the first day.

Then I see Remington Stringer.

And she is not alone.

She is walking over to a guy who looks like a *Sons of Anarchy* dropout, and he throws his arms around her. She accepts his embrace. I can't see his face, but she seems almost nervous, which I guess seems very out of character for a girl who calls out her teacher on the first day of school. They are basically grinding in the parking lot, and somewhere in my head, I know I should put a stop to it. But they're like a car accident that I can't look away from. If I wasn't sure before, it's clear now. She's no West Point princess.

He grabs her ass, looks over her shoulder, and spots the blond kid she walked out of school with. Christian Chambers. I taught him his last period. Obviously gay, but there's no way for the simpleton on the bike to know that from looks alone. Remington's gaze follows her biker boyfriend's, and when her eyes land on Christian, her whole face drops in horror. She schools her features quickly and turns her attention to pacifying him. If the whole scene weren't so creepy, seeing him fall under her spell as quickly as he did would be comical.

He hands Remington a red helmet, and when he turns around to mount his bike, his eyes meet mine for a split second. And that's all it takes for me to recognize him. I stuff my hands into my pockets to keep them from strangling the bastard right here and now. What the fuck is Remington doing with this guy? Ryan Anderson. The man I've been trying to find for the past year. The man who ruined my family. The man I want dead.

The school year just got a lot more interesting. *Thank you, Remington Stringer.*

Chapter Four

Remi

I swing open the chain-link fence in our front yard and make my way past the collection of empty beer cans and mismatched chairs—that have permanent ass prints from Ryan and his good-for-nothing friends—before heading inside. The inside, unfortunately, is not much better. We live in the ghetto of Las Vegas, where the houses are over-run with bionic sewer roaches, and the streets are over-run with tweakers. Ironically enough, all the streets in our neighborhood are named after Ivy League schools. I live on Yale, which I figure is about as close to an Ivy League school as I'll ever get. West Point could change everything, though. And boy, was I off to a great start. *Not*.

Ignoring the mountain of dishes in the sink, Ryan's random tools lying everywhere, and a suspicious wet spot on the old green carpet, I head straight to my room. Let's be honest—this place isn't ever The Ritz, but when Dad goes out of town, it goes from bad to worse. And I can't bring myself to care today. I pause to look at my giant corkboard full of photos above my dresser. I see my mom pregnant with me. My dad taking me for a ride on the back of his old Softail, rocking a Kool-Aid smile and ratty light brown hair. Then the more recent ones of Ella and me smoking weed in her car on an old back road while we were supposed to be in school. And Ryan. So many pictures of Ryan. Teaching me how to skateboard, sitting with me in the hospital after I broke my ankle on said skateboard later that week, putting our tent together on our camping trip with Dad, selfies from concerts we snuck into, and tons of sunsets and scenic shots from the countless times we drove around just to escape the hellhole of Las Vegas. I flop face-down onto the pale blue comforter on top of my old twin bed. I toe my shoes off, not moving from my face-plant on the bed, thanking my lucky stars that Ryan had plans. He disappeared right after dropping me off. *Again.* I'm not sure where or what he's up to, but right now, I'm grateful for the silence. I roll onto my back and stare blankly at the popcorn ceiling above and count the revolutions of the fan blades.

What a day.

Mr. James' face flashes in my mind, unbidden, and I cringe. *Of course,* I'd have the hottest teacher to ever grace a classroom, and *of course,* I'd manage to make him hate me twenty seconds into meeting me. Not that I blame him. My verbal diarrhea was in full effect today. It wasn't all bad, though. The rest of my classes were fucking hard—as to be expected—but it felt good. *Really* good. I was totally overwhelmed and out of my element, but at the same time, I felt like I was exactly where I belonged. Meeting Christian was a plus, too.

I pad out to the kitchen and snatch a Hot Pocket out of the freezer. After wolfing that down, I decide to call it a night. I peel off my knee socks, skirt, and shirt and fold them carefully. I only have the one skirt and one extra shirt, so I'll need to keep them as nice as I can for as long as I can.

I'm too tired to even take a shower, so I throw on a big, white, cotton T-shirt—either Ryan's or my pops'—and hop into bed. I focus on the sounds outside to distract me from my thoughts. I hear the bass thumping from a car a few houses down, a group of teenage boys heckling each other, sirens in the distance, and the rhythmic sound of the wheels of a skateboard hitting the cracks in the sidewalk. And before long, the soundtrack of my city lulls me to sleep.

I don't know how long I've been asleep when I feel two strong arms around me and a nose nuzzling my neck. *Ryan.* Lately, he only sleeps with me when he's fucked up. I can smell the alcohol seeping through his skin, but somehow, it's still comforting.

"You can't leave me, Rem," he whispers into my ear, his voice as rough as his touch. The desperation in his words breaks my heart and reminds me of the wounded boy he once was.

"You're almost done with high school." He continues, "And soon, you're going to go off to college and leave us behind. I can't protect you if you're not here."

"Shh, it's okay." I soothe him, rubbing his arm like I always do when he's like this and avoiding the topic altogether. I know I shouldn't lead him on. I know this is going to blow up soon, but now—when he's drunk, vulnerable, and unstable—is not the time to serve him a healthy dose of reality. I've got defusing the bomb that is Ryan down to an art form, and nothing I say right now will go over well. Not when he's in this state.

He squeezes me tighter, and a few minutes later when his breathing evens out and I know he's passed out, I succumb to the security of his arms and drift back to sleep.

⌐⁓

I reach blindly for my phone on my nightstand, knocking a water bottle off in the process before I finally feel the cool plastic of the case in my hand. I open one eye and try to focus on the time. Once my eyes adjust, I spring out of bed like it's on fire. School started ten minutes ago.

Shit. Why the hell didn't my alarm go off?!

I'm kicking myself for not showering when I had the time last night. I yell out Ryan's name on my way to the bathroom, but I don't get a response. I brush my teeth while I go in search of him. This place is a shoebox, so he shouldn't be hard to find.

"Ryan!" I yell around a mouth full of toothpaste. "Where *are* you?"

I shove his door open, only to find his empty bed.

Jesus Christ. I'm late for my second day of school.

I get dressed in record time and throw my unwashed hair into a messy fishtail braid. I swing my backpack over my shoulder and run outside to see if by some miracle Ryan got up early to work on his old school Firebird that's been sitting on blocks in the driveway for the past year. Nope. No such luck. And even worse, his bike is gone.

Come on, Ryan. Don't fuck me over like this. Not today.

It's way too late to catch the bus now. I'm weighing my options in my head—all zero of them—when I hear the telltale rumble of his Harley in the distance. Halle-fucking-lujah.

Ryan swings into the driveway and lifts one leg like he's about to get off his bike.

"No, no, no, don't you dare! I have to leave, like, five minutes ago! Where were you?" I screech, scrambling toward him.

"Back off, Rem, and get the fuck on. I had some shit to take care of early this morning. I'm fuckin' tired, and I don't got any patience for your tantrums right now."

I don't know what could have possibly gotten him out of bed before noon, short of the world ending, but I don't have time to hound him for answers. I snatch my new helmet off the old metal patio swing and hop on behind Ryan. He takes off like a bat out of hell, and I'm forced to hold his middle tighter. He weaves in and out of traffic and somehow manages not to get stuck behind one single red light.

We pull into the parking lot, and I don't know what time it is, but the horde of students outside tells me that second period is about to begin. I think Ryan is going to let me off, but much to my utter horror, he keeps on going. Straight for the fountain. Straight to where half the school still lingers. He romps the sidewalk and slides to a stop parallel to the fountain, effectively creating a scene.

"Here you go, princess," he taunts. I roll my eyes while I unbuckle my helmet and start to slide off, but his huge hand grips my thigh, keeping me in place. I arch an eyebrow in question.

"Say 'thanks', Rem."

"Thanks, Rem," I grit through clenched teeth.

"Say it sweetly, baby doll," he insists. All eyes are on us, and to them, it probably looks like nothing more than a little PDA. But Ryan's hand squeezes my thigh so tightly that my eyes water.

Who is this person?

"Ryan. *Enough.* I'm already late."

"Not until you *thank me*," he says with venom in his voice and points at his cheek.

Fuck this, I think, and once again, try to get off the bike. His fingers crush my leg, but it's his thumb digging into my inner thigh that causes me to cry out in pain.

"What the fuck, Ryan!" I practically scream, and I'm thankful that most of the other students have gone inside. The fear of being tardy trumps drama—yet, another difference between West Point and Riverdale. Ryan points to his face one more time with a malicious glint in his eye. He's an asshole, but I've never known him to be cruel. This is not the Ryan I grew up with, and this new realization hits me right in the stomach. Gone is the boy who made me mac and cheese and reluctantly let me tag along with him and his friends to the skate park, the boy that I idolized and worshipped. This is a stranger wearing my stepbrother's face.

And this guy plays by different rules, so I better start adapting, fast.

I smack a quick kiss on his cheek, but he grips my chin in place and turns to plant his lips on mine. I squeal and jerk back, but he simply laughs.

"Fuck you," I spit. I jump off and scramble toward the front doors.

I'm almost inside when I hear him yell out, "Bummer

about your alarm, Rem. You should be more careful next time!"

I never told him that my alarm didn't go off. *That motherfucker.*

After I make a quick stop at the office for a late slip, I run through the hall, not even stopping at my locker. Strands of hair have come loose from the ride here, and I rub at the tears that are starting to dry on my face. I'm a mess. I skid to a stop in front of the door to Mr. James' class and take a second to gain my composure.

Get it together. Every second you waste is another second you're late.

I take one deep breath and open the door. Not one person looks up. No one, except Mr. James, of course. He scowls in my direction as I duck my head down and scurry to my desk.

"Miss Stringer, a word?" *Fuck my life.*

He's sitting at his desk while the rest of the class flips through a packet of some sort. He's wearing a plain baby blue dress shirt and black slacks. His hair is pushed back off his face, and his eyebrows knit together as he takes me in. His eyes seem to soften for a fraction of a second, but then the severe expression is firmly back in place so quickly that I wonder if I'm imagining it.

"I'm so sorry," I start. "About yesterday, and being late. It won't happen again," I promise. He hands me a packet.

"See that it doesn't," he bites out. "I don't tolerate tardiness. Now, today is a fresh start. Tell us something about yourself. You didn't get the chance yesterday."

Is he for real? This isn't kindergarten. We don't need to play ice-breaking games anymore. But the expectant look in his eyes tells me that he's serious. And he's waiting for an answer.

"I, uh," I start, articulate as always. I clear my throat and try again. "I like to take pictures." This time more firmly.

Some kid mumbles something about nude photos under his breath, but Mr. James either doesn't hear or chooses to ignore him.

"What kind of pictures?" he asks, seeming genuinely interested, and it throws me for a loop. Yesterday he was callous and aloof, and today he still seems frosty, but almost human.

"I don't know." I shrug. "Sad things. Beautiful things. Everything."

Mr. James studies me for long seconds before he jerks his head in the direction of my desk. I take that as my cue to take my seat.

Once I'm seated, I turn my attention to the papers in my hand. It's a syllabus. Mr. James stands and starts walking the class through the outline for the year, and I know I should be paying attention, but all I can focus on is the way his full lips move when he speaks, the perfect amount of stubble on his face, and the casual way he runs a hand through his dark hair as he leans a hip against his desk. He's such a fucking *man*. And even though it's clear that he's got more class in his pinky finger than I have in my entire body, you can just tell that deep down, he's a bad boy. Or maybe a reformed bad boy. But he reeks of sophistication and wealth. So, why is he a teacher? My mind works overtime trying to make sense of this dichotomy before finally settling on "does not compute".

I wonder if he's married. I wonder what she looks like. I hate her already. Then I imagine him and his perhaps non-existing wife rolling in bed, him eating her out while she tugs at his perfect hair, and cross my legs, squeezing the soft damp fabric between my thighs.

My eyes roam all over his body with shameless appreciation for the way his shirt hugs his chest and biceps. His sleeves are pushed up to the elbow *and who knew forearms could be sexy?* I'm perving on my teacher approximately two seconds after being manhandled by my pseudo stepbrother. Seems legit.

I shake those thoughts out of my head and attempt to focus on the words coming out of his mouth once more. When I look up to his eyes, they're trained on me.

"Write down any questions and fill out the back page," he addresses the class, but he's still glaring in my direction. His jaw hardens, and his eyes narrow as they drift down my body. My heart races, and I feel my ears get hot under his attention. I drag my teeth across my bottom lip and cross one leg over the other. His eyes aren't wavering from my legs, and his expression morphs into one of…anger?

I glance down and immediately know exactly what he's looking at. *Fuck.* Ryan left a little present in the shape of his goddamn hand on my thigh. It's bright red, and the four obvious finger marks leave little question as to what made them. I tug down my skirt and shift in my seat, hating that he must think I'm some sort of helpless victim.

I avoid eye contact for the rest of the period, and when the bell rings, I practically run toward the exit. But Mr. James can't make anything easy.

"Stringer, hang back. I need a word." There is no question in his voice. I freeze in place, not wanting to defy him, but definitely not wanting to stay behind and face him. I'm a street-smart girl. Maybe I haven't seen it all, but I've seen most of it, and God knows I've dealt with a lot of people. Scarier people than Mr. James. But somehow, he scares me more than any of the criminals and creeps I've encountered over the years. It doesn't even make any sense.

I turn on my heels and stare him straight in the eye, because even though I'm uncomfortable around him, it's not in my nature to let this kind of thing show.

"Yes, Mr. James?" There's a bite to my tone. I can't hide it. I'm not sure I even want to. His hands are tucked inside the pockets of his black dress pants, he is standing at his full, impressive height, and his eyes glide up my body, from my toes to my head, halting briefly on my thighs. I suck in a breath and close my eyes. *Goddammit, Ryan.*

"Riddle me this." He takes a step in my direction, rounding his desk, and my heart is in my throat. Danger rolls off of him, and I don't know how to stop my body from responding to his. Because it's there. The electricity. The attraction. The lust.

I can't be the only one who feels it. It feels too big to be one-sided.

Oh, how pathetic would that be if I'm the only one who burns under these clothes.

Mr. James continues, "Yesterday, when I saw you for the first time, you appeared to be in good shape, except for the shoes, of course. Today, I found something different. You're a smart girl, so you don't need me to spell it out for you. Tell me, Miss Stringer, is there a reason to worry about your safety?"

I gulp and look away so he doesn't see what's in my eyes. I'm not even sure what's in there myself. Fear? Desire? Anxiety? All I know is that I need to get out of here, fast.

"No need to worry." I shake my head. "May I be

excused now?"

"No, you may not." His voice is so cold, it provides a little comfort to the scorching hot waves he seems to be making inside my body. "What happened? Explain. With words. Preferably an adequate amount for me to make an educated decision on whether to call social services."

"Funny you should say that, you use so little," I whip out without even meaning to. I have to stop doing that. Taunting him like this, like we're equal. Mr. James lifts a lone eyebrow, a ghost of a smirk finding his perfect lips.

"Miss Stringer," he warns, his ice-cold tone licks at my burning flesh. "You're not getting out of here until you explain."

"I got into a fight with my kitchen drawer handle," I say dumbly. "I lost." I let the lie roll from my tongue, and Mr. James' expression tells me that he doesn't believe me for even a second.

"Put your palm flat against the mark," he orders. My first thought is, *fuck, he knows it's a handprint*. My second thought is even more alarming. *His demanding tone is turning me on.*

I chance a glance at him, and his eyes are half-mast, so I know I'm not the only one who is feeling it. Feeling *this*. That thought hits me like a ton of bricks. Mr. James is a grown *man*, and I affect him.

And suddenly, putting my hand on my thigh doesn't seem so bad. Maybe I'll put those morals of his to the test.

I do as I'm told, not breaking eye contact with him. I don't need to look down to find the mark because it is still searing, even after all this time. His eyes roll down—slowly, I don't fail to notice—until they stop.

Starting just above my knee, I slowly trace my black

fingernails upward, bunching my skirt up my thigh in the process. I lay my hand flat on the mark, not giving away the fact that it still stings to the touch.

His throat bobs on a swallow, and he looks up.

"Are you going to make a habit out of lying to me, Miss Stringer?" He steps toward me, backing me into my desk. I sit perched on the edge with my skirt still bunched. I have the urge to push him further, to spread my legs, and to let him see what he does to me.

"Are you going to keep asking me questions I can't provide the answer to?" I ask honestly, letting my skirt fall back into place. "I'm a big girl. I've been taking care of myself for a long time now."

He takes his final step toward me, erasing the space between us, and now I can see him and smell him and *feel* him. So help me God, I need to keep my knees from buckling and see this thing through, because he makes me want things. Things I shouldn't want to do with my teacher. Things a girl shouldn't ever want to do at all.

"That's the problem," he hisses. "I'll be keeping an eye on you, Miss Stringer. I'm trusting you here. If something happened to you, and I failed to report it, well, I'm sure I don't have to tell you how bad that would be for the both of us."

"Thank you," I say curtly, because apparently, I'm done acting like a brat for the day. "But there is no need."

"On the contrary." He turns around, sending one last look on my thigh. I don't ask if I'm excused. I know that if I don't leave his class now, I'll do something we'll both regret. So, I turn around toward the door, taking tentative steps, both afraid that he will stop me and that he won't.

He doesn't stop me.

He lets me go.

And he should.

Because he's my fucking *teacher*.

But a second before the door closes behind me, I hear him say, "There won't be a next time, Miss Stringer. Not to your tardiness, not to talking back to your educator, and not to putting on your little show. Am I clear?"

"Yes, sir." I swallow as I shut the door behind me and rest the back of my head on its window, closing my eyes.

Holy. Fuck.

Chapter Five

Pierce

I pop open the trunk of my Audi SUV and take out the paper bags of groceries. I will get them all the way to the fourth floor, like I do every month.

I knock and she doesn't answer, but that's nothing new. I don't give a damn. I kick the old door open, which is easy because this building is rotten and everything is decaying, including my sanity, and walk into the apartment. She doesn't greet me, but she'll come out once she's sure it's just me, and for just a couple hours, I'll feel close to Gwen again.

Arranging the peanut butter and jam and bread and pickles on the shelves—Shelly's diet consists of that of a four-year-old mixed with pregnancy cravings—I hear the bedroom door creaking open.

"Pierce? Pierce, baby, is that you?" Her tentative voice followed by a deep cough punctuates the question as she makes her way to the peeling kitchen in her ratty slippers. I turn around and lean my waist against the counter, folding my arms on my chest and taking her in. Shelly is in her early thirties, but she might as well be sixty. She was beautiful once, but drugs, alcohol, and *life* ruined her.

"Who else are you expecting? The Pope?" I quirk a brow, and she laughs and coughs, tucking strands of greasy hair behind her ear. She clasps me into a hug I accept, for no other reason than the fact she was my sister's best friend.

"You look good, kid," she says. *Tell me something I don't know.* If teaching high school girls has taught me one thing, it's that I'm easy on the eyes. Young girls with crushes can be dangerous, so I lay low and stay my asshole self. It seems to be working fine so far.

Things got really difficult when Gwen left me. I would say 'left us', but it's me she left, really. My parents stopped giving two fucks the minute she failed to be the person they wanted her to be. They cut off her cash flow and let her fend for herself instead of helping her with her addiction. For me, it wasn't that simple. Maybe because my parents were always so busy with keeping up appearances and their precious careers, they didn't make the time to actually parent me or get to know me, but Gwen did. Gwen took me to swimming classes twice a week and tried—but failed—to make me birthday cakes every year and mothered me more than my mother ever has. Now that she is gone, a part of me is, too. A part I miss and would really fucking appreciate having back.

"Thank you," I say, exhaling harshly and grabbing a

garden chair—the cheap kind you get for a buck at Dollar Tree—which is a part of her dining area. I plop down on it, throw my head back, and close my eyes on a sigh. "I miss her," I say.

"I miss her, too." Shelly puts a hand on her shoulder. "They say it gets better."

"They lie." I suck my teeth. I hear her laugh, but there's nothing happy about it.

"You're still so young and successful, Pierce. I may not know much about life." She laughs bitterly. "Hell, I don't even know if I'll make it to next month, but I do know you can be happy again. Put this all behind you and live your life before another life is wasted. Maybe find a girl. Have a family of your own one day. Don't you want that for yourself?"

I guess that's the saddest part. Women don't occupy my thoughts. Not for more than one night at a time, anyway. I have no recollection of showing interest in more than a warm body to spend the night with in the last few years. Remington's face flashes in my mind, and I shut it down as fast as she came. I don't even know her, but I find her fascinating. It's like watching a car crash. She is spectacular in a sad, beautiful way. I know there's more lurking behind those big, green eyes. Luckily, I'm not crazy and self-destructive enough to ever find out.

"Thanks for the tip, Mom," I bite out, and that awards me a light punch to the shoulder. "What about you, Shell? Don't *you* want that? How is what you're doing to yourself any different?" Her eyes glaze over with tears that she tries to conceal as she focuses on a piece of lint on her pants.

"You forgot my cigarettes," Shelly says, avoiding my question altogether.

"I didn't forget. Those things will kill you," I retort, even though I know I've found myself smoking more in the past few days than I have in my entire life. Smoking is Shelly's least dangerous vice. We always go through the motions of this conversation. I will most definitely go get her cigarettes. And I will do so because I know she'll be waiting upstairs, taking out the old albums of her and her late best friend—Gwen—and she'll tell me all about their adventures in being young and wild and free. Then, I'll question her about Ryan's whereabouts, and she'll deny me. If I'm lucky, she'll inadvertently give me another small piece to the puzzle.

"Camels. Soft packs. It's crucial."

"They're going to kill you."

"No, baby. The drugs will."

"Is that the goal? To die? If so, you're right on track." I finally get up from the chair.

"At least I'm good at something."

I decide to walk to the Rebel gas station a few blocks away. It's a rough part of town, but I actually like it. How real the streets feel. In Summerlin, it almost feels like nothing bad can touch you with its secluded, gated communities. Which is, of course, bullshit. A lot of bad things touched me. Touched Gwen. They left marks. The permanent kind. Just because you can't see them, doesn't mean they're not there.

I round the corner when I hear the exhaust of bikes behind me. I tune it out and push open the door. The overhead bell dings. A large, sleepy guy with a curly black ponytail lifts his head from a *Playboy* magazine and picks his nose as he follows my movements behind the counter. *Hello to you, too.*

"Three packs of Camels, soft, and a pack of Reds." I point at what I need. I decide to cut my visit with Shelly short this week. I'm in the mood for fucking. To blow off some steam. Especially after today. The fucker who left an imprint to last a few weeks on Remington Stringer's thigh has been occupying my thoughts. Hurting women is not my style. In or out of bed. Hurting people who hurt women, however, is something I'm completely open to.

Especially as I know exactly who he is, and I want to do a lot of things about it, but none of them will benefit her. Or me, for that matter. I need to be patient and play my cards right.

I still don't know what role he plays in her life, and reporting this to Headmaster Charles would drag her into a lot of drama I'm sure she doesn't need. But I can't, in good conscience, turn a blind eye.

The cashier rings me up, and I grab my stuff. Just as I turn around, I bump into a shoulder.

Speak of the devil.

Ryan Anderson, AKA Remington Stringer's ride, is looking me right in the eye. I stare at him hard but impassive, my face not giving away one damn thing. We hold each other's stare far too long for it to be a coincidence, until someone in a leather cut without a shirt underneath and holey jeans grabs onto his shoulder and pulls him away.

"C'mon, Ryan. We have shit to do. Let's get outta here."

I want to kill him for doing what he did, and not just to my sister, but I find myself helpless. For now. Just for now.

"Do I know you from somewhere?" I lift my chin up and inspect him. This part is crucial for me, because I need to know how I proceed with Ryan Anderson. What my angle will be. He doesn't say a thing, just looks at me like I'm speaking a foreign language. If he recognizes me, he doesn't let on. What the hell is wrong with this guy?

"Doubt it," he snorts. "I don't go to no country club."

"I'm Remington Stringer's teacher, Pierce James," I spell it out for him myself, because there's no way this Neanderthal is going to connect the dots without a little help. He gives me a slow once-over, assessing the situation, and his forehead crumples.

"Oh, yeah? I'm Ryan," he spits out, not offering his hand.

"A family friend?" I feign ignorance.

"*Step*brother," he clarifies, adding emphasis on the word *step* as if that makes a difference. "I also own her."

You're also about to get your ass whooped.

"You do?" I smile casually. "And here I thought that was illegal since 1863."

Of course, this idiot doesn't get the reference and stares at me blankly.

"She's mine," he says again, slow this time, taking a step in my direction. I make no move. This asshole doesn't intimidate me. "Make sure you remember that." He delivers the threat directly into my face, the veins in his neck popping.

"I'm her teacher." I bypass him with an easy smile, unaffected. "I will make sure my students make it through the year healthy and safe, no matter the consequences." The edge in my tone doesn't leave room for doubt. I'm returning the threat. "It's literally my job."

Before he comes back with another idle threat—men like him always need the last word—I walk out of the gas station, my hands clutching the plastic bag.

I go straight to Shelly's house, only staying for half an hour this time. I leave out the part about my new connection to Ryan—though, I'm not sure why—and complete my mission for the night. I make a short trip to the bar, pick up a random woman, make use of the condom in my wallet, and end my night in bed alone, smoking and staring at the ceiling.

Ryan Anderson. I now have a way to get to him, and I will.

He is going to pay. I'll make sure of it.

Chapter Six

Remi

Ryan has never been accused of being reasonable or rational, but tonight, he seems to be taking his unstable behavior to a whole new level. I don't know what climbed up his ass, but I can practically hear the time bomb ticking. I'm lying on my stomach on the cold kitchen tile, attempting to cool off while doing my English homework. Ryan won't let me turn the air-conditioning any lower. My hair is sticking to my neck, and even in a spaghetti strap tank top and a pair of hot pink sleep shorts, I'm still on fire. Between the heat, Ryan's angry stare, and his leg bouncing in place, focus is not coming easy.

"Somethin' on your mind, Ryan?" I huff, rolling onto one elbow to meet his eyes.

"You runnin' your mouth, Rem?" he snaps back.

What the hell is he talking about?

"Not any more than usual," I quip.

He nods bitterly and takes a swig of his beer.

"Funny, your *teacher* says otherwise."

My what?

Ryan stands and slowly walks toward me, and I scramble to get out of my vulnerable position on the floor. I stand with the counter at my back and straighten my shoulders. For the first time in a long time, I don't only hope—but pray—that my dad will come back home sooner rather than later from Los Angeles.

"I don't know what you're—" I'm cut off by Ryan slamming his beer bottle against the cabinets above my head. It breaks, dousing my shoulder with lukewarm liquid and bits of shattered glass. I flinch so hard that I slip in the beer that's puddled at my bare feet, but Ryan squeezes my bicep to keep me upright.

"Don't *fucking lie to me!*" Ryan screams, and his spit lands on my cheek. My eyes are wide with fear, but it's not for myself. It's for Ryan. With each passing day, it's getting harder and harder to ignore the fact that something is seriously wrong with him. And I don't know how to fix it.

"Are you fucking him, Rem? Is that how you got into that fancy ass school of yours? Well, if you're selling your ass, then I should at least get a family discount," he sneers, grabbing my waist and squeezing. Not lightly either.

"Do you even hear yourself? There are so many things wrong with this conversation. You're not making any sense, Ryan." I push him away, and this time, I'm not nice either. His eyes soften briefly before turning cold again.

"You keep your mouth shut about me. I don't need any extra attention right now. Don't need anybody breathing down my neck." He brings his fists to the cabinets, boxing me in. "Your pretty boy teacher isn't gonna save you, Rem. You and me—we were meant for this life. We'll never be good enough for people like them. It's time you get used to it. Don't let that pretty head of yours get filled with sweet sounding lies. I am your truth, baby. It's just you and me."

I give a short nod, and he storms off and slams the metal screen against the frame. Once I hear his bike fade off into the distance, I let my tears fall. I cry for me, because a part of me believes Ryan when he says I'm meant for this life. And I cry for Ryan. For the boy he was, and the man he won't get to become. This town is poison that seeps through the veins of everyone who lives here. And the only antidote is getting out.

Ryan is too far gone, I can see it now. And a part of me is scared he won't make it out alive.

A part of me is scared it's already too late.

Ryan and I didn't say a word to each other the entire day yesterday. I was too pissed at how he treated me, and Ryan was just, well, pissed in general. When he called out my name after dropping me off at school, I thought maybe he'd apologize, but instead, I got a stern reminder to keep my mouth shut.

Now, I'm in second period where I've been shooting daggers with my eyes at Mr. James for the past forty minutes. With each passing second, I become progressively irate at him for interfering. I don't even know what went down with him and Ryan, but it's clear that I cannot trust him.

Blinded by sheer hatred—hatred that is dipped in

lust, slightly coated by something feral, and completely heady—I don't even realize that he is talking to me until his voice becomes a low, pissed-off growl.

"Miss Stringer, I asked you a question."

I straighten my spine, military-sharp, and tilt my chin up. "I apologize, Mr. James," I say robotically, and see his features melt into confusion at my tone. "I'm afraid I didn't hear that. Can you kindly repeat?"

I'm not going to let him ruin this for me. I am getting out of this place, with or without Mr. James' help. It's a debate class, for fuck's sake. An elective period. I'm acing everything else so far. I just need to survive this man for the rest of the year.

"We're talking about the subject of same sex marriage. Would you like to contribute?"

"I'm pro," I mutter. "If that's what you're asking."

"It's not a survey, Miss Stringer. Explain yourself."

I look around me, acutely aware to the fact that all eyes are on me. It's not the other students' eyes that I am afraid of. It's those gray-blues that are staring down at me through a furrowed brow. They betrayed me, and now they want my cooperation. I shouldn't be so goddamn angry, but I am. Poised as I could be under the circumstances, I answer, "Equal rights." I part my lips, and his eyes drop to them before moving back to my eyes quickly. *Win.* I'm going to fuck with him a little just to get back at him and show him he may hold most of the power here, but certainly not *all* of it.

"People should have the right to marry whoever they want. It's not my business, anyway."

"Whoever?" Mr. James questions, his hands knotted behind his back as he starts walking the narrow gap between my row of desks to the one near the wall. "So, Miss Stringer, can I marry my pet?"

I scoff. "Of course not. It's not the same thing."

"Enlighten me."

This is so stupid. Why is he doing this?

"People should marry other people. Otherwise it creates...chaos."

"Chaos is bad?" he asks, this time the whole class. A pimpled girl in the back lifts her hand and answers.

"Yes. Because where there's chaos, there's anarchy."

"And where there's anarchy, there's fun," I mutter, not asking for permission to speak. I feel Mr. James' eyes on my back, even though I don't turn around to check. I ignited something there, and I'm going to let it burn until he feels the wrath and flames of his actions.

"Anarchy is fun," he repeats my statement, as if mulling this over.

"If you can handle it." I shrug.

"I can handle it, if you need willing candidates." A preppy, pretty boy from my right snickers, fist-bumping his friend. They are both wearing burgundy varsity jackets and smug-ass faces I can break without even breaking a sweat.

"Mr. Herring, Mr. Schwartz, watch it," Mr. James whiplashes.

"Sorry, sir," the idiot mumbles, deflated.

The bell rings, and students get up from their seats, chairs scraping and books snapping shut. I flip my hair over my shoulder as I bend down to grab my backpack, but a pair of chestnut leather shoes attached to long, lean legs covered in dark denim stop me in my tracks. I pause almost infinitesimally and return to the task at hand. I stand, swing my bag over one shoulder, and attempt to move past him. Mr. James sidesteps and blocks me, our fronts nearly bumping. I roll my eyes and pivot on my feet to walk the other way, but he grabs my wrist, causing me to freeze in place. Adrenaline courses through me at his touch, and I shake out of his grasp.

We're alone. In class. He wants to corner me again, but this time, I'm going to get the upper hand.

"Remington. Stop." He says my first name for the first time with an air of authority that has my belly flipping with desire. I turn around and paint my face with indifference.

"We've got to stop meeting like this, *Mr. James*," I say, biting my bottom lip. "Wouldn't want anyone to get the wrong idea."

"Cut the nonsense. What's going on with you today?" His brows are wrinkled, like he honestly doesn't know that he made my life significantly more complicated by one little conversation.

"You think you know me well enough after a few days to make that assessment? Well, you don't. I'm not some project for you to fix up to make you feel better about yourself. And I'd appreciate it if you stayed out of my business." I could get reprimanded for speaking to a faculty member like this, but I can't stop myself. All I want to do is keep a low profile, graduate, and get into a decent fucking college anywhere but here.

"What do you want from me?" I ask, moving in even closer. "Huh? What's your game?"

Mr. James drops his head back, and he sighs at the ceiling, hands on his hips.

He doesn't know. He doesn't fucking know what he wants from me. Or if he does, he sure as hell doesn't want to admit it to himself.

He is making me crazy. There's no other way to explain my next move. Maybe it's retaliation for him butting into my business. Maybe it's just an excuse to ruffle his feathers. But even as I do the unthinkable, the unimaginable, I still don't regret it. Not even with one bone in my body. I take a step in his direction and place my hand over the first button of my crisp dress shirt, toying with it.

"Do you want this?" I part my lips, my eyes dropping to his mouth. "Hmm? Is that it?"

He takes a step back immediately, and I release the button, exposing milky skin and a hint of cleavage. If I release the next one, he is going to see the valley of my fat, heavy tits that are secured by nothing but my tattered Walmart bra.

"Miss Stringer," he warns, but I know enough about Mr. James by now to know that this warning doesn't hold the usual authority. He knows he should stop me, and he is, but his attempt is half-assed at best.

My finger slides down to my second button, and I take another step in his direction. He takes another step back. We tango. I don't know if I'm fucking with him to show him that I'm dangerous, that he should just leave me be, or because I'm desperate for his reaction. His attention. God, his everything.

"You didn't answer my question, Mr. James." I pop free the second button, and my pushed-up tits are staring at him now, daring him to look at them. He doesn't. His eyes become hooded, and his nostrils flare.

"I didn't answer because I don't want to insult you. Would you really like an answer to your question?"

"Yes." I lick my lips, taking another step, and this time,

he doesn't even realize that he stopped walking backwards. We're almost chest-to-chest now, and I know how it would look if someone opens the door. He does, too, because he folds his arms over his chest and tilts his chin up, his stance guarded and stiff. So unlike his usual self-assured posture. Good thing it's lunchtime, or students would already be pouring in right about now.

"I'm not interested in high school girls, Miss Stringer."

"I think we both know I'm not your typical teenager, *Teach*," I retort. I'm pushing it, big time, but I want to see how far I can take this without getting my ass thrown into detention, or worse.

"Call me Teach one more time..." His face gets into mine, and hell, I see it. In his pupils. They're burning.

Yes, I'm not imagining this.

This is mutual. This is *magic*.

"And what?" I smile, shamelessly pushing my chest between us. "And what exactly are you going to do about it?" My voice turns cold in a second. "Stay out of my personal life. I will be the best student I can, Mr. James, but you don't get to talk to my stepbrother and stir *chaos* in my life." I throw the words we spoke in debate class in his face.

"I wasn't stirring anything, Remington. I was merely dropping a very subtle warning." His lips thin. I'm not sure who is scarier, him or Ryan. They are intimidating in very different ways. And lookie here, he referred to me by my first name again.

"I can take care of myself."

"I beg to differ. Look at your thigh."

"Maybe you should *stop* looking at it, Mr. James. Your job is to educate me, not to ogle me." I just went there.

"That's rich coming from the woman who's throwing

herself at her teacher," he whiplashes quickly. *A debate teacher, after all.*

"So now you admit that I'm a woman?" I smile sweetly, twirling a lock of chestnut hair around my finger, putting on a stupid show he can see right through.

That awards me with a smile, the first genuine smile I've seen from Mr. James. Funny, I haven't even noticed he doesn't really smile until now. But it is glorious and beautiful, and I want this smile to be only for me.

"You should be a lawyer, Miss Stringer," he says darkly, motioning with his head to the door, excusing me. "You'd be dangerous."

"I'm in the right class then." I shrug my backpack onto my shoulder and walk away. He collapses in the chair by his desk behind me and sighs.

"You're in the right class, but you're definitely the wrong kind of student."

⌒

"What's up with Mr. James?" Christian asks as he slings an arm around my shoulder on our way to the cafeteria. I snort and hitch one shoulder up.

"What do you mean?"

"He kept you after class. *Again.*" He wiggles his perfectly shaped eyebrows.

"Ugh," I groan as I toss his arm off of me. "He has it out for me. Not sure why." I like Christian a lot, but the less people I have knowing my business, the better.

"Ah-uh," he says, unconvinced.

"Miss Stringer." I recognize Headmaster Charles' curt voice and look up to see him down the hall, heading toward me. Jesus Christ, I can't catch a break in this place.

"I expect you'll have the proper shoe wear by next week?" I glance down at my Chucks that I've made exactly zero effort to replace.

"Working on it!" I promise.

"Very good."

"Looks like Mr. James isn't the only one who has it out for you," Christian whispers into my ear after Headmaster Charles passes.

"Shut up." I laugh and bump his shoulder with mine.

The cafeteria hall isn't crowded or noisy like Riverdale. God, even social hour is quiet for these people. *How boring.* Christian heads straight for the food line. I don't have lunch money today, so I pretend I'm not hungry. Christian doesn't buy it, but he doesn't press me either. Once we're seated, he tosses a roll in my direction.

"I said I wasn't hungry," I say, catching it with one hand.

"Gotta keep that booty ripe, Remi. *Ripe Remi.* That has a nice ring to it," he muses.

"You're an idiot."

"And you're stubborn. Are you really not going to tell me why he's kept you after class for two days in a row?"

"Can you keep it *down*?" I hiss, my eyes darting around to gauge whether we have any eavesdroppers. "There's nothing to tell."

"Then I guess you're not interested in the rumors about him," Christian teases.

"I wouldn't go *that* far. Show me yours and I'll show you mine?" I bat my eyelashes exaggeratedly.

"I don't usually play this game with girls," he drawls. "But for you, I'll make an exception. Spill it."

Taking a deep breath, I decide that there's no harm in

telling Christian about Ryan. For one, judging by his reaction to him the other day, I'm sure he already suspects something. And two, I just don't see Christian as the malicious type.

"My stepbrother is going through some stuff. He got a little rough with me the other day, and Mr. James noticed. He just wanted to make sure I was safe. Sort of part of the job description, you know?"

Christian shakes his head.

"I knew something was off with that guy."

"Seriously, Christian, I've lived with him for most of my life. He's not a threat. He's...struggling," I reiterate.

"Doesn't matter, babe. Don't be that girl. Don't make excuses for him."

"Listen, I'm not an idiot. I know Ryan, and he's not dangerous." Even as I say the words, I wonder if that's still true.

"Your turn," I remind him, taking a bite out of the softest roll I've ever had in my entire life.

"Okay, here's what I know. His first name is Pierce." *Pierce.* I never knew a name could be sexy, but I stand corrected. He looks like a Pierce. All dapper with a side of darkness. Brosnan has nothing on this guy.

"Twenty-nine years old," he continues. "Perpetually single, but never lacking female companions. He was teaching in California, but came here a couple years ago. Then, in the middle of the year, he left. He never came back," he says, pausing for dramatic effect. "Until now," he adds thoughtfully. "That's all I know."

"You got all of this information in less than a week? I don't even know the school's mascot, and you have everyone's life story."

"People like me." He shrugs. "It's a gift."

The warning bell rings, and we both stand.

"Knights," he says.

"Huh?" I ask dumbly.

"West Point Knights. That's our mascot." He winks.

"Noted." I laugh. "I'll be sure to file that under Things I Don't Give a Flying Fuck About."

Chapter Seven

Pierce

Tick, tick, tick.

She says her boyfriend is a ticking time bomb. That she never knows how he is going to show up. Nice and charming, or drunk and violent. I tell her that that's what you get for dating a junkie and a drug dealer. She doesn't listen. Gwen never listens.

The thing about my older sister is that she can be my parent and a child at the very same time. Like right now, when I see her lying in a pool of her own puke in the apartment that she shares with her roommate, Shelly, all I want to do is throw her into the bathtub, find the idiot who gave her the drugs, and finish him off.

"What's his name?" I take her by the arm and lead her to the bathroom. I wish I could take her home with me, but she'll never come. I wish I could stage an intervention, but my parents don't want anything to do with her anymore and they'll never be there. Standing there by myself, pleading her to take care of herself, will only be a reminder to the fact that no one but me cares.

"He's the best." She smiles to herself as I turn on the faucet and peel her out of her reeking clothes. She complies. A brother should never see his sister naked. Not at this age, anyway. "He is really sweet, Pierce. He is."

"Yeah? Somehow I doubt that. He sold you the drugs?"

She shakes her head. "Gave it to me for free. I'm sampling for him."

"You're sampling drugs for him?" I repeat her words, dumbfounded. The worst part is that she is a smart girl. Smart girls, I learned with time and experience, sometimes do very stupid things for men. Gwen ran away from California after she went to UCLA. She has a degree and speaks three languages. She could have been a very successful, very happy woman, if she wanted to be. But she doesn't. Instead, she followed me to Las Vegas and let herself get caught up with the wrong people. The wrong lifestyle.

What she wants is to defy our parents. And what she fails to understand is that they're not wired the same way as us. They cut all ties to her and moved on. They didn't care enough to raise us. Why would they care enough to look after us when we're grown?

"Rehab," I say, throwing her clothes to the trash. There's no point in washing them. I'll just buy her new ones. They're two times too big, anyway. Gwen has become rail thin and scarily bony the last couple of months. She's fading, and it physically hurts to watch. "You need to go to rehab, or I'll go back to California and cut all ties. I mean it, Gwen."

"Sure." She laughs. "Leave me. Just like them. It's not like I raised you."

"You did raise me," I agree. "You raised me, and now it's my turn to take care of you. Something that's a little hard to do when you're hell-bent on destroying yourself."

She laughs more hysterically, bordering on maniacal. I throw her into the bath, and it's ice-cold, and she deserves it.

"I hate you!" she screams, spitting in my face. I stare at her through leveled eyes.

"That's fine. Give me his address," I say. I'm ready to do something stupid, but I don't even care anymore.

"No." She crosses her arms over her chest, sitting in the full bath like a toddler.

"Gwen."

"No!"

"Fuck!" I punch the tiles.

"You won't take him from me!" she yells.

"Oh, we'll see about that."

Ryan Anderson.

I'm sitting in my car, staring at him from across the road as he works, bare-chested, on his motorcycle. I pulled Remington Stringer's address from the contact list online, and I did just so I could see where he lives. It has nothing to do with Remington and her advances, though I know that, logically, at some point I will need to make sure she knows that she can't pull that kind of stunt again.

It's not about Remington—not in the way Remington wants it to be about Remington—and she needs to know that. But I have plenty of time to clarify that to her. Right now, I'm more interested in Anderson.

Taking into consideration the fact that my car is probably going to stand out in his neighborhood, I parked around the corner of his street, where he can't see. But I can definitely see him and his inked chest glistening with sweat. The asshole doesn't look bad, and for some reason, that bothers me. The images of him touching and doing things to Gwen morph into ones of him with Remington, and the thought stirs something in me that I never knew existed.

I want revenge. Justice.

But I don't know the whole story, and it's killing me.

Remington Stringer is not emancipated, but I sure as hell don't know if her father or mother is around either. A Daniel Stringer signed every single school document for her. I assume that's her father, but I don't know how present he is. For all I know, Ryan is the only consistent person in her life.

That doesn't deter me from hunting him down and bringing justice to my sister's case, but for some reason, it gives me pause.

Beyond the tough exterior, Remington Stringer is a teenage girl who still needs to be taken care of, and I reluctantly recognize that.

I'm about to kick my vehicle into drive and leave. This was obviously a mistake. Stalking Ryan Anderson is not going to do me any good. If anything, it's just going to make me angrier about my inability to act on my desire to throw him in a cell. I know where he is now. That's what's important.

My hand is on the console, and I twist my head to see that the road is clear when I hear her voice and still.

"Dinner's ready, Ryan. Get your ass inside."

She jumps the three steps down from her door to the yard, wearing an oversized shirt—and just the thought of it being his has me clenching my jaw—her bare, naked legs are long, and her brown, wavy hair is flying everywhere from the hot wind. I shouldn't look. I don't *want* to look. My gaze drifts to the house next door, but then she speaks again.

"Ryan, I need a favor, and I really need you not to be crappy about it."

I can see her from my peripheral standing slightly above him, and he is peering down toward her shirt where her undergarments should be. I want to kill him and find my eyes following them again. It's not the fact that he is looking down Miss Stringer's shirt that bothers me. At least that's what I tell myself. It's the fact that he sees her as another victim. Just like Gwen.

"What do you need?" Anderson asks, his muscles flexing. Idiot. He is trying to seduce his stepsister, and for all I know, he might have already succeeded.

"Money for new shoes. I know you said you picked up some extra shifts at the shop…"

That actually makes me snort. If she really thinks that her stepbrother holds a legitimate job, she is dead wrong. I've been trying to find him everywhere in Vegas ever since Gwen died to no avail. And while it's a fairly small city, it is what you call *chaotic*. Vegas is the perfect place to disappear. All the lights, parties, tourists, and temptation. He did a great job.

Until now.

"What's wrong with your shoes?" Ryan puts his hands on his hips, scanning her legs. He stares at her in a way I can easily decode, even from across the street. I know this look because I sometimes give it to women, two seconds before

I rip off their underwear with my teeth.

"They have a dress code at West Point." She shrugs, moving her fingers through her hair. "Headmaster Charles has been bugging me about it. You know how they are. Stuck up and all."

"Well, money is tight this month."

"I thought you said you're going to buy a new toy hauler to go spend the summer in California." She clears her throat, and my heart breaks. It shouldn't, but it does. This girl is a far cry from the brazen one in my class.

"You keeping tabs on me?" Anderson asks, pushing his chest toward her. It reminds me how she pushed her chest to me earlier today. I was a little taken aback at how bold she was, but I didn't take into consideration the fact that it's all she knows. She doesn't know subtle. Wouldn't know it even if it hit her on the head.

"Not keeping tabs, Ry. Just trying not to get into too much trouble at my new school."

"Maybe you should get in trouble," Ryan retorts. "That way you can stay here and quit eating up all those fantasies about leaving they've been feeding you there. I know your game, Rem. Know it well."

Rem.

"Dinner's getting cold," she snaps, turning around and heading back into the shack they call home. I drive away, straight to the nearest mall.

Three, four, five pairs of smart, black-laced Oxford shoes in a few different sizes, just to be sure.

They'll be waiting in her locker first thing in the morning.

Miss Stringer is not going to end up like my sister did. I will make sure of that.

Chapter Eight

Remi

"Well, hello, Cinderella." Christian pretends to bow down for me when I meet him in the hallway, stuffing my textbooks into my locker and throwing it shut. I huff, rolling my eyes. This day can't get any worse.

"You heard," I deadpan.

"I don't think there's a soul on campus who hasn't heard yet." Christian is matching my steps, and he looks extra bouncy today. His smile extra wide. "So, who is the secret admirer?"

"Maybe it's not an admirer. Maybe it's a joke at my expense because I'm not fucking loaded like everyone else." I shrug, stretching my toes inside my beat-up Chucks. Whether it was a way to taunt me or not, I don't care. I refuse to wear them. When I got into school this morning, an arsenal of new shoes waited inside my locker. I'm not going to lie. I was tempted to try them on, but my pride—and general mistrust of basically everyone here besides Christian—wouldn't let me. Unfortunately, a few students roaming the hallway caught a glimpse of it, and word got out that someone bought me shoes. I became a charity case. The one thing I refuse to ever be.

"Whatever. Look at you. You're a head turner." Christian smiles, stopping by his locker and twisting the lock until it pops open. He checks his phone discreetly, and like the nosy bitch I am, I peek over his shoulder.

"What the hell is that?" I screech, reaching for it with my hand, but Christian is faster.

"Remi!" he barks.

"What?" I laugh, because he is blushing, and I didn't think it was even possible for him to get flustered by anything. "Please tell me that was a dick pic."

"It's nothing." He looks down to his shoes.

"Why are you acting so embarrassed? Christian Chambers, you are *blushing*!" He rolls his eyes. "Is this, like, a random Tinder guy, or are you seeing someone?"

"I'm *talking* to someone."

"A secret someone?" I hedge, leaning closer, my ears perking up. He nods, looking somewhat defeated. My smile disappears, melting into a frown.

"Someone who is still in the closet," I guess.

No response. Oh, that *is* juicy, but also not any of my business. The only part I really hate about this whole conversation is the fact that Christian doesn't confide in me. I gave him all the information about Ryan, so I thought maybe he'd open up for me, too. But then, to be completely honest, I didn't tell him the whole truth about Mr. James or my little Alicia Silverstone a la *The Crush* act either, so I can't be too mad.

"Okay, we don't have to talk about it." I pat his arm awkwardly. "Just let me know when you do. I'd be happy to be a shoulder for you to cry on, or, you know, listen to some steamy gossip about you and your boy toy."

"Thanks."

We go our separate ways, and I make a quick stop into Headmaster Charles' office. An office aide delivered a slip informing me to stop by his office on my lunch break. His secretary gives me the green light, and I'm about to enter when a familiar voice has me pausing. The door is cracked, and my heart stops when I see Mr. James. I start to turn around to leave, but against my better judgment, I stay. I can only see a sliver of him, sitting in the chair in front of the desk, and I can't see Headmaster Charles at all.

"I just wanted to make sure you're holding up, considering—" Headmaster Charles' voice is low and concerned.

"I'm fine," Mr. James cuts him off sharply.

"Well, that may be true. And if it is, I'm glad to hear it. I just don't want to have another repeat of last year."

What happened last year?

"That won't happen," Mr. James assures him. I hear movement, and then Headmaster Charles stands next to him, clapping him on the back.

"Let me know if you need anything."

Mr. James nods, then stands, and I take that as my cue to bail. I tiptoe to the chairs waiting outside his office and sit down just before they open the door. I plaster on a fake smile that fades once I see the expression on Mr. James' face. He looks angry and uncomfortable, and even though I'm not sure what that conversation was about, I have the urge to hug him. I'm not even sure why I'm so affected by him, but my red face betrays me. I shouldn't have pulled that shit on him yesterday.

"Miss Stringer." Mr. James nods curtly, his mask slipping back into place.

"Yes?" Headmaster Charles peeks at me over Mr. James' broad shoulder. I imagine what those shoulders would look like as he holds himself up on his forearms and thrusts inside me. My thoughts can't be healthy, but at the same time, it's natural. I'm willing to bet that I'm not the first student with a schoolgirl crush.

"Headmaster Charles." I ignore Mr. James completely, choking the door handle and flashing a flaccid smile. "I was told you wanted to speak with me."

"Actually, Miss Stringer, I was just checking in to see if you've managed to correct your shoe situation," he says, glancing down at my feet. "But I can see that's a no—and to see how you are otherwise adjusting."

"I'm still working on it," I explain, avoiding Mr. James' penetrating stare. "And I can't complain. Everything else is going well."

"Very good." He nods.

"Is that all?" I ask hopefully. I can feel him looking at me accusingly, as if he knows I was eavesdropping.

"You're excused," he says, walking back into his office.

Chapter Nine

Pierce

"**P**ierce, you have to help her! She's barely breathing, and she's not responsive. She's fucking blue, Pierce! Please, hurry! I don't… I don't know what to do!"

That's the voice message that's waiting for me from Shelly three months after my sister starts going out with Ryan Anderson, and I have to take the rest of the day off and run to her place. I take her to the hospital. Stay with her for the whole period—two whole days—never leaving her side.

Anderson never bothers to visit her. Not even once.

Can't say I'm half-surprised.

She isn't exactly in a coma, but she is out of it for long hours. When she finally opens her eyes, she smiles at me apologetically, and for one heartbreaking minute, she looks like the girl I used to know, the one who took me for an ice cream every Friday and helped me decorate the Christmas tree we had to order online because our parents never bothered to buy one.

"It wasn't Ryan, Pierce. It was me. I did too much. He told me it was laced with something, that it wouldn't take as much to get me high, but I guess I got a little carried away."

I'm not a religious person, but if there's a God, he needs to kill Ryan Anderson. Strike him down here and now. I clasp her hand in mine and smile, pretending not to give a damn, even though I do.

"It's okay. Can I have his phone number?" I gave up on getting his address a long time ago, and now the only thing stopping me from finding out the information myself is the stupid loyalty I have for my sister. "I just want to let him know you're okay."

Gwen frowns, seeing through me, even in her state. "Pierce, no. I told you. This one's on me."

No, it's not, Gwen.

No, it's not.

After they discharge her, I lock her in my apartment. She doesn't have a key, and I guess she can try to jump from the second floor I live on if she really wants to, but she won't. That's the only thing that gives me hope. Gwen doesn't want to die. She just wants to be loved. Too bad she is looking for that love in the wrong place. From the wrong person.

I go to work, come back, and find out that my lock has been doctored. It can't be Gwen because she is still a rich little girl from California at her core. But I know who it could be, and I'm glad I finally get to meet him.

Walking into my apartment, I find them lying on my sofa. Naked. Looking dead to the world.

I now have a face to the name. Ryan Anderson still looks

like a kid. But also like a thug. He is tall and tan with trouble written all over his face. And he is slowly killing my sister.

I grab him by the throat and squeeze. His eyes are slow to adjust, and it takes him a minute to come out of his drug-induced daze.

"If you give her drugs again, I am going to fucking end you." I smile, my voice easy. He's so high off whatever the fuck his drug of choice is that he doesn't seem to know where he is or what's going on. I doubt he even knows what planet he's on.

"What the fuck," he says, scrambling and tripping out in slow motion.

I throw his clothes out the door and kick him out, hoping he'll never come back.

⌒

"Is age an important factor in a relationship?" Samantha asks, tapping her chin with her pencil. Every Friday, I let my students pick the subject they'd like to debate. I find it makes them more interested and engaged in class, and it also keeps me in touch with their interests. I'm not that old. Twenty-nine is not exactly ancient, but I don't have the time or the need to read their magazines and watch their stupid movies and shows to stay in the loop. So I take it. And every year without fail, this subject comes up.

"All right, Miss LaFirst, let's hear your introduction to the subject." I lean on my desk and listen to her. Herring, the preppy fuck who sits to Remington's right, is slipping notes to her. I ignore them, if only to remind myself that I don't have a particular interest in Miss Stringer herself, but in her brother. I better remember that, because the lines are beginning to blur, just a tad, and that makes me somewhat uncomfortable.

LaFirst talks. She makes sense. The class starts the discussion.

"I would not date an old dude." A girl from class, Tiffany, snorts, widening her eyes. "I mean, what would be his motivation? Is he just a creep after fresh meat? Or does he want someone he can manipulate because I'm not as experienced as he is?"

"I would totally date an older guy!" another girl, Faith Matthews, exclaims. "In the end, it's all about the connection and the chemistry between two individuals. Right, Mr. James?" She held herself back from winking at me. *Just.* I lift a brow.

"There are many issues you still haven't touched. I want you to dig deeper into this subject: laws, expectations, stigmas, interest, and goals," I answer dryly, my eyes scanning the class. I see Herring—the idiot—slipping another note into Remington's palm. I haven't even seen her open any of them, so I can't pick on her. Not that I should want to, but it's making me irrationally angry.

"Mr. Herring, anything to contribute to this conversation?"

He raises his head and grins slyly. This kid is a tool, and if it wasn't for the fact that Mommy and Daddy are loaded, he wouldn't have a single friend here.

"What? How I feel about dating a MILF? I think I would. I mean, why not? Though for now, I'm sticking to high school girls. I even have my eye on one in particular." He winks and pretends to elbow Remington, though they are too far apart. Remington's expression is bored and apathetic. It placates me a bit, even though it shouldn't.

"Yeah, like your *girlfriend*?" Mikaela Stephens snaps,

and Herring doesn't even look a little sorry.

"My bad, babe. I forgot you were here." He laughs, and his friends follow suit. *Dumbasses.*

"Miss Stringer?" I ask, before I can stop myself. Not that it looks suspicious. She regularly partakes in these discussions, and everyone is expected to participate. It's because I am too fascinated with this girl, and it unnerves me.

"I wouldn't care about the stigma," she says, her eyes still stuck on the board behind me.

"And the expectations?" Herring asks. The class laughs, and I find I'm actually curious to know her answer.

"I'm fine with the expectations, too." She doesn't even blink.

"Well, you look like a ride or die chick." Schwartz laughs.

"You look like a biker chick," Miss Matthews mumbles.

"No need to sugarcoat it. The term you're looking for is 'white trash.'" Mikaela Stephens snorts. My head snaps up.

"Stephens, come again, please," I say, as indifferent as I possibly can be. She lifts her head from the doodles on the notebook in front of her and opens her mouth, at a loss for words. She didn't think I'd hear. Mikaela Stephens. The senator's grandchild. A cheerleader. The poster child for everything empty and superficial herself.

"Sorry, Mr. James," she mumbles.

"That's not what you said." I smile easily. "And that's not what I asked. Repeat your last sentence, Miss Stephens."

She looks left and right, clearly uncomfortable. I chance a glance at Remington. It doesn't look like she cares too much, and that not only puts me at ease, but makes me feel a misdirected sense of pride.

Mikaela repeats her words, looking down, looking guilty.

"Miss Stephens, a word after class," I say. She nods.

We continue the discussion. The bell rings. Everybody stands up but Stephens. Remington, included. "You, too, Miss Stringer."

"Again?" Herring mutters, annoyed, as he flings his backpack over his shoulder and stalks to the door. I need to stop. I need to stop this, but the prospect of revenge is too much to resist. I tell myself it has nothing to do with this invisible pull I feel when it comes to Remington.

I sit behind my desk.

"Stephens, come sit next to Stringer."

She does without hesitation. For a split second, I think she might challenge me, but then I remember that Remington Stringer is the only girl at West Point who ever would. And the only one crazy enough to get off on it.

"Apologize to Miss Stringer."

"I'm sorry," she tells Remington, who doesn't even acknowledge her. She continues picking at her chipped black nail polish. "I didn't mean that."

Yes, she did.

"Miss Stephens," I pull out the detention slip, "two days."

"Oh my God! Are you serious?" She flings her arms in the air, exasperated.

"A week," I say easily. "Starting Monday."

She cups her mouth with her hand, her eyes wide, shaking it back and forth. She knows what's going to happen if another word slips between her lips. I scribble on the detention slip, tear it off the pad, and hand it to her with a smile. "In my world, your actions today in class classify as bullying. I will not tolerate bullying, in any shape or form. Am I clear?"

"Yes, sir."

She stands up and walks out of the classroom, slamming the door behind her. Remington is still in her seat.

"You can go now, Stringer," I say. What I fail to add is I don't want her to. What the hell is wrong with me?

She lifts her face from her hands finally and smiles.

"I've been thinking about you this week."

Oh, fuck no. I get up and gather my things. Laptop, notebook, wallet, and keys.

"You're excused, Miss Stringer. Don't test my patience. Not again."

"Do you like my shoes?" she asks, parting her legs open a few inches. Not a lot. Enough to make me want to peek and see what's between them—the way her stepbrother did the other day—and that thought makes me feel like a scumbag.

I don't know why she's still wearing her old shoes, and she's obviously baiting me, but I don't give anything away.

"Not particularly," I say shortly. "If you don't evacuate my room in ten seconds, I will take it as a sign you would like to join your good friend, Stephens, in detention."

"I don't mind." She shrugs. "It's not like I have a ride home today. My stepbrother is out of town."

I swallow.

"Stringer," I warn.

"*Pierce*," she retorts.

Reluctantly, I move my eyes to look at her. My desk is clean, and it's time for me to move my feet and *go*. Her legs are wide open, and all I have to do is scroll down and see her panties. She smiles. She knows what she is doing to me, and it makes me want to break all the rules and show her that she's not the only one who can be brazen. *Fuck, I invented brazen, sweetheart.*

"Close your legs." I blink away, fast. "If you pull this kind of shit on me one more time, I'm telling Headmaster Charles. You claim to want out of your situation, but you know what I think? I think you're scared." On the surface, she appears unfazed, cocking a sardonic brow. But I know my words are getting to her if the pursing of her lips is any indication. Her lower lip trembles just a tad. I show no mercy. She needs to hear it.

"You're scared," I repeat. "You have a chance here, and now that it's a real possibility, you have no idea how to handle it. So, here you are, seducing your teacher. Sabotaging your opportunity because this life, in this city, is all you know."

"Is that what I'm trying to do?" Her red lips curve into a smile, her walls rising back up, higher than ever before. God, this woman. Yes, *woman.* Little girls are not my type. Never have been. But Remington Stringer is only technically a teenager. She is so much older than her years.

"I don't care what you're trying to do." I take a step toward the door, tilting my head, signaling her to join me. "I just want you out of here."

"Why can't I stay? Maybe you're the one who's afraid?"

"I'm locking the door behind you."

"Maybe you should lock it with us inside." She grins.

Blood rushes to my dick, and I really need to get out of here.

"You just earned yourself a week of detention."

"Fine." She pouts her pretty lips in a way that makes me think she just got exactly what she wanted. When she stands, I allow myself a quick fix, checking out her creamy, long legs and hourglass figure. I need to blow off steam tonight. This girl is trouble of the worst variety.

I hold the door open for her, and she finally leaves, swaying her hips exaggeratedly. *Fuck. Me.*

I watch her leave, resisting the urge to offer her a ride once school is out.

We're not even going in the same direction.

Not only geographically, but in life.

Chapter Ten

Remi

I sit, dangling my feet from the bench at the bus station with my camera on my lap, still stuck on my exchange with Mr. James. Part of me finds his attempt at psychoanalyzing me annoying, but the way he looks at me—like I'm every rule he's ever wanted to break—gives me a high like no other.

I check my phone for the time. I don't even know when the bus hits this part of town, and I'm just hoping I'll get home in time before it's too dark to walk the streets. Ryan is not around today—said he was going to check out a toy hauler a few hours away from home—and I really should have thought this one through. Maybe I should get some mace. Or pepper spray. Something to make me feel a tad safer. Even though, I argue inwardly, most of the people I should stay away from are the ones that usually hang out on my front lawn.

At least I have that going for me.

I didn't care too much about Mikaela's jab. Surprised Mr. James did. Then again, maybe it was just another way for him to embarrass me. And it seems like every time he does, I try to one-up him and beat him at his own game. Pushing back has always been something that I liked doing. It's a daily struggle to stay neutral.

You're playing it smart, Remi.

Listening to Queens of the Stone Age and mouthing the words to "No One Knows," I still when I hear a familiar voice.

"Get in."

I look up and see Mr. James. I'm more than a little shocked to see him here. Though he doesn't look happy about seeing me at all. I see the indecision warring on his face.

I stub a finger to my chest. "Me?"

"Yeah, you. It's just a ride. I happen to know you don't live in the best neighborhood, and it is my duty as an educator to keep you safe."

Again with this bullshit. Is he trying to convince himself or me? I smile and hop from the bench. "You give me detention and then a ride home? Whatever you say. You're the boss."

I grab my bag and head toward his SUV.

"Sweet minivan," I joke as I slide into the smooth leather seats that burn the backs of my thighs. This heat is no joke. He only looks mildly irritated at my jab.

"It's an Audi Q7," he explains as he pulls away from the curb, like I'm supposed to know what that means. I raise my eyebrows questioningly, causing him to sigh, exasperated. "Never mind."

"So, am I just supposed to ignore the fact that you know where I live?" I can't assume that he sought me out. Not when he's vehemently shut down my advances. But, I can't seem to come up with another explanation either.

"Buckle up," he deadpans, giving me a sideways glance, avoiding my question. *Interesting.* Maybe he did look me up. I do as he says and buckle my seatbelt, stealing a glance at him, and literally feel my stomach flip. From his black Wayfarers and his perfectly disheveled hair to the way his forearm flexes when he grips the gearshift, he's fucking flawless. I wish I could reach into my backpack and pull out my camera to capture him in this moment. And I decide to do just that.

Mr. James doesn't even notice at first, but the sound of the shutter has his head snapping in my direction, his brows furrowed.

"What are you doing?" he asks, suspicion lacing his voice.

"Calm down, Teach. It's just a picture." I take a few more. His hand on the gear, my feet up on his dash, the new mural on the freeway.

I put my camera away, and my eyes trail their way back up to his. I can't tell for sure through the sunglasses, but I'm pretty damn sure he's zeroed in on my thighs, and his throat bobs with a hard swallow. My hands fist the edge of my skirt nervously, and I adjust my legs that are sticking to the hot leather seat. His head jerks up, and he clears his throat and focuses back on the road. I'm flushed and on fire, but it's not from the Vegas sun.

I bite my lip to keep from saying something stupid

and rest my forehead against the window. Flirting comes as naturally as breathing to me, but it's one thing to bait him at school. This little game feels all too real off school grounds and in the intimate space of his car.

As we get closer to my house, my stomach is flipping for a very different reason. I don't want him to see where I live. He says he knows, but *knowing* my address and *seeing* where I live are two completely different things. I hate that I'm ashamed of something I have no control over, and at that I feel a twinge of guilt. My dad works hard to keep a roof over our heads, and there's no shame in that. I half expect Mr. James to ask for directions, but sure enough, he knows exactly where he's going.

I don't notice him at first, because our street is lined with shitty cars parked every which way, blocking my view of the driveway, but when I see Ryan and his friend Reed in the yard, my whole body fills with dread. And when I notice the beer in his hand, that dread turns into panic. What the hell is he doing home? And why wasn't he there to pick me up if he was in town? I whip my head around, my wide eyes pleading with his to understand. Mr. James' jaw flexes, and he shakes his head imperceptibly. He's not going to make this easy on me.

"Thanks for the ride. See you tomorrow?"

He unbuckles his seatbelt, and I turn to see if Ryan has noticed our arrival. Oh, he has, all right, and he's marching straight toward us.

"Don't," I implore before Ryan is in earshot. "I don't have the energy to deal with this tonight."

"Deal with what, exactly, Remington? I thought you said you weren't in any kind of danger?" I roll my eyes and hop out, coming face-to-face with Stepbrother Dearest.

He's in a muscle tank and grease-stained jeans, his massive ink-covered arms crossed over his chest.

"You play chauffeur to all your students?" Ryan flicks his chin in Mr. James' direction. I don't dare look at him, but I feel him come stand behind me and I sigh, knowing this isn't going to end well.

"Just making sure she gets home safe since no one else cared to," he says as he presses his palm to my lower back. It's meant to be a polite gesture, I'm sure, but I know Ryan, and he's not going to see it that way. I can't even pretend that the weight of his large, warm palm on the small of my back doesn't affect me. His pinky finger rests on the small space of skin above my skirt, where my shirt has ridden up, and if we were anywhere else, I'd be tempted to ask him to show me how good his hands can make me feel on other parts of my body. But Ryan notices the placement of his hand, and I know I have about two seconds to act before shit hits the fan.

Annnd here we go.

Ryan grips my bicep and pulls me out of the way. My foot catches on a rock in the yard, causing me to stumble into him.

"Get in the house, Rem," Ryan says as he chugs the rest of his beer and wipes his mouth with the back of his hand. He tosses the empty bottle into the graveyard of bottles in our yard.

"Ry, he's my *teacher*. Don't be ridiculous."

"Remi. House. Now."

"She's not a dog, man." At that, Ryan lunges at Mr. James, but I manage to jump in between them before he makes contact. My hands are on his chest, and I know he could flick me away like an insect, but he doesn't. His breaths are coming out short and fast through his nose, and I know I need to diffuse the situation before he loses control. Once again.

Tick, tick, tick.

"Ry, take me inside." My voice is steady and calm, belying the anxiety swirling in my gut. He doesn't answer me. Ryan seems to be shooting daggers out of his eyes while Mr. James appears almost bored.

"Yo. Let's go." Ryan's arm wraps around my hip possessively, and I know I've gotten through.

"Don't touch my fucking girl again. Don't talk to her. Don't even *look* at her unless she's in class. I won't tell you again."

I lead Ryan toward the house, and this time, he lets me. Reed tags along behind us. After we're inside, he goes straight for the fridge and grabs another beer. I set my backpack on the kitchen counter and look out the window, only to lock eyes with Mr. James. He's leaning against his car, arms crossed over his chest, and a scowl on his face. I bite my lip and look back at Ryan who is already firmly planted on the couch next to Reed, downing another beer, oblivious to our little staring contest.

"Thank you," I mouth silently. Mr. James nods once and heads back to the driver's side. Despite the drama, I feel a smile tugging at my lips. He feels something. He has to.

"What the fuck are you so happy about? I mean it, Rem. Stay the fuck away from him. He's bad news." At that, I have to laugh.

"He's bad news? You're the one who bailed on me, leaving me to find my way home, and for what? To get drunk with this asshole in the middle of the day?" I fling my arm in Reed's direction. "No offense, Reed."

He burps and wiggles his eyebrows. "None taken."

"It was just a ride. And stop telling people I'm yours. It's creepy."

"It's the fucking truth," he seethes. "And I had a change of plans. Shit happens, Rem, and believe it or not, my life doesn't revolve around you." *I wish that were true.*

"Dick," I mumble and turn back to the kitchen.

I make myself a turkey sandwich, grab a water bottle, and head to my room for the night. I'm not making dinner for those fuckers. I have a feeling they're drinking their dinner tonight, anyway.

⌒

I wake up to rough hands pawing at my chest through my tank top and the scent of beer invading my nostrils. "Ryan, stop," I croak out—my voice still groggy from sleep—as I throw an elbow into his gut. These middle-of-the-night meetings are becoming more frequent, and it's equal parts irritating and alarming.

"C'mon, Rem. I need it." I feel his hard-on pressing into my ass, and I wiggle away.

"You're drunk. Get out of my bed."

"Make me," he slurs as he flips me onto my back and pins me with his weight. "Have you been giving this sweet little body to your teacher, Rem? Is that why you don't want me anymore? That pretty boy can't make you feel like I can. Let me show you." He starts tugging at my sleep shorts, and that's what has me snapping out of my sleepy haze.

"Get off me!" I thrash beneath him and manage to heave his drunk ass off me, and he lands on the floor with a resounding *thud.*

"Fuck, Rem!" he yells, still laid out on the tiny space between the wall and my bed. I know he could easily overpower me and take what he wants, but he doesn't. He won't. I know deep down, Ryan would never hurt me like that. He pounds his fist into my wall three times before standing up and storming out. I don't even say a word. I stare at the ceiling, wondering how we got to this point. My stepbrother, best friend, and childhood hero has turned into someone I don't even recognize. Every pivotal moment in our lives plays out in my head, and I dissect them all—wondering what we could've done differently—until the sun comes up. When it does, I've come to two conclusions. And it's nothing I didn't already know.

Ryan needs help, and I need to get the fuck out of here.

Ryan was gone all weekend, and my dad called to let me know that he was picking up another route, so I was home alone. Extreme boredom had me calling Christian, and he came to my rescue. I spent two full days drinking poolside in a house more gorgeous and luxurious than I ever knew existed. His parents weren't home, so we had access to their endless supply of alcohol. Christian seemed to need the distraction about as much as I did, but we had an unspoken agreement. Don't ask; don't tell. I decided to save my interrogation for Monday, which is today.

I expect to have to drag Ryan out of bed to take me to school after I get ready, but to my surprise, he's pacing the hall outside my door, fisting his greasy hair with both hands.

"I'm sorry, Rem. I'm sorry I'm fucked up." He pulls me in for a hug, and I revel in the familiarity. No matter how unstable he becomes, I think his arms will always feel like safety to me. It doesn't make sense, and it's certainly not healthy, but it's us. I run my hand up and down his back in a soothing manner, and he keeps talking.

"I've got the weight of the world on my back. I don't know how to fix things. The things I've done…" he trails off. He's rambling, not making any sense. I can feel his heart pounding in his chest, and his eyes look crazed.

"What do you mean? What did you do?" Ice fills my veins. As if he suddenly realizes what he said, he stands up straight and disconnects from me.

"Come on. You're gonna be late for school," he says, effectively changing the subject. I nod slowly, not knowing what to say or do for him, and grab my backpack off the counter. I stuff a banana and a water bottle into my bag and head outside.

"Have you slept at all?" I scan him, worry tugging an invisible string in my heart. He looks like complete shit. His eyes are red, and his skin looks clammy.

"I'm fine. Mind your business."

Ryan is fidgety on the way to school, tapping his handlebars at every stoplight and jiggling his knee. Even when he pulls into the West Point parking lot, he can't seem to get me off his bike fast enough, and he takes off before I can even mutter a 'thank you'. He seems nervous. Paranoid, almost, with the way his eyes dart around, constantly surveying his surroundings.

After first period, I can't find Christian anywhere, so I head to second period early. When I see that Mr. James is the only one there, I rethink my decision. I stop short in the doorway and hesitate a minute being turning around to leave.

"Come in, Miss Stringer. Have a seat," he says casually, not giving any indication if Friday made things weird for him or not.

"I, uh, didn't know you'd be here already," I say lamely.

He gives me a brisk nod before returning his attention to his laptop.

I make my way to my desk and notice that our papers from last class are graded and waiting. I spot the B minus on mine and roll my eyes. That was an A paper, no doubt. I flip to the second page and notice a sticky note attached that reads:

Remington,
If you ever find yourself in trouble.
702-639-0628

Holy. Shit. My teacher just gave me his number. Part of me wants to do a happy dance in my desk, but my giddiness dies when I realize that it's for all the wrong reasons. Or, I guess, the *right* reasons. He feels sorry for me.

"What the hell is this?" I ask, waving the note attached to my finger.

"It's exactly what it says it is. You don't seem to have a parent around. Your source of transportation is your unreliable, unstable stepbrother. And you live in the roughest part of Vegas."

"And? That's your business, how?" My wounded pride has me acting like a snot, but I can't help it.

"It's not. I just…" He sighs and scrubs a hand across his jaw. "I've seen firsthand what can happen to girls in your shoes," he says cryptically while he gets a far-away look in his eyes. It's an unexpectedly candid moment free of any

sarcasm, and some of my irritation melts away. I don't
know what to make of it.

"You know many poor girls with absent but well-mean-
ing fathers and borderline obsessive stepbrothers from the
hood, do you?" I push my lower lip out and nod. His usual
aloof mask falls back into place at my teasing, and the bell
rings.

"Save the damn number, Miss Stringer."

"Yes, sir," I say sardonically. When he looks up at me
again, I swear I see a hint of a smirk, but he wipes it away
the second students start to pour into the classroom, and
the moment is gone.

During class, I sneak my phone under my desk and
program his number. In a moment of bravery, or maybe
temporary insanity, I scrawl out my number on the back
of the Post-it. He's standing in front of his desk when we're
dismissed, and I take my time packing up so I'm the last
one out. As soon as the last person stands, I follow and slip
the Post-it into his palm. His warm hand squeezes mine,
and he rubs his thumb over my wrist before jerking his
hand away, pocketing my number with a quickness. His
eyes dart around to make sure no one else saw, then he
looks at me expectantly.

"In case *you* ever need *me*," I explain, unable to hide
my grin. His eyebrow cocks in amusement, and I walk
away, my hand still burning from his touch.

"Somebody got laid," Christian jokes upon seeing the
stupid grin still firmly fixed on my face. He hooks an arm
through mine.

"I wish."

"I can help with that," Benton Herring—the kid from
second period that likes to harass me—says as he takes my

books out of my hands.

"No thanks," I snap, reaching to snatch my books back.

"Whoa, whoa, whoa, I'm just trying to be a gentleman here." Benton laughs as he holds my books over my head.

"Dude, come on," I whine. "I have first lunch today, and it's pizza day. *Pizza*," I stress. "I'll never forgive you if they run out before I get a piece. Or seven."

"Agree to go out with me tomorrow, and I will."

"Ew," I say, crinkling up my nose, because it is the only appropriate response to that.

"Tick-tock, baby girl. Pizza goes pretty quickly."

Before I can even roll my eyes at his little game, Christian steps in front of me and shoves Benton. Hard. His back hits the lockers, and he looks almost as confused as I am.

Well, that escalated quickly.

"Quit being a dick and give her the fucking books," Christian demands through clenched teeth. Benton throws my books down and pushes Christian back.

"What the fuck's your problem? If I didn't know you were gayer than a bag of dicks, I might think you're jealous." Benton looks smug, but it doesn't last long because Mr. James is now walking toward us looking his tall, imposing, sexy as fuck self.

"Break it up, ladies," Mr. James says, sounding bored as he looks between Dumb and Dumber. Neither one says a word.

I don't even know what the fuck just happened. Up until now, Benton was a harmless douche. A cocky little fucker who's annoying but never malicious. But even more shocking is Christian's behavior. I don't even know *what* triggered that reaction.

When Mr. James is tired of their silent act, he orders everyone to get moving.

I bend over to grab my scattered books and head to lunch.

⌒⌐

"Hey, Remi, right?" I turn toward the voice, and a little raven-haired Hispanic girl is hurrying in my direction.

"Yeah, what's up?" I ask as I adjust my knee sock in the hall. School is out, but I still have detention. *Awesome.*

"I'm Samantha LaFirst. Or just Sam. We have second period together?" she states it as a question.

"Oh, yeah, that's right. I think we have English together, too."

"Yep." She nods. "You need a poncho for the first row in that class." She laughs.

"So I've noticed," I grumble.

"Anyway, I'm an office aide for my third period, and Christian told me to tell you not to wait up. He went home."

"I figured as much." Something's up with him today. "Thanks for letting me know, though."

"For sure. See you tomorrow."

My phone buzzes in my hand, and I see a text from my dad.

Hey, Hurricane. Just stopping for lunch and thought I'd check in. Staying out of trouble?

Dad calls me Hurricane Remi. Says I'm a force to be reckoned with, like my mom, and always causing trouble. *If he only knew the kind of trouble I was looking for.* I decide to respond later because I need to get to detention. Just as I turn the corner by Mr. James' class, Mikaela comes into view.

"What are you looking at?" she snaps.

"I'm not really into snap judgments, but if I had to guess, I'd say I'm looking at an entitled, narcissistic little girl who is threatened by anyone other than herself getting attention and wears her mean girl mask to hide her insecurities. But, like I said, I'm not into snap judgments."

Mikaela's mouth drops open, but I don't give her a chance to respond. I walk directly to my seat in Mr. James' class. Mikaela steps in behind me, all but pouting.

"Ladies," Mr. James greets from behind his desk. "Read. Do your homework. Contemplate the meaning of life. I don't care. No phones and no talking."

I give him a mock salute and pull out a notebook. His mouth twitches. Mikaela sighs dramatically and studies her nails. It's going to be a long week.

⌒

I don't know what I was expecting to accomplish or achieve with detention, but whatever it was—it didn't happen. Maybe it was Mikaela's presence in the room—it had to be, I convince myself—because Pierce James has never been so cold and disinterested in me in our entire short relationship.

It's been five torturous days of detention. Five days of being in the same room as Mr. James and having to act unaffected. Five days of ignoring death stares from Mikaela. Five days of watching her shamelessly attempt to flirt her way out of detention and resisting the urge to strangle her. It's been five days of hell, so why don't I feel happy that it's over?

"All right, Miss Stringer, Miss Stephens. Detention is officially over. Let's try not to waste any more of each other's time in the future." Mikaela is out the door before he even finishes his sentence. I take a slower approach, contemplating my next move.

"Everything okay, Miss Stringer?" Mr. James asks as I study the doodles in my notebook.

"Everything is fine," I mutter, tapping my finger against my full lips. The truth of the matter is, detention is not all that bad. I get to stare at him, which probably isn't healthy, but it's nice, and when you're in my position, you take every little good thing that comes your way. I get to do my homework. Ryan is always late to pick me up anyway, so it's not like I'd be getting more free time if I didn't have detention. Oh, and let's not forget—it's not like I'm in a hurry to get home.

"Well, time to pack a bag," Mr. James says, leaning forward, his palms flat against his desk. "And. Leave."

Reluctantly, I gather my things. I see his eyes scanning me. I see him contemplating, too. He wants to ask me if I have a ride. I do. But I would ditch Ryan somehow if he'd ask. Only Mr. James doesn't ask. He turns around and leaves.

⁓

I stand corrected.

I don't have a ride—not for another forty minutes. Ryan texted me saying that he worked at the auto shop 'til late and is just now on his way, so I have time to burn.

At first, I loiter by the fountain at the entrance, but then I spot Mr. James walking to the nearest convenience store by foot. Since I'm an idiot with no self-control, I do the only thing I absolutely shouldn't be doing—take the camera out of my backpack and follow him.

It's not such a big operation to pull off, when you think about it. West Point is bang in the middle of a vast, broad, tree-lined street that looks like it's been copied and pasted from a movie—the complete opposite of where I live. Suburbia-galore and packed with preppy, middle-aged women in obnoxiously big sunglasses, shopping with their daughters. In other words, I manage to follow him without being noticed. I stand behind a tree and ogle him as he enters the store. Through the glass, I see him plucking out a can of Cherry Coke and walking to the register.

Click, click, click.

He points at two things behind the guy who rings him up, and the latter throws a pack of cigarettes and condoms into his bag.

Click, click.

Slowly, I lower my camera and squint. My heart is galloping, slamming into my ribcage, and now it's not just because I am borderline stalking the man who teaches me. Condoms? I mean, logically, I shouldn't be surprised. He's gorgeous. What exactly am I expecting him to do? Turn down women his own age for his student? Nonetheless, it feels like betrayal.

He shouldn't be with anyone else.

Hell, I know I'm talking crazy—thinking crazy, to be exact—but he just shouldn't.

It's a dangerous game, but apparently, I'm still playing it, because when he leaves the store with his bag of sex and the cigarette after, I follow him still. He doesn't walk back to the school grounds. He goes in the other direction, toward a small café. Seeing him like this, in broad daylight, outside of school, gives me a new perspective on Pierce James. I see how people look at him—how women look at him—and realize that whatever draws me to him captures other women, too. He is so tall, so commanding—you can't not look. And I really should stop looking. He's made it very clear that he wants nothing to do with me, and even if he did, what the heck am I saying? I need to focus on getting out of here, not on screwing my way into another problem.

Click. Click, click.

My camera captures him shaking a guy's hand. I don't recognize the other man, but why would I? A crazy thought hits me. Maybe Pierce is gay. Maybe he bought the condoms so he can go to town with this dude. Unlikely. He wouldn't look at me the way he does if that were true. They meet by the café, and the man hands him a manila envelope, which Pierce takes. I'm dying to know what's in there, but I settle for taking a few more pictures. They talk some more, then five minutes later, he is walking back toward West Point. I wait a few minutes before I follow back to sit at the stairs and wait for Ryan.

And spend the rest of my waiting time going over the new images I have of Mr. James.

I'm in trouble.

Deep trouble.

Only difference is this time, I didn't get dragged into other people's woes.

I created it. All. By. Myself.

Chapter Eleven

Pierce

Ducky Woods is the best private investigator in town. You better believe it, because he's helped take down some of the biggest gambling gangsters in Las Vegas. His services aren't cheap. I usually don't like to dip into the trust fund from my grandparents. With the exception of my house, I live a pretty modest lifestyle. I bought it because when Gwen died, I wanted a place further away from the city so I could effectively hide from the world. Paying my own way, even on a teacher's salary, is a pride thing for me, but I don't give a shit. He is worth every penny, and he is going to help me come up with a bulletproof case against Ryan Anderson. Something that will throw him in prison for life without parole, preferably.

Ducky has already started coming up with evidence.

Auto shop, my ass. Ryan has been dealing everything from prescription meds to heroin for the last five years of his life. It's a full-time job, but he's recently found the time to expand and start dealing weapons, too. Nothing too big. Dirty Harry-style unregistered guns. I'm not sure where he is getting them, but I sure hope that he is not keeping them at his house. Remington deserves better. A lot better.

That place is not safe.

Which brings me to why I decided to go for it in full force. For a second there, I had a little guilt trip over the fact that I was going to take away the only person in her life who actually cared. Only to realize that in the grand scheme of things, if the only person who loves you is being physically and mentally abusive to you and sells drugs and guns for a living, then you're better off without them.

Because this asshole is not going to do her any good. For one thing, he's already responsible for one death. He wouldn't be so lucky to get away with killing two of them. Not under my watch, anyway.

Tonight, I dragged some random I met at a bar to my bed and fucked her senseless. It was a calculated move on my end, and I very rarely feel the urge to have sex with strangers. Sometimes you have so many things to take care of in your life that sex is just not worth the trouble and you'd rather rub one off instead of making the effort. But ever since the school year started and Remington Stringer bulldozed into my life with her pouty lips, wide, green eyes, and long, brown hair, I need an outlet. Today was the worst, because when her detention was over, she didn't want to leave. And neither did I.

After Mikaela left, it dawned on me that I could walk over to the door, lock it, amble in her direction, flatten her against her desk, and eat her until she screamed my name. And she would let me. And hell, she would love every single second of it, maybe more than I would. The thought was so real, so vivid, and most dangerously—*so possible*—I had to act fast. So I did. I slept with someone else.

Did it help? No.

Do I still think about her? Hell, yes.

I should stop.

This won't have a happily ever after.

But I can't.

I won't.

⌐⌐⌐

The next day drags. Speech and Debate is the kind of class that is very hit-and-miss. If you have a few intellectual students in class, it's the most fulfilling and exhilarating thing that can happen to you as a teacher—which is why I picked this subject over anything else. But if you are working with a bunch of idiots, you're kind of wondering why the hell you were so hell-bent on becoming a teacher in the first place. My undergraduate degree is in law. I'm very good at what I do. I can make a good living out of it. A living that includes a six-figure salary, sports cars, and friends in high places. Instead, I made a conscious decision to teach others the art of debate. Hopefully, by the time my job is done here, every student of mine will be able to bullshit their way out of a murder case without breaking a sweat.

I stride in the hallway at the end of the day toward my class, ready to grade some papers. It's going to be a long evening, but I have my can of Cherry Coke and my cigarettes for my break—shit, I smoke full-time now, since I discovered Ryan was right under my nose—I can't even complain when Shelly asks me to buy her a pack.

I open the door to my classroom, lock it for good measure—I hate to be interrupted when I read and grade papers—spin around, and see Remington Stringer sitting in the front row, her designated seat, looking me straight in the eye.

"School is over," I growl, perhaps a little too aggressively, but we need some space between us. Fast. This is getting out of control. The last thing I need right now is more Remington time, but I guess that's the least I can do seeing as I'm about to take the only person who is there for her soon.

"I know." She shrugs, popping a fruity gum that sends shivers down my spine. She smells damn good, and that's another problem with her sitting so close to me. "But I've decided to keep my detention time with you. You're here, anyway, so why do you care?"

"Because it's both inappropriate and pointless," I shoot out, scrubbing my two-day stubble.

"I would have to disagree with both assessments, Mr. James. There is nothing inappropriate with me doing my homework in your class while you're grading papers, and it actually does have a point, because as you're well aware, I have enough distractions at home. It's hardly a suitable environment to study in."

She does well in my class, and I know exactly what she goes home to. I'll give her that. And I'm too tired to argue, anyway. At least here, I know she's safe. *From him, anyway.*

I walk over to my desk and dump the stack of papers. Her eyes are following me. I arrange my red and black pens, take out my laptop, then check my phone for messages from my parents and Shelly. All throughout, she is still watching me. And I like it. I shouldn't, but I do.

"Eyes on your work, Stringer."

She licks her bottom lip slowly and blinks once. I do the same, but hell if I meet her gaze. Not going to give her that power over me. She's just a goddamn kid.

Only she doesn't seem like a kid.

"I'm wet," she murmurs. My eyes snap up.

"What the hell did you just say to me?"

"I *bet*," she corrects, her smile casual, "that you're not as cranky after hours, Mr. James."

"You won't find out either way," I mumble, dropping into my seat.

"I already do. You gave me a ride, remember?"

Of course, I remember. I wanted to walk right into her house and rip Ryan to shreds. To reach right into his chest and stop his heart from beating. But I say nothing. I should kick her out. The protocol would advise me to do so, very strongly. Actually, I'm already crossing boundaries just listening to her dirty little mouth telling me that she is aroused. I should be dragging her by the ear to the headmaster's office and slapping her with detention for the rest of the year. But I don't play into her game. She wants me to do just that. Wants more detention. *More attention.* Honestly, she should and would be expelled for the type of shit she's pulling if anyone else knew.

"Miss Stringer, I'd hate for you to kill your only chance of getting into a decent college without having to strip your way through, and for what? A crush? Cut the bullshit."

I stripped myself from niceties and hit her with the uncomfortable truth. Because that's the reality of things. Remington Stringer is going to be stuck here forever if she doesn't snap out of it, and she does have a crush on me.

The fact that the feeling is mutual is beside the point.

She doesn't submit under my stare, nor does she seem fazed. Any other student would be in tears by now. I don't take shit from anyone. And I've made more than one student cry when I crushed their little student-teacher fantasy. But this girl is not scared. She is programmed differently. I can see that.

"You wouldn't jeopardize my future." Her big, red smile widens, and she slacks against the back of her seat, drawing lazy circles with her black fingernails over the flash of her cleavage.

"Oh? And why is that?"

"You like me too much."

"Miss Stringer, I barely tolerate you. If you think I'll give you special treatment…"

"You already do." She leans forward and props herself on her elbows, pressing her tits together, and *fuck*, I am hard as stone. This cannot happen. I need to stand up and open the door. But I can't risk her seeing me tenting like a schoolboy. I'm not Herring or Schwartz. I'm a goddamn teacher. "You already do, *Pierce*. You gave me a ride. And your phone number. And here you are, letting me stay with you after school. You're responsible for this thing just as much as I am. Maybe even more. Because I'm just reacting. You were a willing party in all this." She stops stroking her flesh so she can circle the room with her finger. "And now there's no stopping it."

The days after are much the same.

Remington Stringer comes back every day for the detention that she doesn't have. We're already straddling the line of appropriate student-teacher relationships, and if we keep this up—whatever *this* is—we're going to jump so far over it that we can't even remember what the line looks like. *But still, I let her stay.* I tell myself it has nothing to do with the way she makes my cock twitch from one look at those pouty lips and everything to do with the fact that I know she's safer here than at home. But the truth is more complicated than that. Remington Stringer is not safe with me. She's not even safe from herself. Remington Stringer will not be safe until she goes away. She knows it. I know it. The clock is ticking.

Tick, tick, tick.

Day after day, she comes to my class, until four thirty, under the pretense of doing her homework. Sometimes she reads. Sometimes she listens to music with her earbuds. Sometimes she bothers me with her incessant questions. But always tempting. Always pushing boundaries. Every single shift of her legs, lick of her lips, and twirl of her hair is so effortlessly seductive, so deeply ingrained in her that I'm not sure she's aware that she's doing it.

She's a temptress through and through, but the bad girl act, I suspect, is just that. An act. She's an innocent wrapped in a body made up of every sin I've ever wanted to commit. A good girl with bad intentions. Remington isn't thinking about the consequences of her actions. I'm the adult—it's my job to do the responsible thing. So, that's precisely what I do. I provide a safe, calm environment after school, all while ignoring her brazen flirting and fighting the urge to accept what she's offering. To take her. To use her. To claim her.

This unspoken arrangement has worked out fine for us, if you don't count my internal suffering. Until today.

Today, when it's so hot that she's gathered that long hair into a messy ponytail on top of her head. Today, when the ivory expanse of her neck is exposed and I count the beauty marks sprinkled across it. Today, when her pen is cushioned between her ample lips as she nibbles on the tip. Today, when her long legs bounce to the beat only she can hear. Today, when she stares at me, challenging, under thick lashes. It's as if she knows my senses seem to be heightened and I'm all too aware of her allure and my resolve could snap at any moment. *Fuck today.* She needs to leave.

"It's Friday, Miss Stringer. Don't you have anything better to do than hang out with your teacher?"

"I could ask you the same question," she taunts. "A guy like you can't be short on companions. And yet, here you are. With me. Why do you think that is?"

"Well, clearly, I'm a masochist," I say dryly. Being around her is painful, but not in the way she must be thinking. She bites her lip and looks down at her desk in an uncharacteristic display of vulnerability. If I didn't know any better, I'd say I just offended her. It doesn't make any sense that this girl, who's tougher than most grown men I know, has her feelings hurt over a flippant remark.

Without even making a conscious effort to do so, I'm at her desk in two long strides. I've seen Remington Stringer take on many faces. Pissed off. Turned on. But this one is not one I want to be responsible for.

"Look at me," I order softly.

Always the rebel, she keeps her eyes pointed down. I lift her chin with two fingers, and fuck if her sharp intake of breath and the sight of her pulse jumping in her neck don't do something to me.

"You're always welcome here." And that's as close to a compliment I can give her, because I certainly can't tell her what's really going through my mind. She rolls her eyes in that self-deprecating way of hers, and I squat down, now eye level with the source of my torment.

"I see you, Remington. Beneath all that bravado is a girl who is wise beyond her years. Someone who is too damn smart and too damn beautiful for her own good." I didn't mean to say the last part aloud, and judging by the way her lips part, letting free a small gasp, I don't think she expected it either. Our eyes lock, both our minds working overtime trying to figure out how to navigate this uncharted territory.

Her phone rings from her desk, breaking our trance. I clear my throat and walk back toward my stack of papers. She hesitates for only a second before answering.

"Hello?" A pause. "Jesus Christ, Ryan, I'm coming. I said I'll be right out," she snaps, exasperated. She sweeps her belongings into her backpack and heads toward the door. She hesitates in the doorway before looking back at me from over her shoulder. She bites her bottom lip—again—and my eyes follow the movement.

"Thank you," she says softly. And then she's gone.

I've given up on fucking other women to get my mind off Remington. And since I can't fuck her out of my system, I'm resorting to the lesser of two evils. I'm in bed at ten p.m. on a Friday night fucking my fist to thoughts of my student. *Pathetic.* This is becoming a nightly ritual, and every night I hate her a little more for it. For making me want her. For making me question my morals, my humanity, my general taste in women. But most of all, I hate myself for liking it. On some level, I like this game we're playing, even though I'm the one who has everything to lose. She has no skin in the game.

I'm imagining her straddling my lap as I sit behind my desk at school. I imagine her inching up her skirt before freeing me from my pants. I imagine her sliding her panties to the side and sinking down onto my cock. I'd try to stay still. To not be an active participant—as if that absolves me of my crimes—while she uses me to get off. But I wouldn't be able to stop my hips from thrusting upward. I wouldn't be able to stop my hands from smoothing up her thighs to grip her ass and guide her movements. And when I feel her clenching around me, I wouldn't be able to hold back from—

A violent buzzing from my nightstand interrupts my depravity right before I blow. I consider ignoring it and finishing what I started, but something tells me to answer. It's a number I don't recognize—even more reason for me to ignore it—but curiosity gets the best of me, and I pick it up.

"Hello?" A sniffle. Muffled music and yelling in the background.

"Mr. James?" *Remington?* "I know it's late. I know I shouldn't call you, but I need you and—"

I need you. Those words coming from her mouth affect me more than they should.

"Tell me where you are," I say, cutting her off.

"I'm at my house. Ryan and his stupid friends—"

"Did anyone touch you? Are you okay?" I practically growl.

"I'm fine," she whispers, avoiding the question. "I

locked myself in the bathroom."

"Stay where you are. I'm coming."

"Okay." And the fact that she's being cooperative, compliant, tells me that she's not fine at all.

Knowing what I know about Ryan, I don't take the time to do anything besides shove my cock back into my gym shorts and throw on some shoes before I'm on the road. In Vegas, there's always traffic and *always* construction. But on a Friday night? I'm fucked. It takes me almost forty minutes to get to Remington's house, and each passing minute feels like hours. A sense of déjà vu overwhelms me, making me feel even more anxious. How many times have I done this very thing? Except, it wasn't a student who needed rescuing. It was my sister.

I scroll through my call log—I never saved her number because I was *trying* to do the right thing—and shoot out a quick text.

I'm almost there. Don't move until I come in to get you.

I toss my phone into the passenger seat, looking for Remington's street. I know it's one of these college streets... *Yale.* I swing a hard right and spot her house immediately. It's hard to miss. Cars and motorcycles litter the driveway and road. Music blares from inside. I'm forced to park a few houses down. I almost leave the engine running in my haste, but I know we wouldn't have a way out of here when I got back if I did that.

I force myself to appear calm, to walk and not run. I walk right past the people sitting in the yard drinking and throw the front door open. No one even notices my entrance. I see a hallway with four doors. I'm not sure which one is the bathroom, but that's all there is to the house, so I know she's close.

I try one door, and it seems to be her bedroom. There's a man draped over a girl, moving between her thighs, and I throw him off by the back of his shirt.

"What the fuck!" the guy yells, adjusting his crotch. I look back at the girl on the bed—not Remington, thank fuck—and walk out without an explanation.

Door number two is locked, so I pound on it. "Remington? It's me! Let me in!" I yell over the music. The doorknob twists, and I slip in and close the door behind me.

"What's going on?" I ask as my mind tries to keep up with what my eyes are seeing. She's on the floor with tear-stained cheeks and bloodstained thighs. Next to her are two towels with splotches of blood on them and little shards of glass are sprinkled around her.

"I'm fine," she says again. "I mean, I got nicked up, but I'm okay. What I saw…" she trails off, her lower lip starting to tremble.

"What?" I ask her. "What did you see?"

"Can you just get me out of here first? I'll tell you everything." I nod and extend a hand to help her to her feet. Her palms look like they have cuts, too, but I resist the urge to question her until we're back in my car.

"Ready?" I ask instead. She nods once and tucks her tiny hand inside mine. I open the door and keep her close to my side as we walk out. Just when we're feet from the front door, Ryan stands from the couch. It's then that I notice the glass coffee table is shattered. There are beer cans and fast-food cups that have poured out onto the carpet and dollar bills coated in a white substance.

"What the fuck are you doing with my girl? In my *house*?!" Ryan yells, working his jaw back and forth. He's shirtless and sweating profusely, which on its own doesn't mean much—because it's August in Nevada—but the fact that he can't keep still, bouncing from foot to foot along with the dilated pupils are a dead giveaway. I know the signs better than anyone. He's definitely using. "You're not fucking him, right, Rem? Isn't that what you said? Little lying ass bitch," he spits.

"She's coming with me," I inform him through clenched teeth. I'm trying to stay calm, but firm, because I know from experience how volatile and irrational this shit can make people.

"Fuck this!" Ryan roars, crunching over glass and trash to get to us. I tuck Remington behind my back.

"One more fucking step, and not only will I beat the living shit out of you, but I'll call the police and let them know about your little *extracurricular activities*." My voice is menacingly low. I should have already called the goddamn cops. I won't—not yet. But he doesn't need to know that. I will get revenge. I will get justice. Just a little bit longer...

I see the hesitation in his eyes. He's wondering if I'm bluffing.

"Just let me go, Ry. Don't do this to Dad," Remington says as she comes to stand between us.

Ryan throws his hands up in the air and spins toward the small crowd of people watching us, ignoring her altogether.

"You hear that, guys?" He laughs. "He's gonna call the fuckin' pigs!" He turns back to me. "Didn't you know? I.

OWN. THIS. TOWN."

Such a bunch of bullshit, but he's so fucking strung out, he probably believes it.

Remington tugs on my arm, pulling me toward the door. I keep one eye on Ryan, letting her lead me outside. I open the passenger door to let her in, and when I'm walking to my side, I look up to see Ryan standing in his doorway, arms braced on the frame. "And I own her, too, motherfucker!" he yells and chucks a beer bottle at my car. He misses and that pisses him off even more. He turns to go back inside, throwing some girl off him when she tries to hang on him and ask if he's okay, then slams the door.

"You need to get out of there," I point out dryly, reaching across the console to buckle her up. She's out of it. Completely. I don't like this new Remington. I like the one who looks at me like I'm her next meal, even though it's bullshit we both don't believe in. The Remington from school can deal with what I'm about to throw her way when I lock her brother away. This one? No way in hell.

She's still in her uniform with her knees pulled to her chest, tear tracks dried to her flushed cheeks. And maybe it makes me a sick bastard for thinking so, but she's never looked more beautiful than in this moment. She's vulnerable and bleeding, but still she has fire in her eyes.

"Why do you think I called you?" she snaps.

"I mean for good. You need to leave for good."

Chapter Twelve

Remi

Ryan's paranoia knows no bounds. He's been even more suspicious of me lately, but I haven't exactly been discreet. I knew staying late at school every day wouldn't go over well. But, I couldn't—can't—resist the urge to be anywhere but home lately. The fact that I'm spending all that extra time in Mr. James' class—well, that's simply a bonus. I love pushing his buttons almost as much as I love watching him squirm, but somewhere down the line, I didn't know who I was torturing anymore. Him or myself? Today, in my self-induced detention, I wanted him to put his hands on me. To grip my waist and show me how a *man* touches a woman. Not a fumbling boy. I wanted to feel his skin on mine, to taste his tongue. What would he taste like?

Then Ryan called and reality came crashing down on

me. He gave me the usual third degree about fucking other guys. I informed him that I could fuck whomever I wanted. He didn't like that. Instead of going home, he made me tag along on his errands—one of which included stopping by his friend's house to pick up a "package". In hindsight, I should have known before that moment—the signs were there all along—but I've realized that sometimes we're blind to the truth when it comes to the people whom we love most. It's our heart's way of protecting itself.

Ryan denied doing drugs, said that he was "just selling them"...because that's so much better. The rest of the day was spent putting the pieces of the puzzle together. The paranoia. The mood swings. The late nights. It all made sense. My brain worked overtime, trying to figure out when it began, *why* it began, and wondering what I could've done to stop it.

When Ryan started calling people over to party—a prime opportunity to expand his clientele, I'm sure—a sense of dread swirled in my gut. I knew it wouldn't end well. He told me to stay in my room, which was the norm on nights like this. Usually, I was happy to oblige. The last thing I wanted to do was hang out with a bunch of randoms. But tonight was different. I needed to pull the blinders off when it came to Ryan. To see the truth. And now, I wish I hadn't.

He was sitting on the couch with something tied around his arm. His long, greasy blond hair hung in front of his eyes, and the girl on his lap angled herself toward him to inject something into his veins. At first I was frozen in place. But the sight of the syringe broke through my trance.

"What the fuck, Ry?!" I yelled, and the tears that I

didn't know I was crying started streaming down my face. He stood up, letting the girl on his lap fall on her ass.

"'Just selling,' huh? What is this?" Before I made a conscious decision to do so, I was in his face, shoving at his shoulders, smacking wherever I could land a hit. He grabbed me by the shoulders, shaking the shit out of me.

"Fucking stop, Rem. Go back to bed!" But I didn't budge. My heart was breaking. Instead of breaking down, I held on to the other emotion fighting its way to the surface. Rage. How could he do this? To me, to my dad, to himself? All we've ever done is love him.

"You're a piece of shit, Ry! Nothing but a junkie, just like Darla. Congratulations, big brother. You're your mother's son," I ground out through tears.

It was that comment that did it.

One shove from Ryan and I fell backwards onto the glass coffee table. It shattered, and a chunk of glass stabbed my inner thigh. I braced myself for the fall with outstretched hands when I landed. A couple of pieces of the coffee table were embedded in my palms, but the only pain I felt was for Ryan. Ryan's friend Reed stepped in then, and one of the girls tried helping me up, but I smacked her hand away. When I tried to go back to my bedroom, I found a girl jerking off a dude in my bed. That was the last straw. I had to get the hell out of there. I haphazardly threw some shit into my backpack—a change of clothes, my camera, and God knows what else—all while they carried on like no one was watching.

After twenty-seven million unanswered calls to Christian, I finally caved and called Mr. James. After all, that was exactly why he gave me his number. He probably wouldn't even answer. Except he did. And more than that, he cared. This teacher of mine was more concerned for me than anyone else had been my entire life. There was something terribly sad about that fact, but I can't deny that it felt good to be cared for.

Mr. James burst through the bathroom door, somehow looking more intimidating than a house full of bikers and junkies in only a pair of mesh gym shorts and a tight white V-neck. And he protected me. Defended me. Rescued me. I wasn't usually the type of girl who needed saving, but Pierce James in white knight mode was a sight I won't soon forget. His eyebrows were drawn together, his nostrils flaring. His skin was glistening from the hot, summer night. His usually tamed hair was an unruly mess, and he never looked better to me.

Now I'm in his car—once again—except this time, I have no idea where we're going. I sense an internal battle going on with him, so I don't ask. Anywhere is better than home. The glass barely even broke the skin on my palms, and the cut on the inside of my thigh has stopped bleeding, but I try to pull my skirt down further so I don't get blood on his seats, just in case. Mr. James glances over and shakes his head.

"What happened?" he asks gruffly.

"I—"

"Never mind. Don't tell me. Not yet," he interrupts.

I swallow wordlessly, feeling my age for the first time since we met. We're both quiet as he drives us out of the city limits, toward the Hoover Dam. I still don't ask where we're going. Wherever it is, I trust him. A few minutes later, I see a sign that reads *Lake Mead Marina*. He parks and we silently walk toward the docks. Finally, he stops and gestures for me to enter a houseboat tied to the dock.

It's a modest houseboat, and there's not much going on inside. A tiny white table with a blue booth wrapped around it in a U-shape and a little couch with an old quilt bedspread that's sitting behind it. Mr. James walks straight for the mini fridge and grabs two beers. I reach for one, and he snatches it out of my grasp.

"No way." He shakes his head. "It's bad enough that you're here. I'm not giving you alcohol on top of it. These are both for me."

I've been drinking beers with Ryan and my pops since I was sixteen, but now isn't the time to argue, so I hold back the eye roll. He downs both beers within minutes and gets another. He sits in the booth and gestures toward the bed with his bottle.

"Start talking," he orders, gesturing for me to sit with a head tilt. I feel his demanding tone right between my thighs.

"You mean about tonight?"

"I mean about everything. Don't spare one single detail, Remington. I want to know how you got to where you are, what happened on the way there, and how can we make it better for you."

I sit down on the edge of his bed, and I tell him the whole story, start to finish. I tell him about my mom dying, my dad meeting Darla and taking in Ryan. Darla running off. Dad being on the road all the time, and how Ryan was my brother, best friend, and my parent, all at once. I tell him how lately I feel more like the parent. I tell him about how I got into West Point. I tell him how Ryan has been a loose cannon—hence the reason for hanging out at school more than any sane student should want to. Lastly, I tell him about the drugs. When I get to the part where I fell through the table, I think his teeth might crack under the pressure of his jaw.

"I'm fine," I insist, parting my legs slightly, absently tracing the dried blood. "It's just a little cut."

"It's not the first time he's been abusive to you. Physically," he says, not asks. His hard stare penetrates my self-confidence. I stare down at the floor.

"If you mean the marks on my thigh…." And when I see the look in his eyes, the designated grown-up who doesn't believe me, my voice is firmer this time. "Mr. James, I know how to take care of myself."

"When is your father coming back?" He ignores my statement.

"Next week. Tuesday or Wednesday." I try to remember, but it's really not that easy to get my brain to work under the watchful eye of this Adonis of a man. He taps his lips, as if contemplating the whole situation, and my eyes zoom in on his perfect lips. God, he is hot.

"Do you have anywhere else to stay?" he asks. I give it some thought. Not a lot. I already know the answer. *Nope.* That would be a big, fat no. The only person I would consider an actual friend is Christian, and he won't be able to explain my presence in his house for a few days. I don't even feel that comfortable telling him. Despite our friendship, it is still difficult to admit just how bad things have gotten at home. My life is so different than the lives of West Point's other students, that I think it's sometimes difficult to comprehend.

I don't answer, but look away, outside through the window of the little boat. It's cozy in here. There's a medium-sized yellow couch that looks old but comfy, a small kitchen, and a bathroom you can climb down to.

"Remingt—" He starts again. I cut him off.

"What do you want me to say, Mr. James? That the answer is no? I have no one to rely on when things go south. I called you, didn't I?" I blow a lock of hair away from my face, frustrated. "That should tip you off about my overall situation. I don't want you to save me. I want you to make me forget."

My voice breaks at the last sentence, and I hate it, and I hate me, and I hate *this*. I wanted to have fun with Pierce James. I wanted him to be a distraction from life, and instead, somehow he's become my whole life, and everything else is a distraction.

"You can stay here."

"I don't need your charity."

"You're not getting any." It's his turn to snap and push off his chair, walking over to me. He is assertive. And big. All man. My assumption was right the first time I saw him. He shouldn't be a teacher. He is too menacing to be one.

"If you were a charity case," his eyes narrow at me, "I would throw your case on the headmaster's desk and look the other way. If you were a charity case, I would follow protocol. You. Are. Not. A. Charity. Case. You need a place until this blows over. You need to be honest with your dad about what's going on with your stepbrother. If he's a smart man, he may throw your stepbrother out once you explain. I'm counting on it. Until then, you stay here. Understood?"

There's a pause in which everything is completely silent, save for the distant hoots and hollers from the surrounding party boats.

I hang my head, knowing he's right and hating it. "Yes."

"Good girl."

Only thing is…I'm not good. And I'm about to become

even worse than he had ever imagined, because this—right here—his compassion, is driving me nuts. Without thinking about the consequences—something I never do when I'm around him—I push him to the chair in front of me and hop on the wooden counter of the small kitchenette. I part my thighs, ever so slightly. Pretend to check the bloody wound.

He swallows hard, and my eyes catch the movement in his throat. His eyes drop—finally, *finally*—between my legs as he takes another swig. *Victory.*

My heart is doing cartwheels in my chest, and even though he hasn't so much as touched me, I feel myself growing slick. His eyes stay fixed on me, and it gives me the courage to take it a little further. I slide my fingers up toward my plain white bikini underwear and graze my clit over the fabric. For half a second, I'm insecure about my less than sexy undergarments, but the look in his eyes—a little pissed off and a lot horny—squashes that thought.

I'm afraid he's going to turn me down again. Tell me to stop. Throw me in the fucking lake, I don't know. But he doesn't do any of those things. Instead, he stands and grabs a beer—once more—then returns to the booth. This is the last thing I should be thinking about doing after tonight, but this is the first time he hasn't shut me down, and I need to know I'm not the only one feeling this. I need to know I affect him as much as he affects me. He sits forward, with his elbows on his knees, the bottle dangling between two fingers as he studies me.

He wants to watch.

I lean back on my elbows and bring my knees up so my feet are resting on the edge of the counter. Now my legs are spread wide. If anyone walked in right now, he'd appear to be disinterested. But I know the truth. He wants this. But he wants me to take the choice from him. I rub myself over my panties, slowly circling my clit again. Touching myself is nothing new, but with Mr. James watching me, it's never felt better. A moan slips out, and my hips start rocking into my touch. He licks his lips and takes another drink. When he sits back in his seat, I see exactly how much he wants me through his gym shorts. But he doesn't make a move to touch himself.

Challenge accepted.

I take a deep breath and pull my panties to the side, showing him the parts of me no one else has ever seen. I've never been exposed like this. Even with my ex, Zach, it was only twice, and only ever in the dark, under the covers. I'm spread out on display for my teacher, and the thought only gets me hotter.

This. This is what I've been waiting for.

"Fuck," he breathes, and I take that as a win. I slip two fingers inside, and they slide in easily with how wet I am. My head drops back, and I fuck my fingers harder, rubbing at the tight bundle of nerves with the heel of my palm.

"I picture you touching me like this almost every night," I admit breathlessly. "And in class. It's all I ever think about." He bites down on his plump bottom lip, but doesn't respond.

I palm my breast over my tank while I rock into my other hand, and I feel it building. I'm not going to last much longer. I glance at him again. He stares at me like I am nothing and everything at the very same time. I have no idea what's going through his mind, and that just makes it so much hotter. This is all a mind game. He could just be playing me, and thinks I'm nothing but a stupid little girl—a cheap, soon-to-be-broken toy. Jesus, I'm not even sure if he is hard for me or for the situation. The sheer desperation that I exhibit as I offer him myself like a sacrifice.

I want to break that control. I stand and walk toward him. When I'm standing next to the table in front of him, I slide my underwear down my legs, letting them fall to the floor.

"Remington," he warns, his voice still hard and gruff. It's the same stern voice that tells me to stop touching myself. To go to the headmaster's office. *To behave.* Only tonight, I will misbehave until I break him.

Before he has the chance to object, I sit on the corner of the table, swinging one leg around him so he's in between my thighs. His breath comes out ragged, and I prop myself up on one elbow, while my other hand snakes its way back down. His eyes are glued to where my fingers slowly work their way in and out. In and out.

"I wonder what you taste like…" I whisper. "Your lips. Your cock. Do you ever wonder what I taste like?"

His jaw ticks once. "What do you think?"

"Why don't you find out?"

I pull my fingers out and swirl them around the rim of his beer, then I bring the wetness back, rubbing faster, harder. I'm close, and when he brings the bottle to his lips and takes a long pull—his eyes never leaving mine—I'm done for. A primitive growl leaves his lips after he is done, and his tongue darts out, swiping over his lower lip to lick the remainder of my arousal. His lips are glistening with how I feel about him. With how much I want him.

"Pierce." His name comes out as a whine, and then I climax long and hard, my mouth falling open in a silent scream. I start to close my legs out of reflex, but I feel two strong hands grip my knees, keeping me spread open for him. And then I'm coming again, long and hard.

"Fuck," I whisper, still jerking from the intensity of my orgasm.

"Shit!" he roars, dropping his hands from my knees like they're on fire. I'm still floating when he stands abruptly and walks away, slamming the door to the little bathroom behind him.

It gives me time to make myself comfortable in my new domain.

The one I will reign, if only for a few days.

The one where I will make him my king.

Chapter Thirteen

Pierce

I always used to frown upon men who let their dicks dictate their behavior.

Maybe it's because my father dipped his into anything with a pulse when I was younger. He didn't limit himself to his mistresses or to one-night stands when he was gone on one of his many business trips. He liked underage kids, too. Boys and girls alike. And fuck, I wouldn't be surprised to find out, at this point, that he fucked sheep too if the opportunity presented itself.

Gwen was the one who had found out about it. Out of all people.

She was a good girl, begging to be acknowledged by my father. Thing was, he never really cared too much for us. Not that it deterred her from trying.

One day, when he got back from Zurich and dumped his suitcase in the middle of the foyer like the fucking useless sack of sperm that he was, she took it upon herself to unpack for him. Put his dirty laundry in the wash and rearrange his shoes on their rack.

She found some dirty laundry, all right. Mixed in his luggage were photos of him with countless women and boys in compromising positions.

Psychology 101—kids either want to grow up to be exactly like their parents, or the complete opposite. I sure know where I stand.

That's why it rubbed me the wrong fucking way when I found myself prying my student's thighs open so I could see her slick, pink cunt glistening for me while she was climaxing on my table. In my boat. In the middle of the night.

What's wrong with me? Shit, everything. Everything is wrong with me.

As soon as I closed the door to the bathroom behind me, I started jerking off like a sixteen-year-old on Ecstasy. I didn't even have the half-assed dignity to get into the actual shower. No. I propped one leg over the toilet seat, one hand against the wall, and went to town with the image of her fingering herself.

The blood on her thighs.

The look in her eyes.

Her desperation. *My* desperation.

I needed to get her out of that mess, but I couldn't risk her knowing my real address. We were already crossing lines and limits at a dangerous speed.

Even now, as I stare at her sleeping figure, I know that it's wrong. I don't look at her like a concerned teacher should look at his student. I look at her like a hunter who is about to devour his next prey.

I need to fight it. Every brain cell in my mind screams at me to put a fucking stop to it while I still can, because the doors leading out of this mess are closing one by one at an incredible speed. But then my instincts, my body, my whole being, is screaming at me to take her.

I want to mark her.

I want to fuck her.

I want to do things that I cannot justify. Not as a lawyer. Not as a teacher. Not as a man. And not as a decent human being.

Her eyes flutter open ever so gently. I sit in front of the couch she is sleeping on. I spent the night upstairs on the deck staring at the mountains and didn't sleep a wink. I can see that she is confused. It takes her a few seconds to remember what happened last night. The party. Ryan losing his shit. Me taking her to the boat. And then…

Don't even think about it, bastard. Erase it from your goddamn memory, as you should.

"Good morning." She is the first to speak. The smell of the soap she uses still clings to her skin. Apples or something. Simple. Natural. So unlike the girls she goes to school with who reek of Pradas and Valentinos. And yet there is something so real about this girl precisely because of that. I rake my fingers through my hair and look away from her.

"I left you money on the table. There's a Kmart at the end of the block and a few convenience stores around the area if you need food or toiletries. I will pick you up on Monday morning and get you to school…"

She bolts upright and stops me, raising her hand.

"Wait, you're leaving?"

"What did you think was going to happen, Miss Stringer? I would stay here and take you on a boat trip with flowers and champagne?" Jesus Christ. Even to my own ears, I know that I sound like a first-grade douchebag. I'm trying to throw her off. To get her to stop seducing me. Because the truth of the matter is, people have power over you only if you let them. Dozens of women *and* girls have tried to seduce me in the past. Not one succeeded. Until her. Until Remington Stringer.

"Maybe not champagne. You made yourself clear about me drinking." She yawns, stretching. Her nipples are erect. Her hair is a mess. I stifle a groan. I need to get out of here.

I stand up.

"I'll see you Monday."

"I have nothing to do here, Mr. James. No books. No laptop. No nothing. What am I supposed to do?"

"I'm sure you'll find a way to entertain yourself."

"You liked watching me entertain myself. Why don't you stay, anyway?"

Goddammit.

I blink twice, a casual smirk still spread all over my face.

"Watch your mouth, Miss Stringer."

"Watch your hands, Mr. James," she retorts, raising her green eyes to meet mine, then licking her luscious lips. "They seem to wander to places they have no business going when you finally let your guard down."

"I need to get out of here," I say, this time to both her and myself, because fuck, not only is she a step above every other girl in her class—her *school*—it's been years since I've felt like I met my match.

"Stay," she insists, her voice sharp and bossy.

"I can't promise decorum if I do."

"That's what I'm counting on."

I start walking toward the door leading upstairs to the dock. The small boat moves to the rhythm of my feet. It smells like dust and negligence in this place, but I love it too much to let it go. This is where Gwen and I went to in the Hamptons every day during the summer to sit around, drink beers, and make plans. When she moved to Nevada, I followed suit and took it with me.

"You say you want to help me." She raises her voice, and I still, one hand on the doorframe and the other in my hair. I close my eyes. I shouldn't listen to her. Know better than to do it. And yet here I am, all over the place, allowing her to sway me. "You say you care, but what you do is no better than what Ryan does. You dump me in a strange place I don't know with a few bills and expect me to fend for myself the whole weekend? I'm better off staying at home kicking stones with my neighbors, waiting for my dad to arrive."

She has a point, and it kills me. I want her to be argumentative and cunning, and she excels in my class even when we're not in session.

"You know the implications," I say without turning my back to look at her.

"I'm aware, and I'm responsible enough to face them." There's a grin in that voice, and I'd like to wipe it. With my lips all over hers.

Finally, I spin on my heels, slow.

"No one can see us together." My voice is steel.

"No one will." She gives me half a shrug. "But we're not staying on the boat today. I'm taking you on a ride."

"Do you know how to drive?" I cock an eyebrow.

"No, but you're going to teach me, *Teach*."

⤳

Remi

I'd never been in a vehicle like Pierce's before I met him. I was used to beat-down cars and things that looked like you dragged them out of a junkyard. The seats here smell like real leather, and the a/c seeps chill to my bones. I choke the steering wheel like it wronged me somehow, my knuckles snow white. I stare ahead, afraid to let my eyes wander left or right.

Dad is too busy to teach me how to drive, and Ryan would never entertain himself with the idea of giving me a tool to independence, so I've never had a chance to learn how to do it before.

"Any pointers?" I ask as the GPS fires directions at me. I knew exactly where I wanted to go after I convinced him to spend the day with me. It ticked all the boxes. No one was going to spot us, and I've always wanted to visit there.

"First and obvious one is to breathe," he mutters, seemingly entertained. "You look anxious."

"I don't want to ruin your car. It's really expensive."

"It was your idea to drive it."

"Ideas seem better in theory than in practice," I admit.

"You should keep that in mind next time you try to seduce your educator."

"Not the same thing." I tsk. "I'm very much on board with being with you, Mr. James. I think we both need this distraction in our lives."

After we agreed on the place we wanted to go to, I

grabbed my backpack that Pierce had managed to grab from my room before he ushered me to his car last night. It contains my most important possession—my camera. Other than that, Pierce went to a food mart down the road before we hit the road and bought us food for the trip. Basic stuff. Plastic-wrapped sandwiches, chips, and soda. Everything is thrown in the backseat as we zip through the golden roads and dusty mountains.

An hour after we start driving, Pierce tells me to pull over. He wants to drive the remainder of the way to St. Thomas, the ghost town that was demolished by the very Lake Mead his boat floats on. It's an historic site I always wanted to see, but Ryan never wanted to go, and Dad was always on the road. The last thing he wanted to do on his days off was more driving.

I take a sharp right to the shoulder of the deserted road. There is something naked and intimate about sharing the desert with no one but him. No one can see or hear us here. We can get away with anything.

With everything.

With what I want to be able to do with him every. Single. Day.

I unbuckle my seatbelt, throw the door open, and hop out. He does the same, sans the jumping, because Pierce is like six two. I walk around the car and meet him halfway by the trunk. Our shoulders brush, and he clasps my arm out of nowhere. My eyes shoot up and meet his. He squeezes my bicep lightly.

"What's your game, Remington Stringer?"

I shake my head. "Just a poor girl from the wrong part of town trying to claw her way out. What's your *secret*, Pierce James?"

"I have no secrets." His throat bobs with a swallow.

"Bullshit. You already have me, and I'm a secret. What's your other one? The one that's eating you alive? You're not the first privileged person I've met. But you are the first who's tried to save me."

He doesn't answer. I shake my arm away from him.

"If you want to touch me, make it good for me."

"I don't want to touch you."

"Is that why you jerked off after I fingered myself yesterday?"

"How the fuck would you know that?"

"You let out a groan I heard from across the room. You're lucky I didn't open the door to help you finish the job. I'm patient, Mr. James. But I have my limits, too."

"We should make a U-turn," he snaps.

"We've already gone way too far to go back now," I say, and I'm not just talking about St. Thomas.

The rest of the drive is silent. I clutch my camera to my chest and look at my surroundings, snapping pictures all the while. I've never come face-to-face with nature before. It's always been concrete and dirt for me, from day one. And I decide here and there that I want more of what life with Pierce James would offer, even if he isn't offering.

When we get to St. Thomas, he parks the car, and we both step out. It used to be populated by Mormon settlers in the mid to late 1800s before the waters of Lake Mead submerged it. The lake lowered back in the early 2000s, and the town resurfaced from its watery grave. We walk around for a while, taking in the crumbled beige remains of the town's buildings. It's crazy to think they were under water and stayed somewhat intact until just fifteen years ago. The desert wind is hot, and it moans against my skin. I

peel off my top, but I'm in my sports bra, so it's no big deal.
It looks more like a cropped shirt than anything else. We
don't speak much. But it's a comfortable silence. We don't
need words. I think we are both reveling in the feeling of
being with each other like this.

"The Chamber of Commerce looks like a hand giving
you the finger," I comment dryly, and Pierce chuckles beside me. I shrug. "It's true."

Click, click. I take some pictures of what's left of the
building. Nature has a way of destroying beautiful things.
I wonder if that's what happened to Ryan. If he was ruined
or if he himself corrupts others. Or maybe both.

"You let your imagination run wild," Pierce comments,
tucking his hands inside his pockets. He is athletic. I can
see it now. Bulging biceps and a broad back. He's wearing
khaki pants and a black V-neck shirt I would love to rip off
of him. That means that he has some clothes on the boat, I
realize, since he was wearing something else last night. My
mind *does* run wild.

What if he stays the night again?
What if this time we sleep together?

"Where I come from, dreaming is what saves you." I
kick a little rock. We're not really going anywhere, but we
keep walking.

"And where I come from, too many dreams destroy
you," he says bitterly. I perk up. He's never said anything
about his past, present, or future to me before. "How so?"

"Well, you know the term helicopter parents? In
Orange County, they are pretty much F-16 parents. They
will push you to be better than the neighbor's kid, no matter the price. Even if the price is the sanity of your child."

"Am I supposed to feel bad for you?" I snort and

immediately regret it. I don't know his story. All I know is
that something went wrong along the way. Pierce James is
not a happy man. He is gorgeous, feared, and well-liked,
and smiles so rarely.

"Giving you the pros and cons of every situation," he
says, undeterred by my attitude.

"Forever the debate teacher," I say, which is again,
dumb. I shouldn't be reminding him that he is my teacher.
I should be making him forget.

"Bad things happen in neighborhoods like mine," I tell
him, changing the subject.

"Bad things happen in families like mine," he retorts,
sighing.

We stop in the middle of nowhere, nothing but dust
and dirt for miles. His stare makes me feel uncomfortable,
and I shrug it off by smiling, but that just makes his brooding expression grow even madder.

"Are you having sex with your stepbrother?" he asks.

"What the fuck!" I push him away, my palms slapping
against his chest. I spin on my heels and power-walk toward the car. What a prick. Who asks that kind of question, anyway? I race back to where we came from, but
Pierce is taller and faster than me. He grabs my shoulder
and spins me around. I lose it. Every ounce of self-control
that's left in me.

"Get the hell away from me!" I growl. His eyes are
blank. He doesn't give a damn about my little hissy fit.

"It's a yes or no question, Remington."

"Why do you care? You're just my teacher, right?"

"We both know that's not true."

"Then what are we?" I put one hand over my jutted
hip, my body language seductive, but my tone betrays me.

I'm annoyed and embarrassed, but most of all, ashamed.

"You don't get to ask me questions before you answer mine."

"Why, because you're my teacher?"

"No, because I'm a lot more than your teacher."

That shuts me up. The nerve he has takes me by surprise. I want to laugh in his face. To tell him that he's tripping, but he is right. He is a lot more than my teacher, and we haven't even touched each other yet.

I wet my lips and huff. "I'm not sleeping with my stepbrother."

"Have you ever?"

"No."

"Have you done anything else inappropriate with him?"

"No."

"At all?"

"We've kissed," I admit, feeling blush crawling up my neck and settling in my cheeks. Even the roots of my hair are burning with shame. Jesus Christ. Why must I be such a fuck-up?

"When?"

"A day before school started."

"Did you like it?"

I shrug. No point lying. But that was way before I knew of his existence.

"Are you seeing anyone else?" He is asking now, his voice strained. He takes a step toward me. It's almost invisible. Like he floated toward me. But he is close. Closer than he's ever been.

"No," I answer. "You?"

"No," he says.

Silence. Our lust is thick and heavy in the air. It's not just me, I know. It's *us*. He wants to kiss me. He wants me to seduce him. Wants to pin this on me. Not this time. This time, he will own up to wanting me. To wanting this.

"What are we?" I whisper. I inch closer to him. Just a tad. Lean forward. Feel him. Smell him. I can almost *taste* him. This man…this man is salvation.

"I don't know," he admits, the tip of his nose touching mine for a brief moment.

"Me neither."

"But whatever it is," his hand moves in my peripheral, but I don't dare disconnect my gaze from his, "it's already happening, and I can't make it stop."

Just like that, his mouth comes crushing down on mine. It's feral, and wild, and completely insane. He fists my hair in a way no one has ever done before, in a way *a man* would, deepening our kiss. My mouth parts for him instinctively. He walks me back, and I'm losing my balance until my back hits his scorching hot car. It burns, and I couldn't care less. I grab his face with both hands and allow our tongues to dance together frantically. They're swirling, teasing, chasing each other, saying so many things we aren't able to say in class.

Pierce James is kissing me.

Pierce James wants me.

Pierce James is going to be mine.

I chant this in my head to make it more real, but it still feels like a dream. Like I could wake up at any moment— like I do any other school day—and find my hand shoved inside my panties and a confused, sleepy, disappointed expression on my face.

I decide to test reality. If this really is not a dream, he

won't let me to take it any further. I know it. I lift my legs and wrap them around his waist.

He lets me.

His raging hard-on presses against my navel, and I moan loudly when I realize that I've never had such a vivid dream in my entire life.

"Pinch me," I cry out into his mouth. It's ridiculous, but I need it to be true.

He doesn't answer me. Just grabs me by the jaw and plunges his delicious tongue into my mouth again.

"Pinch me," I say again. And this time, he presses his firm body against mine—he is all tight abs and manhood—captures my lower lip between his teeth and pulls it slowly to a point of delicious pain before he frees it.

I sigh.

I would wake up from something like this.

But I didn't.

It's really happening.

"I'm going to hell for this," he says.

"I'll follow you down."

Chapter Fourteen

Pierce

I have six missed calls, which I don't bother checking until we get back to the boat. Remington hopped into the shower, not before offering me to join her. I drew the line there. It had to be somewhere, after all.

Two from my mother. She could wait. Two from Shelly—she probably ran out of food and cigarettes—one from Guy, a friend I see once in a blue moon for the odd beer just to prove to the world that I'm still alive, and one is from the private investigator I hired to bring Remington's brother down.

I don't return any of them, but make a note to check on Shelly soon. I haven't been there in a while, and since she probably wouldn't leave her house even if it were on fire, she's come to depend on me. But reaching out of this boathouse and facing the real world is inviting reality back into my weekend, and I'm not ready for that yet.

I grab a notepad hanging on the small, old fridge and scribble Remington a message saying I'm going out to pick up some pizza. There's nothing to eat here but canned food and chips.

As I drive the short distance to the pizza parlor, I wonder how the hell I am going to explain to Remington what I'm about to do to her stepbrother. It was a relief to hear the bastard didn't go as far as getting into her pants, but I know she is still attached to him. Does she love him? Maybe. Hopefully not. One thing is for sure—I need to tell her before shit goes down.

Because I don't want her to be there when said shit hits the fan and everyone gets dirty.

When I get back to the boathouse, she is sitting at the settee in one of my shirts I keep in the small closet there and scrolling through her phone with her thumb. I open the door, and she doesn't notice me. Her eyes are down, and from that angle, she is your typical teenager.

The typical teenager that I dry-fucked in the middle of the desert today. *Fantastic.*

I dump the pizza box onto the table instead of announcing my arrival, but it's mainly because I'm mad at myself, not her. Her eyes shoot up, and she blinks.

"Something wrong?" she asks.

I don't answer. I set up the table with whatever silverware we have here and take out two cans of Cherry Coke. She said she doesn't drink soda, and I laugh. She asks me what's so funny as we both plop down to our seats at the table.

"I'm addicted," I admit.

"To fizzy drinks?" She smirks.

"To everything. Pop, cigarettes, alcohol..." I leave the sex part out. I shouldn't be going this route. That would be encouraging her, and I'm not that type of dick. "You?"

"I don't have any addictions," she admits, and I believe her because Remington Stringer isn't the type to be controlled—not by drugs, and not by her stepbrother. "I don't smoke, I drink a beer every once in a while, and I normally opt for water or O.J."

"That's healthy," I note.

"I'm a sensible girl."

"A sensible girl wouldn't share a kiss with her teacher," I say dryly, picking out olives from my pizza instead of looking at her. It's still difficult to come to terms with what I did.

"It's not just a kiss that we shared. There was more there," she insists, looking into my eyes.

"More what?"

"More everything. More us."

And that night, when she goes to sleep on the little couch and I can't bring myself to leave, I make myself comfortable in a sleeping bag underneath her and think, *you're right, Remington. We share a lot.*

Your stepbrother has tainted us both.

But it ends soon.

⌒

Remi

Sunday morning, we take the boat to a secluded cove on Lake Mead. When he takes off his T-shirt, exposing that long, sculpted torso and cut as shit V, I can't help but break his no pictures rule. I dig my camera out from the bottom of his waterproof bag, which earns me a disapproving look…one that I ignore. I bite my lip, then saunter over to him, pouty lip and puppy dog eyes in full effect, and he groans dramatically.

"Whatever it is, the answer is no," he growls.

"Come on," I whine, batting my eyelashes. I wrap an arm around his neck, stand on my tiptoes, and bring my mouth close to his ear. I can smell him and almost taste the salt from his sweat. "Just," I whisper, inching even closer. "One. Little…" I nip at his earlobe, and he sucks the air between his teeth. "Selfie!" I yell, extending my arm to snap a quick picture before he can stop me. He breaks out of his trance, and I laugh like a fucking hyena at the expression on his face. Suddenly, his face morphs into a sinister grin, and my laugher dies off into a nervous giggle.

"You're going to regret that, little girl," he says tauntingly. He plucks the camera out of my hands before tossing it into a pile of towels. Then he charges me, and I panic because I have nowhere to run.

"Pierce!" I squeal, and somewhere in the back of my mind, I think how out here, alone and away from school, being with him feels as natural as breathing.

He scoops me up honeymoon style as I kick and scream in his arms—even though Pierce James' arms are not a bad place to be. Not. At. All. It's more about where I'm *going* to be in about two seconds.

"Please don't, please don't, please don't! I'm sorry!"

"Too late for sorry now." He adjusts his hold, as if he's preparing to throw me in.

He wouldn't dare. I'm fully clothed, for fuck's sake.

But I should know better than to underestimate him. He launches me into the air effortlessly, and I hit the water screaming.

"Oh, you son of a bitch!" I yell back up at him as I fight my way through my hair that's threatening to suffocate me. The water is nowhere near as cold as I thought it would be, but I guess I shouldn't be surprised. It's at least one hundred ten degrees today. I dip down into the water to smooth my hair back and come up just in time to see Pierce jump in after me.

I shriek and race toward the cove, but it's no use. He swims like a shark, and I guess that makes me the bait. My heart is pounding in my ears, and when I'm almost inside the cove, I turn around to gauge his distance. Except I don't see him anywhere, which means...

"Ah!" I yelp, feeling a firm hand tug my ankle. I turn around to see him emerge through the water—flipping his dark hair out of his face—and kick off his abs, but he doesn't so much as grunt.

"Don't run from me, Miss Stringer. I'll always catch you," he says, cornering me inside the cove. He means it as a threat, but I wish it were a promise. "Now, apologize." He's so close now. His strong forearms are on either side of me. The water is shallower here, and he can reach, but I'm still too short.

"I'm not sorry," I whisper, and in a bold move, I wrap both arms around his neck and my legs around his waist. His hands find my hips reflexively, and both of us are breathing hard. His expression is one that others would find intimidating, but I know this is the look he wears when he's waging an internal battle. I feel his bulge between my legs, and I rock into it without even thinking. He drops his forehead to mine on a sigh.

"Remington," he warns, but his hands sliding down to squeeze my ass say something entirely different. He opens his eyes, and then he zeroes in on my lips. He inches closer, ever so slightly, and I close my eyes. I feel his mouth ghost against mine, and I open for him. His hot breath mixes with my own, and his wet lips graze mine. And then Pierce James shows me just how much fun "just kissing" can be.

We eat seafood for lunch in a darkened corner of a diner that shouldn't be serving more than a cheeseburger and talk about our lives. He grew up in Orange County, and I've never left Las Vegas.

"I don't get why you're here. The world is big, and you're well-traveled. This place is a shithole."

"I can't bring myself to leave this shithole." He's wearing a fitted hat that's the opposite of his usual attire, but equally hot, and a stern expression. His folded arms over his chest make his muscles pop out. I try to ignore it because we definitely can't make out in public.

"Why?"

"I moved here after college. Blew off my career in law to become a teacher. My sister followed me here to escape my parents. She only lived here for a couple years, and I want to move back to California eventually, but I have some loose ends to tie up here first."

He wants to move back? It doesn't even make sense to feel disappointed, since I don't plan on being here after graduation, but I feel it nonetheless.

"She moved away?" I munch on a French fry as I stab my fork at a poor, shrunk shrimp swimming in an unidentified white sauce.

"She died," he deadpans quietly. My eyes dart up in horror.

"Jesus. I'm so sorry."

"So am I." He looks relaxed, calculated, and dark. His usual self. You'd think he is telling me that he was slightly late filing his taxes.

"How did it happen?"

"I'd rather not talk about it right now."

"Okay." I feel extremely uncomfortable, and he can probably see it by the way I shift in my seat. He pops some fried calamari into his mouth and chews, taking a sip of his watered-down Coke.

"Do you think you'll come back here after you finish college?" he asks. I need to shake my head from side to side just to make sure I hear him correctly. That was abrupt. Also, I'm not sure what my plans are. My immediate plans are to make out with him some more. Other than that, I'll take pretty much whatever crumbs life throws my way as long as they lead somewhere else.

"Doubt it," I say. "Maybe I'll visit every once in a while to say hi to my dad and Ryan. But other than that…"

"Why Ryan?" He cuts into my sentence. "Hasn't he done enough damage? Guys like him are poison to women."

There's something about his tone. Something edgy that makes me freeze in place and examine him for a second. What do I know about Pierce James, other than the dry facts? Suddenly, his presence here seems suspicious.

"Why are you still here, Pierce?" I call him by his first name, even though I'm not sure how he feels about it. I lean against the table, my fingers lacing together. "Tragically, your sister is no longer here. Then why are you here?"

"Remington." He does this thing again where he warns me simply by saying my name. I don't budge. He chuckles darkly.

"Are you being a bad girl?"

"Are you evading the subject?"

"Are you asking me questions without answering mine first again? I think we both agreed that that's something I will not tolerate."

"I'm not being a bad girl." I keep my tone casual. "But I'm not sure what to make of your fascination with my brother."

"*Step*brother," he corrects.

"Tomato, tomahto." I shrug.

"He doesn't deserve you in his life."

"That's not for you to decide." I grind my teeth together.

"I like it when you're mad." He cocks one eyebrow. I immediately melt and hate myself for it. *Goddammit, Pierce James.*

His eyes are still on mine as he signals the waitress to bring us the check. He pays. We walk out. We walk together, but we don't touch each other. There's something sizzling in the air, and I cannot wait for it to explode. When we both get into his Audi, he starts the car and drives outside the town limits until he reaches an old, deserted dirt road, then kills the engine.

I wait.

He reaches a hand to the side of his seat and presses a button. His seat moves back a few more inches from the steering wheel. He pats his lap.

"Come." It's an order.

Don't mind if I do.

I don't waste any time. I swing one leg over the middle console and straddle him. His hands immediately find my waist, gripping almost painfully hard. I meet his eyes and bite my lip under his close proximity. He grips the back of my neck and rests his forehead against mine, exhaling raggedly.

"Fuck the consequences," he mutters, and then his lips are on mine again. His tongue dips past my lips, and he tastes like Cherry Coke.

"Mmm," I moan, sucking his tongue into my mouth. He groans, and I feel his hard length twitch between my legs. Instinctively, I grind on him, selfishly seeking the friction that I need. He slides both hands down the gap at the back of my cut-off jean shorts and pulls me into him. He's fucking my mouth with his, and I never want this to stop. This feeling. Right here. It's so perfect, I could cry. He squeezes my ass, controlling the rhythm, and I pull away from our kiss to gasp at the sensation. He licks and nips and bites his way down my jaw, down to my collarbone, and everywhere in between.

His lips are on my neck, but my heart is in his teeth.

I want more, so I lift the plain white T-shirt I stole from him over my head and toss it into the backseat. His eyes drop to my sports bra, and my nipples grow impossibly hard. Goose bumps prickle my skin. And he hasn't even made a move yet. I cross my arms over my chest to remove my bra, too, but right before I'm about to spill out of the bottom, his hands stop mine.

"Remington, wait," he says, like he can't believe he's stopping me. *That makes two of us.* I drop my hands, and he rights my bra, pulling it back down over my chest.

"We can't go any further than this," he explains.

"But I need you," I almost whine. "I need you to make me feel good."

"Fuck, Remi. You can't say things like that," he growls, thrusting his hips upward. I want to melt against him. I feel like I might. My lust for him is smeared all over my underwear. Every nerve in my body sizzles with desperation.

Remi. That's the first time he's referred to me other than Miss Stringer or Remington or pain in the ass, and I die a little at him using my nickname.

"For how long?" I don't need to specify. He knows what I mean.

"I don't know." He shakes his head, scrubbing his face with his palms. "Jesus Christ. Look, I don't want to ruin you."

"You're giving yourself an awful lot of credit, Mr. James," I tease, raising a brow, masking the fear that's creeping its way into my head. He *could* ruin me. I *could* ruin his career. This game that we're playing… it's not going to have a happy ending. And if we're not careful, the consequences will be grave.

He smirks, but when I start to move on top of him again, the smile disappears.

"So, just kissing?" I ask.

"Just kissing." He nods faintly.

And that's what we do, until the sun goes down.

Pierce

At nighttime, I roll my sleeping bag under the couch and stare at the ceiling, wondering at what point in time

I voluntarily gave my balls to a seventeen-year-old, and when, if ever, I am going to get them back.

Telling myself that I'm staying here to protect her from whatever bullshit is lurking in the shadows of her life is a poor excuse I don't allow myself the luxury of believing. After all, I didn't shove my tongue into her mouth trying to protect her. I didn't grind against the damp fabric of her jeans to make sure that she was okay. I didn't bite down on her soft flesh like she was my favorite meal to save her.

I want her.

I want more of her.

And it's either caving in or handing my resignation letter tomorrow morning, first thing on a Monday, and get the hell out of there.

I could do it. Resign. I can do it in a heartbeat, if I were so inclined. Before I decided to help the youth of America with my brilliant educational skills, I was an intern at Rosenthal, Belmont, and Marks in Los Angeles. I have the résumé to do whatever I want. I don't even have to be a teacher if I don't want to.

I roll to my side and prop my head on my forearm, staring at her through the small light the moon provides. She is beautiful, but that's not it. A lot of girls at West Point are. And that's just what they are. *Girls*. Remi Stringer is not a girl. If she were, she wouldn't have snorted in my face when my dick was firmly clasped between her thighs and told me I don't have the capability of ruining her. Not like *this*, anyway.

I roll the last two days in my head in slow motion, and before I notice, the sun comes up. At six, I get up and make her breakfast. At six thirty, I shove lunch money into her backpack. At six forty-five, I wake her up.

"Time to go to school, Remington." I try to sound firm, but it's gone now. That shield is no longer there. And it's always there when I talk to my students.

She stretches on the couch like a lazy cat under the sun, a smile on her luscious lips, and my dick jerks inside my pants.

"Mmmm, but I don't want the weekend to end."

"Too bad, it's already ended."

"Sunday felt really short."

"That's the thing about weekends. They're short," I snap, even though my weekends used to feel very long before the last one I spent with her.

"And weekdays are long and hard. Just like—" She reaches out to palm my cock over my pants.

"Remington," I cut her off, throwing a pile of clothes—her school uniform, which she brought over with her—at her face just so she won't see the raging hard-on I'm sporting. Her nipples are erect, and her body is the smoothest, ripest thing I've ever seen. How can she only be in high school? "Five minutes or I'm driving without you."

"That actually sounds like a plan to me." She giggles into her arm.

"Don't sass."

"Or?"

"Or I'll take the role of responsible adult in your life, and then you'll really be in trouble."

"I kind of like getting into trouble when it's with you," she says, righting herself on the couch and clutching into the new clothes I threw her way.

"Then I'm happy to report that we're both royally and

completely fucked."

Her hip connects with my waist as she swaggers her way to the bathroom to change. What she doesn't know is that if she got naked here and now, this time I wouldn't stop her. "Good," she whispers.

And that's that.

Chapter Fifteen

Remi

Everything is a production when it comes to Pierce James.

First, we had to stop by his house before we drove to school because he had to pick up his dress clothes and whatever the hell he needs for his class. I stayed in his SUV, examining his house from the window. Pierce lives in one of those new developments on the outskirts of Vegas, the plush, rich ones. This one is called El-Porto, and all the houses are cookie-cutter, ranch-style homes with perfectly manicured lawns. One is decorated with a giant "It's a Boy!" sign that stretches across the lawn, along with a blue stork that has the baby's name, birthday, and weight. Jesus Christ. *Might as well give out your social security number while you're at it.* It feels like we live on two different planets.

I feel strangely breathless. Like this is monumental in a way, though I don't know how it could be. It's just a house. A really gorgeous house, but still *just* a house. And yet, there's another piece of him that now belongs to me. That only I have, out of all the girls in school. Pierce gets into his house—not even bothering to shut the door—and appears twenty seconds later clasping his brown leather bag. When he fastens his seatbelt, he says, "You should probably erase this place from your memory."

"Jesus, Pierce." I shake my head, peppering the gesture with an eye roll. In reality, I'm pretty pissed, and I might not show it, but the sting in my eyeballs suggests I want to cry, too. It's getting old. This whole I-don't-want-you-in-my-life act. I clutch my backpack tighter into my chest and look out the window. He sighs beside me, throwing the vehicle into drive.

"That's not how I meant it."

"Enlighten me, then," I say, but my voice loses that interest and enthusiasm I usually keep for him.

More sighing. He doesn't say anything, and my heart stops beating in my chest before he finally groans, "Fuck. I guess I meant it."

"Okay," is all I say.

He tries to make small talk the rest of the way to school. I shut it down. This is not happening. I'm done chasing after him like a little puppy.

When we're two blocks from school, I motion for him with my hand to stop. "No point coming in together, right? I'll walk the rest of the way."

My voice is dry and lacking. Lacking emotion, lacking interest, lacking a soul. He stops by the curb, angling his body to look at me and say something, but I'm already out the door.

I don't look back to watch his confused face.

I don't give him the opportunity to boss me around.

I sling my backpack over one shoulder and race to school, leaving him to feel how he makes me feel day in and day out.

Small.

⌒

Remi

When I see Christian in the hall before class, I don't ask him why he didn't answer me over the weekend, because I don't have to. I can see for myself. He went through some sort of transformation. Got a septum piercing and dyed his hair green. Not bottle green. Dark and mysterious. I'm talking The Joker green. He looks…extreme.

"Faggot," Herring coughs as he passes by Christian and me in the hallway, straightening his varsity jacket over his broad shoulders. His minions are following him, their backwards ball caps and stupid smirks on full display. I put a hand over Christian's back.

"Fuck him. What's up?"

Christian takes a long look at Herring before he slams his locker shut and locks it.

"Fucking straight boys," he grumbles.

At least I'm not the only weirdo here.

I cock an eyebrow. He shakes his head, and we both walk to the entrance. We are going to a café across the street. Even though Pierce sneaked some money into the smallest pocket in my backpack—the Benjamins fell to the floor with a soft thud when I opened it to get a piece of gum in English Lit—I'm still not going to use it. I'm tired of feeling like his pet project, and even though I'd kill myself before going back to Ryan and admitting defeat, I also don't feel like going back to the boat.

"Do you have secrets, Remi?" He jerks his head to look at me as we descend the stairs to the street level. I try hard not to blush, which ironically makes me blush even harder.

"Sure. I mean, everyone does." Sometimes the best moments in life are the ones you can't talk about.

"Well, I do. And it's a big one."

"Okay." I lick my lips, keeping my steps and my voice and everything about me extra casual, because I know how weird these things can be. It's hard to be out of the closet at Christian's age. It's hard to be out of the closet at any age, and I have a feeling that even though he's in, the guy he is interested in is not.

"And every time I have to see him in the halls, pretending to be someone he's not, it's a constant reminder that he'll never be mine. He'll never come out. He doesn't even want to be seen with me anymore."

I don't ask if it's Benton Herring. A part of me knows the answer to that. Another part doesn't want to believe it. But Christian's voice hit home nonetheless, because this conversation can be about Pierce and me. A secret that's too big to shoulder. A love story that isn't meant to be written. A script that anyone can know—from miles away—is not going to have a happy conclusion.

After first period, I reluctantly attend my Speech and Debate class. A part of me is dying to see him again. To smell him. To get a fix of the man I can't get enough of. The other part dreads it for the very same reasons.

I sit at my desk, and when Benton Herring passes me by, he slaps a paper to my desk. I don't even bother to look at what it is. I'm still scrolling my thumb through my Facebook, trying to figure out through the updates if my stepbrother is still alive. Looks like he is, and he checked in somewhere in Reno. Fun times, but at least I'll be able to go home today after school. The fact that I don't have to be dependent on Pierce today is a small victory.

"Pssst, Remi." Benton is now leaning across his desk toward me. He smells of too much Abercrombie and Fitch cologne and desperation. I ignore him.

"Remi. Remi. Remi. Remi. Remi."

"What?!" I turn around and snap at him, probably looking like a psycho, but I don't even care. I don't like him very much right now. Not that I did in the first place.

"I invited you to a par-tay. A special party at my house. The deets are all on the page. Mikaela made special invitations because she's cute and hot and talented. Right, Mikaela?" He twists his head and winks at her.

"Should've added that no skanks are allowed in the fine print." She pops on pink bubblegum while concentrating deeply on putting on a coat of hot red nail polish.

"Not interested," I say, ignoring Mikaela.

"Why?" Benton asks.

"Because I don't like you or any of your friends," I say honestly. "And because you called Christian a faggot, and frankly, I find your behavior, if not your entire existence, appalling."

Benton throws his head back and laughs. "Oh, Jesus, Remi. Get some chill. Chris is used to it. It's just banter. Stop being an uptight bitch."

"Oh, yeah?" I smile sweetly.

"Yeah." He swipes his eyes along my bare legs under my desk.

"So, can I bring him along?"

His cocky smile collapses into an annoyed frown. *Busted.*

"Remington," Mikaela warns in her nasally voice behind me. "I'm sorry to break it to you, but Christian is gay. You can't get knocked up and leech on his family money. You're better off placing your bets on someone else."

I can't take it anymore. I turn around, holding onto the back of my chair, and hit her with my own brand of nastiness.

"Jealous much?"

"Why would I be jealous of *trash*?" She giggles and elbows one of her mean girl reject minions.

"Because your boyfriend wants *me*, and you couldn't catch a dick if it hit you in the face," I say simply. I strongly suspect that Benton is Christian's secret hookup, but my jab worked, because Mikaela looks like she is about to spontaneously combust.

"BURN!" One of Benton's friends slaps his desk, and the sound rings in my ears.

"Fucking bitch!" Mikaela roars, standing up, and before I know what's happening, she's launching herself at me. I'm still seated when she clasps the collar of my dress shirt and throws me across the room. I land on Benton's desk and watch his smirk as she leans between my legs to slap my face. I snap out of it. Fast. As her arm comes down at me, I take ahold of both her wrists and twist them like you would a doorknob, applying as much pressure as I can, and hear her little bones squawking together. A shrill scream leaves her mouth. It echoes between the walls, and

I push her off me. In the background, I hear people yelling, "Fight! Fight! Fight!" "Catfight!" and "End that bitch, Kae!" She throws herself at me again. I step away, letting her hit the wall. People around us laugh. I was in a lot of fights as a kid. With girls. With boys. Ryan always says I'm a "scrappy little shit," and that if I had more discipline, I could totally be a fighter.

When the laughing and yelling around us die, so does the fight. Mikaela and I look up—I'm not sure when exactly I pinned her to the floor, everything is a fog when the adrenaline takes over your body—and see Pierce, I mean Mr. James, staring at both of us coldly.

"Up," he says, standing behind his desk, the tips of his fingers splaying across it. He looks like a stranger now. He sounds like one, too. It's hard to believe that this is the man who kissed me like I'm the only thing that matters. That told me things, personal things, about his family and sister and life. The heat in my face is unbearable. There's an argument to be made that Pierce James is a chameleon. He changes his colors all the time. He has so many hats— teacher, lover, brother, savior, enemy—he always throws me off balance when he looks at me, because I'm never sure which Pierce I'm getting.

We both right ourselves, leaning against a desk and a chair. Mikaela has a fat lip from a punch I threw, and her hair is a tangled mess. I have bloody scratches on my arm, but that's about it. I know how to dodge a slap or a punch. I'm my stepbrother's sister, after all.

"Sir, I—" Mikaela starts, but Pierce waves her off, looking bored more than anything else.

"Sit down. Both of you."

The whole class is staring at him like he had just

ordered us to French kiss and fondle each other on his desk. That is unacceptable at West Point, and in general. You don't just break up a fight between two students and not send them to the headmaster.

"You mean…" Mikaela's mouth drops.

"I mean I will deal with this later. This class is important, and I don't want either of you to miss it. You will be punished, Miss Stephens."

"Oh." Her voice drops with disappointment.

"Oh, indeed."

I look around me before I hurry to take my seat. I don't dare look at Pierce. I'm not sure where we stand, but I don't regret acting the way I did this morning. I'm tired of this hot and cold game. Tired of him giving me a little taste and then denying me in the next breath. Denying *himself* of what we both want.

I see him in my periphery opening a thick, red book with yellow pages but keep my eyes trained on my desk. I want to keep my head high but can't. Not right now. Benton Herring is high-fiving his friends to my left like the dickhead that he is. They probably thoroughly enjoyed the show. Especially the part where our skirts parachuted and everyone could see our underwear in the process. Goddamn Mikaela.

"We dance around the ring and suppose, but the secret sits in the middle and knows. This is a quote by Robert Frost. Today, we're going to discuss secrets. I'm sure you've all watched the news at some point this month, so you know about the affair between our president, John Holloway, and Secretary of State Elsa Dickenson. They were both single. Holloway is divorced, and Dickenson was never married before. Yet, this type of relationship is considered taboo.

Wrong. A misconduct.

"Secrets. We all have them. Some of them are big. Some of them are small. How do we determine what's big and what's small, and do secrets hold a moral weight on us? Today, we will discuss all those things."

I press my forehead against the cool desk and squeeze my eyes shut, seeking comfort. I don't want to hear him talk. I especially don't want to hear him talk about secrets. About *our* secret. I don't want to hear that what we're doing is wrong. My only comfort is that Pierce doesn't normally voice his opinions in class.

"I think secrets are morally corrupting." A girl, Jasmine, pushes her glasses up the bridge of her nose in a huff.

"There's not even one person in this world that doesn't have secrets," Schwartz, Benton Herring's friend, says loudly. I chance a look at Benton himself. He's gone all quiet now. I'm not surprised, yet I am.

He and Christian? Really? Shit. But he seems so… *douchey.*

"Miss Stringer?" Pierce asks. I shake my head solemnly.

"No need to shake your head. You haven't been offered anything. You're required to contribute to the debate," he says coolly. I maintain my position. Literally and figuratively. My body is stiff and ready for battle. My heart, on the other hand… it feels like it has already lost.

"I'm not feeling well, Mr. James. I think I need to go to the nurse."

I start to get up when he says, "You're not excused."

"Excuse me?" I ask. Ironically, I should point out.

"I said you're not excused. You're staying here. Yes? Hannah? I see you raised your hand."

Hannah begins to talk, and I glue my ass back to my seat, wondering what the hell is going on.

"Secrets scare me," Hannah says. "What if they come out? A lot of people can get hurt."

"Secrets are human nature. We all want to keep some things to ourselves."

"Secrets can get you killed."

"Secrets are what keeps this world moving."

"Secrets…"

"I don't want any secrets in my life," I announce, out of nowhere. I'm folding my arms across my chest now, looking resolute. "Secrets make you feel…*dirty*. And alone."

"Are you saying that you don't have any secrets?" Pierce strokes his chin like he is deep in thought, and even though his voice is light and aloof as always, I know that the answer to this question holds a special weight for him. I play along, looking him dead in the eye.

"Not anymore."

"Is that so?" he asks. Again conversationally, but this time I see the flash of irritation in his eyes. Maybe even hurt.

I nod.

"I don't think I could ever give up my secrets." Another girl, Amanda, giggles nervously. But Pierce is still looking at me and I'm still looking at him. The bell rings. Neither of us budges. Students begin to collect their stuff. Mikaela stays in her place. The tension is tangible and heavy in the classroom. Both she and I are waiting to see how he is going to react to what he saw earlier in class.

"You both get off with a warning," Pierce says, pretending to go through the papers on his desk. I almost choke on my tongue. Mikaela looks between him and me, not moving an inch. She looks too shocked to be a bitch, so at least I have that going for me.

"Am I… Is she…" She points at me, and I know that she hasn't done anything wrong per se, but I still want to kill her for it.

"Don't test me, Miss Stephens. I don't know what happened today, and frankly, I won't lose sleep wondering. But I'll tell you one thing…" His voice is low and menacing. "This is your last chance. Keep the drama off campus and especially *out of my class*, and we won't have any problems. Are we clear?"

"Yes, sir." Mikaela nods eagerly, too relieved to question him, as she gathers her things. I, on the other hand, am pissed.

"Are you *fucking* kidding me?" Mikaela looks at me with wide eyes, afraid that I'm going to make Pierce rethink his decision, and Pierce looks at me with a blank, bored expression. "She fucking attacks me in class and gets off with a *warning*? This is bullshit!" Why would he do that?

"You can leave, now, Mikaela. It seems Miss Stringer wants her punishment right now." He says it almost playfully, and despite my outrage, my panties are damp again. Oh, shit.

The door closes behind Mikaela, and I'm still looking at my desk. This is all so stupid. If he is actually going to punish me, I am going to lose my shit on him. But right now, getting suspended is not even on my mind. Something else is, and I bet it's throbbing between his legs.

He slings his arm over his chair and stares at me, sitting down with his legs spread. More like a student, less like a teacher. Every inch of him like a man. My lower belly tumbles, and yet again I wish he wasn't so easy to look at.

"No secrets?" He cocks an eyebrow, his fingers laced together on the table.

"Am I getting suspended?" I pretend like I care. Like anything other than him matters.

"No. You're not." His voice is even. "Is she bullying you, Remi? I need to know. And I know you can hold your own, so it doesn't matter that you can take it."

"Mikaela doesn't bully me," I answer flatly, raising my gaze to meet his. "But she does deserve to be suspended for what she did today."

He doesn't even ask me what happened. He knows Mikaela and knows me. And somehow, even though I don't want it to, it makes me feel so much better about everything. To have someone by my side who believes in me. In my character.

"She should be," he snaps, like this doesn't matter. Like nothing matters other than us. "But if she gets punished, so will you. I walked in on you on top of her, Remi." Hearing him say my name at school seems so wrong, but so right. "I was doing it to protect you. But then you had to go and run that beautiful mouth of yours," he says, walking up to my desk to drag my lower lip down with his thumb.

I try to act unaffected, but my breathing picks up, and I feel my nipples harden.

"That mouth of yours is going to get you in trouble," he says more to himself than to me. "So...no secrets you said?"

"No more secrets." Our eyes are boring into one another. He swings another chair around in front of me and sits forward with his elbows on my desk. There's heat sizzling all around us. It's the feeling he got me hooked on, my very first addiction. My only vice. The universe disappears again, and we're being sucked into a small, white capsule that's floating. I feel the *pop, pop, pop* in my belly. Pierce James can make my body dance without even moving. I don't think I've ever met someone who holds such power over me.

He slides his leg toward me and laces it with mine. Ankle-to-ankle. We're still staring at each other.

"Don't play with me, Stringer. I'm older, wiser, bigger, and more powerful than you," he hisses, and a little moan escapes my lips. He's too serious to even care about that. I sober up, shaking the weight of the lust from my shoulders.

"I can't keep doing this. Begging for crumbs of affection when all you do is tell me how wrong we are. I can't do the hot and cold thing. If you want me, *take me.*"

He pushes his leg between both my thighs, and because I'm a masochist, I spread them apart. My skirt is short, and there's a nagging ache for him between them. The need to be filled with everything Pierce James to the brim, until I howl in pleasure and pain, is taking over every single inch of my body.

"You are a part of my life," he says, almost with annoyance. Like he doesn't want it to be true. And he doesn't. I know that. In fact, he wishes he could still tell me to close those legs, take my backpack, and fuck off from his classroom. But he can't, so instead, his angle travels upwards. That's as much connection as we can get with a desk between us, and the door may be closed, but it isn't locked.

"Not enough," I say, looking at him under my thick, long lashes. My voice is a tender rasp, and his throat bobs in reaction. My hand drops between my legs, but I don't touch myself this time. No. This time, it's him who is going to pleasure me.

"Don't do this," he warns.

"Do what?"

"End this."

"End what?" I press, blinking at him, doe-eyed and oh-so-innocent.

And just like that, without a warning, he storms up to his feet, bolts to the door, locks it from the inside, and turns around, still holding the knob with white knuckles.

"Sit on my desk," he orders. Everything is strained suddenly. Everything. My nipples are tight and begging for me to touch myself to subdue some of the lust. My center is throbbing. My panties are completely wet. I want to keep still and play with him a little more, but my desire overrules every morsel of pride I was hanging onto. I walk over to his desk, hopping on it with my face toward the dry erase board. The word *secret* is still written there in red, circled with sunrays pointing out to other words: *scandal, morals, mystery,* and *consequences.* All the things we talked about in class.

It dawns on me that this is real. People are passing the locked door in the hallway. I hear shouting, the pinging of iPhones across the floor, and a few girls giggling and protesting when a bunch of guys dribble a basketball inside the school premises. I swallow hard, my eyes rolling backwards as I think of what's about to happen.

He walks over to me. Slowly. He is still in charge. Or at least he makes me believe that he is. Pierce stops when his whole body is between my legs, his waist level with my sex.

"End what?" I repeat myself, because he still hasn't answered me.

He leans forward and bites my lower lip with his

straight, white teeth, whispering into my mouth, "Our secret."

Then I feel his fingers—just the tips of them—drawing lazy circles on my knees. Like he's in no hurry. Like it's not a possibility that someone will try to open the door any minute. Like what we have is *real*. Shivers break down my spine and make my skin prickly when he deepens our kiss, and I lean backwards, my hands slapped on his desk, trying not to get crushed by him. His tongue devours my mouth, and he tastes like peppermint gum and the man I want inside me. One of his hands travels deeper into my inner thigh, and the other one clutches onto my hip, nailing me onto the table like I'd ever try to run away.

"I like our secret," he growls into my mouth, his fingertips dancing in the sensitive area between my sex and my thigh. He pinches that bone there—or maybe it's a muscle—and my whole core is about to explode.

"Why?" I rasp into his mouth, and his grasp on my waist only tightens, and it's beginning to feel downright rough. Like he is trying to own me in some way. "Because it's a dirty little secret?"

"There's nothing dirty about it." His fingers hook the damp fabric of my underwear, and I don't even have time to feel embarrassed about my arousal that's pretty much smeared all over his desk. "There's nothing *wrong* about it." He sucks hungrily on my throat, his stubble and teeth scratching my sensitive skin, and I'm about to lose it. "There's nothing, Remington Stringer, but you."

His fingers dive into me. Not one. Not two. Three.

And it's not dirty. It's filthy, and we both know it.

He plunges into my hot center, in and out, not rhythmically, but in a way that lets me know that he is nowhere near as in control as he wants to be. I slide forward and ride his hand, taking over the situation. His hand between my legs is heaven, and now I know why his hand is on my waist. It's either that or unbuckling himself and fucking me raw and senseless on his desk.

"Fuck, fuck, fuck, fuck." His voice is barely audible, nothing but a frustrated whisper, every time I dive in and he is knuckles deep inside me. He fills me. He stretches me. He consumes me in a way no man would ever be able to, and it's not a stupid high school crush that's saying this. It's the reality of things, and we both know it.

"I'm going to come," I moan, and it's the first time I look down to see his massive tent of an erection pointing at me. I look up, and he is tortured. Every curve of his face gives it away. He loves it, and he hates that he loves it. He is fucking his student with his fingers, and he is disgusted with himself. Good. He sure made me feel like shit for asking for it this morning.

"Come." He inhales deeply, his nose in my hair. "Come, my favorite secret."

And I come, collapsing under him.

Everything becomes brighter.

The earth shatters beneath us.

And when I'm done, I stand up, smooth the hem of my skirt, rearrange my panties underneath it, sling my backpack over my shoulder, and pat his chest.

"Thanks for that, Mr. James. Oh, by the way, I won't be needing a ride home tonight." I unlock the door and leave. Just like that.

Two can play this game, Teach.

Chapter Sixteen

Remi

After school, Christian is waiting for me by the steps outside, leaning on a pillar, looking all kinds of broody.

"You're taking me home, and then you're hanging out with me until you tell me what's going on," I inform him, sticking my index finger under his nose to wiggle his septum ring. He bats my hand away and rolls his eyes.

"Fine. But, I saw you pull up to school today..." he trails off, waiting for my reaction. "With Mr. James. Seems like we both have some confessing to do."

Well, shit.

My eyes dart around, looking for anyone who may have overheard.

"All right," I concede. He kicks off the pillar and hooks

an arm around my neck.

"Remi, Remi, Remi." He tsks, shaking his head. "I have a feeling your sins are far worse than mine."

"And probably a lot more fun," I joke, wagging my eyebrows suggestively.

"Mmm, that's debatable." Christian laughs, then pulls me in to give me a quick peck on the forehead.

We walk to his Range Rover, and when he starts the engine, I burst out laughing. He looks at me, confused.

"What?!" he demands.

"I'm sorry," I say, covering my mouth with the back of my hand. "You look ridiculous driving this now. You're way too punk rock."

"Shut the fuck up," he mutters, pulling out of the parking lot, but he can't keep a straight face either. "You're just jealous of my sweet ass ride."

"Hell yes, I am," I admit. "So, are you going to tell me what's up with Christian 2.0?"

Christian sighs, running a hand through his dark green hair. "It's complicated." I shoot him a look that says *fucking duh*, and he continues.

"Benton and I—"

"I knew it!" I point at him triumphantly, nearly jumping out of my seat.

"Yeah, yeah, you're a regular Sherlock Holmes," he mutters. "Anyway. We…you know. We're together. Or we were. I don't know now. Benton is bisexual, for one. And I can deal with that. It's not like he's really with Mikaela, despite what she may believe. But he just cares so. Fucking. Much. About what everyone thinks. When it's just us, everything is fine. Perfect, even. But then once he spends time with his older brother or his douchebag friends, it's like a switch flips. He's cold, distant…*hateful*. The day that we fought in the hall?" he asks, looking over at me before turning his eyes back to the road. "He was flirting with you to piss me off. The night before was the first night we hooked up, and the next day, it was like he wanted to punish me for it."

Sounds all too familiar.

"I can't even pretend to know how hard it must be to not only admit to yourself, but your family and friends that you're gay, but he can't treat you like that, dude. It's bad enough being someone's dirty little secret," I say, thinking back to my conversation with Pierce. Sometimes secrets are necessary.

"I'm just so sick of giving a shit about what anyone thinks. So, to, I don't know, prove a point or something, I decided to do something I've always wanted to do," he says, gesturing to his new look. "My parents hate it. My mom doesn't even want my grandfather to see me. Benton *really* hates it. But I don't care. I'm fucking free."

"Such a drama queen," I tease.

"Guilty."

"You know when Benton lashes out like that, it's not about you, right?" I add more seriously. "He hates himself and takes that out on you."

"I know." He nods somberly. We pull up to my yard, and Christian lets out a low whistle.

"Damn, Remi. There's a lot you haven't told me."

I gasp as I look up to assess the damage, and my stomach instantly drops. I expected more beer cans and trash, but this is so much worse.

The yard is full of broken chairs, discarded beer bottles, and Lord knows what else, but what's really concerning is the broken screen door—lying on its side, completely detached from the frame—and my front door that's cracked open.

Inside is even worse. The table is flipped over, and the glass still sits scattered across the floor. Alcohol containers, cigarettes, and empty pizza boxes cover every surface. My feet stick to the tile floor, and it smells like straight death in here. It's as if Ryan hasn't been home in days. That thought sends a shiver down my spine, and I internally panic about something happening to him. But I push the fear aside. This is Ryan. He's invincible. The only one who could hurt him is himself, and if there's one thing I can say for sure about Ryan, it's that the boy is a survivor. Always has been.

I scan the rest of the house, looking for anything missing or broken. The bathroom mirror is shattered, but other than that, the other rooms seem to be mostly untouched. Thank God.

I walk back to the kitchen, ignoring the way my shoes stick to the floor with every step, and grab the trash bags from under the sink. I take one out, toss the box to Christian, and start sweeping stuff off the counter and into the bag.

"Spill it," Christian says, bending over to pick up the bigger pieces of glass.

"It's a long story." I sigh. "I don't even know where to start."

"Look around, Cinderella. We've got time."

"I called you Friday night," I start. "You didn't answer, so this whole thing is basically your fault," I tease, but my smile doesn't reach my eyes. "Long story short, Ryan had a party. I caught him doing drugs, and I don't mean smoking weed. I called him out. He pushed me into the coffee table.

I needed to get the hell out of here."

"Shit, Rem. I'm sorry I didn't answer. Benton—"

"It's fine." I shake my head. "Mr. James had given me his number. He knows how Ryan can get. So, I called him. And he came to get me."

"No fucking way." Christian grins like the cat that got the canary. "Tell me he came up in here all Captain Save a Hoe."

"He totally did. If I hadn't been so upset, it would've turned me on."

Christian cocks a brow at that.

"Okay, so I was a little turned on."

"Obviously. Proceed." I take a deep breath before continuing. Saying this out loud makes it real. Part of me wants to gush, but a much bigger part feels protective of our secret. If I have to tell someone, Christian is the best bet. He's got too many skeletons of his own to go around exposing mine.

"He took me to his boathouse. We kissed. A lot. But he doesn't want it to go any further than that. We spent the whole weekend together, but then this morning, it was like he wanted nothing to do with me." I tie the full bag of trash and toss it outside the front door, then come back to fill another one. I don't tell him about the classroom incident from today. Hooking up in class is probably the worst thing we could've done.

"He's probably spooked. I don't exactly blame him either, Rem," he says unforgivingly.

"Whose side are you on?"

"Yours. Always. But he could lose his career. His reputation. He could go to jail. What do *you* really have to lose in this situation?"

Everything. I'm already in too deep. And that's what I'm afraid of.

"Stop making sense with your stupid logic."

"Just keepin' it real, baby girl. But I do think he cares for you. Call me crazy, but I don't think he'd risk that for a piece of ass."

"Or maybe he realized he made a mistake, and now he's trying to do the bare minimum to keep me quiet."

Christian snorts.

"Come on, Remington. I'm gay, and even I'm a little in love with you."

"*What?*" I laugh.

"You're hot." He shrugs. "Not to mention cool as shit and intelligent. The perfect trifecta."

"Well, thanks, but I think I'll go back to dating fictional characters. Everyone knows boys in books are better."

Christian rolls his eyes and dumps a stack of dishes into the sink. "I wouldn't be so sure about that," he says, staring out the window.

"I'm serious. He's made it pretty clear that he regrets it."

"Is that why he's creeping outside your house right now?"

What?!

I whip around so fast that my ponytail smacks my face. I look out the window, and sure enough, there's Mr. James, pulling away from my house.

I don't know why, but this has me feeling both triumphant and irrationally angry. He wants me to forget where he lives, but he can show up at my house whenever he pleases?

I snatch my backpack off the kitchen table and dig out

my phone. It died over the weekend, so I plug it in near the counter and wait for it to turn on. Once it lights up, I ignore the onslaught of incoming texts from Ryan from the past two days and shoot off a quick message to Pierce.

Me: Are you spying on me now, Teach?

My phone pings not even ten seconds later.

Pierce: Yes. I figured our relationship wasn't dramatic enough, so I've decided to add stalking to the list.

Reluctantly, I crack a smile at that.

Me: What relationship? You're just my teacher, remember?

Pierce: The fact that I can still smell you on my fingers says differently.

Oh holy Jesus. I feel my cheeks heat at the memory of those talented hands on my body just an hour ago.

Me: Go home, Mr. James.

Pierce: Just making sure you're safe. Boathouse is still all yours.

Me: Won't be necessary.

I toss my phone onto the counter, ignoring Christian's knowing smirk.

"Yeah, you're totally right. He doesn't care about you at all. In fact, I think he hates you," he says sarcastically. I chuck an empty beer can at him, but he dodges it.

"Less talking. More cleaning."

⌒⌒

"I can't believe you talked me into ditching again," Christian complains. "You know, you're kind of a bad influence."

"I get that a lot," I say, hopping out of his beast of a car.

Last night, Christian helped me clean the entire house before informing me that we were having a sleepover. He ordered us a pizza, and we stayed up late talking about the mercurial men in our lives and how much they suck.

I didn't want to go to school today for a couple of reasons. The first being that it's my birthday. The second, well, I'd be lying if I said I didn't want to see Pierce, but the desire to punish him was stronger than my urge to see him today. Barely. When Christian fought me on skipping the entire day, I pulled the birthday card. He caved and took me to breakfast before wasting the whole day drinking Bloody Marys and playing video games at his house. I wanted to have a pool day, but the sky was dark and gloomy, the air uncharacteristically sticky. A storm is coming, and it's the best gift I could've asked for. I love monsoon season.

Now, we're a few drinks in, and I have a couple of hours to kill before my pops comes home.

"So, what now, birthday girl? Movie? Prank phone calls?" Christian waggles his brows.

"I turned eighteen today, not twelve." I laugh. Even though prank calls never get old.

"Okay, tough girl. Let's go buy you a pack of cigarettes. Better yet, get a tattoo, or go hit up a strip club," he jokes.

"Oh my God, you're a genius!" I say, suddenly excited about the idea.

"I was *joking*! I don't wanna see floppy titties. Even if I wasn't gay, it's the *day shift*." He shudders, and I laugh.

"Not the strip club. The tattoo!" I laugh. I still have the money Pierce stashed in my bag, and I'm feeling just childish enough to spend it.

"Fuck yeah, baby girl, let's do it," he says, grabbing his phone.

"What are you doing?"

"Calling an Uber. I'm buzzed." Oh. Right.

Thirty minutes later, I'm flashing my I.D., and then I'm lying half naked on a black leather tattoo table at some shop near the strip. We figured they'd be pretty lax on tattooing drunk people, but my nerves and the drive have sobered me right up.

The guy about to tattoo me is named Dylan. He's tall, tattooed, and lean, but gorgeous.

"Is it going to hurt? That's a stupid question. I bet people ask you that every time," I babble nervously.

"Yup."

"Yes, it's going to hurt, or yes, you get that a lot?"

"Both."

Okay then.

I take a deep breath and tell him what I want it to say.

"Easy enough." He nods thoughtfully. "All right, beautiful. Roll over onto your left side and let's get this party started." He snaps his gloves, and I feel a little relieved when I see that his own ink looks legit. Not that he does his own tattoos, but at least he has good taste.

Christian grabs the hand that's extended above my head from his stool next to me while I clutch my shirt to cover my chest with the other hand. I hear the buzz before I feel it and I try not to jump when the needle hits the thin skin underneath my boob and near my ribs. At first, it's not bad, but try scratching yourself in the same spot over and over. It gets raw fairly quickly.

"Fuckballs, that hurts," I hiss.

"Such a lady." Christian chuckles next to me.

"How long has it been? Like an hour?" I whine. Christian rolls his eyes.

"Not even twenty minutes, drama queen. What's that from, anyway?" He nods at the words being etched into my skin.

"It's from one of my favorite songs. And, also, one of my dad's nicknames for me."

I feel Dylan swipe a cloth against my ribs, and then the buzzing stops. "Hop up and check yourself out," he says, holding out a mirror.

It's perfect. Two lines starting right underneath my right boob written across my ribs in the prettiest, daintiest script I've ever seen.

I'm the violence in the pouring rain.

I'm a hurricane.

"I love it!" I beam.

"Super hot, babe," Christian says, pulling some cash out of his wallet.

"What are you doing?"

"Giving you your birthday present." He smirks.

"Chris, no. I have money." Pierce's idea of "lunch money" was over a hundred bucks. Plus, I had a couple bucks of my own. *God, I really need a job again.*

"Keep your sugar daddy money." He smiles knowingly.

"I hate you," I say, shoving his shoulder. "But I love you. Thank you."

Dylan slathers some type of cool ointment over my tender skin and bandages me up.

"Okay, leave this on for six hours. Don't touch it. I mean it," he warns, pointing a stern finger. "Once you remove the bandage, wash all the ointment and junk off with a mild soap, like Dove. Keep it moisturized with something that doesn't have any fragrance. Don't cover it up again after the six hours. Let it breathe. No swimming or submerging your ink until all the scabs fall off. Use common sense and you'll be golden."

"Uh, can you write all that down?" I'm too excited to focus on anything he just said. He laughs and hands me a baggie with instructions and a sample of some ointment to rub on it later. I carefully pull my shirt back over my head, and then we're off.

After forcing Christian to snap some pictures of my tattoo with my camera and stopping for coffee—my treat—I ask him to drop me off at home so I can wait for my dad. I need to talk to him about Ryan. I'm dreading this conversation, but I know Pierce is right. I need to give my dad a chance to be a dad. And even though Ryan will most likely hate me afterward, it's the only way he has any hope of making it to thirty years old. He's only been gone a couple of weeks, but it seems like a lifetime. Everything has changed.

"Good luck with your dad. Text me later, birthday bitch," he yells out the window.

"See ya."

When I walk in the door, my house is completely as I left it. Which means Ryan still hasn't shown his face. I don't think I've ever gone this long without seeing him, and when I think about how we've drifted apart and how much he's changed, I feel a pang of sadness. And not just a little guilt.

Every year on my birthday, my pops and Ryan take me to Freemont Street to see the light show. I didn't exactly expect Ryan to show up like nothing happened, but it hurts not having him here. I pick up my phone to see if he's sent any more texts—nada.

My dad is late—big shocker—so while I wait, I eat, shower, and look for last minute things to clean. When I run out of things to do, I lie down on the couch and pull up a book on my kindle app. The unmistakable sound of an eighteen-wheeler eventually interrupts my reading, and I run outside. The monsoon is moving in hard and fast. The sky is almost completely black, and the wind is howling.

"Pops!" I squeal, throwing my arms around his neck, inhaling deeply. He smells like coffee and chewing tobacco, and I know if he turned around, I'd see the telltale circular imprint in his back pocket where he keeps the aforementioned chew.

"Hey, Hurricane," he says tiredly, using his nickname for me. When he spots the screen tossed haphazardly against the side of the house, he shoots me a look, but surprisingly, doesn't ask any questions.

"I have to talk to you about something," I say as we take our time walking to the door. We aren't in a rush to get out of the storm. Almost all my favorite memories with my dad take place on nights just like this.

Once we're inside, he surveys the damage. It's as clean as I could get it, but we're still down a coffee table and gained a few extra stains.

"Yeah, I'd say so, sweetheart." He lifts his hat and wipes the sweat from his forehead with his forearm before tossing the hat onto the counter. "Let me make a pot of coffee first." He sighs.

"Already took care of it." My dad doesn't care if it's fifteen or one hundred fifteen degrees. He still drinks coffee twenty-four hours a day. I bring him some in his favorite Harley Davidson mug before taking a seat at the table across from him, knotting my fingers together and leaning on my elbows.

"Ryan needs help, Dad," I start off, subtle as always. "He's struggling. Now more than ever." He takes a sip of his drink, not showing any sign that he's heard what I've said. I swallow before I continue. "This weekend, he finally just… exploded. That's what happened to the door, and, well, everything else," I say, gesturing around the room.

"Remington." He sighs. "I think you're the one who needs help." His voice is a flat line. It takes a second for that to sink in. I couldn't be more surprised if he decided to haul off and punch me in the face. It certainly feels the same to me.

"What are you talking about?" I ask, my eyebrows pinched in confusion.

"Ryan told me everything. I thought this school would be good for you. A new start. But it seems to have backfired." He sets his mug down and smooths a hand over his short beard, a nervous habit of his that tells me he's feeling uncomfortable.

Oh my God. It makes sense now. His lack of enthusiasm. His non-reaction to seeing the damage. Ryan got to him first. I feel my blood heating in my veins, simmering with rage.

That son of a bitch.

"And what exactly did he tell you, Dad?" I say, crossing my arms defensively.

"He's made his concerns known for a while now. Since you started at West Point. But he said after this weekend, he couldn't watch you self-destruct anymore. Said you had a party and that drugs were involved."

"What?! That fucking liar."

"That boy is a wreck worrying over you, Remington!

He's probably still out looking for you. You're all he has. Why would he lie?"

"Because I caught *him* doing drugs! It was *his* party and *his* shitty friends!" I hold out my arms, showing him the healing cuts and bruises. "He pushed me through a freaking glass table!" I scream. There were a dozen witnesses. Maybe more. But knowing Ryan and his friends, they are going to say whatever suits them. I'm completely helpless. It's my word against so many others. The world is so unfair. It's a juvenile thought, even naïve, but it hits me in that hollow place in my stomach where I keep the bad shit. And it stays there, digging deeper.

"Ryan said you were drunk and fell into the table."

I throw my hands up in the air.

"Well, you just have an answer for everything, don't you?" I shake my head. Un-fucking-real.

"Tell me something, Remington," Dad says darkly, his brows creasing. "Is he lying about you running around with an older man, too?"

"You have got to be kidding me!" I yell, not even trying to control my outburst. This is insane. I stand up because I need to do something with my body, and I'd prefer it if that something isn't tossing the coffeepot in his face.

"Answer the damn question!" he roars.

I'm pacing back and forth in the small kitchen that feels like it's physically preventing me from running away. There's no way I'm throwing Pierce under the bus. I've never really had to lie to my dad, but for this? It's not even a question. He thinks I'm a liar, anyway. Might as well act the part.

"No," I say evenly. "I called my friend Christian—my very gay, very teenage friend—and he picked me up. He let me stay with him so I didn't have to be around Ryan. He's changed, Dad. He *hurt* me. More than once."

"Whatever happened with you two, I'm sure he didn't mean it. It sounds like this was a big misunderstanding. You know how he is when it comes to you. He's just being an overprotective big brother."

"Because he *wants me*, Dad! There's nothing *brotherly* about his love. Trust me." I've completely lost it. Knowing how Ryan has been treating me will only break my dad's heart, but I'm beyond thinking rationally at this point. And I've got a broken heart of my own right now.

"Don't you say one more goddamn word. I don't know what's going on with you two, but I won't have you talking like that. Your brother has been through a lot. The last thing he would do is hurt either one of us."

There's no getting through to him. I see that now. I hold my head between my palms, legitimately afraid that it is about to explode.

"If you want to stay oblivious, then that's fine. But I'm not going to stick around to watch." I slip on my shoes near the door.

"You're not going anywhere," he says, crossing his arms.

"Happy fucking birthday to me," I croak out through the tears fighting their way to the surface. And with one look at my dad's face—the way he sighs heavily and squeezes his eyes shut like he's mentally kicking his own ass—I know. He's not here for my birthday. He didn't even *remember* my birthday.

I shake my head disbelievingly and open the door.

"Remington, wait," Dad says almost sheepishly, rubbing at his forehead. But I can't wait. I'm losing Ryan, and not only does my dad seem unconcerned for his own daughter, but he'd rather pull the wool over his eyes than to admit that Ryan needs help.

"Remington," he says again, sharper this time. "You can't go out in that!" He gestures outside where the weather fits my mood. Dark, stormy, haunted.

With one hand on the doorknob, I look at him over my shoulder. "Watch me."

I pull open the front door, the heavy, metal screen already banging against the side of the house repeatedly. The wind is howling, but the air is hot and oppressive. My hair whips in front of my face as I try to figure out my next move. But I already know where I'm going. It was never a choice.

Pierce.

I take off running toward the bus stop. I don't care that I have nothing on me except a few wadded-up bills in my pocket or that the rain is coming down hard and I'm only in a tank top, my cut-off jean shorts, and my Chucks. I don't care that I don't have my phone, and I'm running around a seedy part of town alone at night. None of it matters. I can think only of getting to Pierce.

The bus ride is a blur. No one talks to me or looks at me curiously. No one wonders why a young girl is soaking wet and visibly upset on a bus alone at night. This is Vegas. I'm probably the most normal thing this bus has seen all day. I stare out the window, seeing but not really absorbing until skeevy gas stations and liquor stores start to turn into gated communities and manicured lawns. The long ride does nothing to calm me down. With every minute that passes, I feel more desperate, more defeated.

Pity party for one, your table is now ready.

The rain turns to hail that pings against the bus, and the driver swerves to avoid a three-car pile-up at an intersection. Thunder sounds in the not too far off distance. Finally, the bus rolls to a stop a mile from Pierce's place. I take a deep breath before stepping out into the monsoon. I run in the general direction of Pierce's house, splashing through the flooded streets, and once I get to the gates outside his neighborhood, I realize I don't even have the code.

"Fuck!" I kick the gate and immediately regret that decision when pain radiates through my foot. The wind blows the hail sideways, sending a thousand bullets into my naked legs, and a stoke of lightning lights up the sky. Mentally, I try to remember what my dad taught me about gauging the distance of a storm.

"All right, Remi, watch for the light, then count the seconds until you hear thunder."

"One Mississippi, two Mississippi, three Mississippi, four Mississippi, five Mississippi…"

Thunder booms before I get to six.

"Five seconds," I tell him, sitting on the counter with my chin on my dirty knees, staring out at palm trees threatening to fall over in our yard. I hope they do. I love storms. But even more than watching them, I love playing in the wreckage afterward.

"That's right. So, to figure out where lightning struck, you divide the number of seconds between the lightning and thunder by five. How far away is the storm?"

"Five divided by five is one, so…one mile?" I look up at him, excited that it's so close. He musses up my stringy hair with a proud smile.

"Bingo," he says and tips his beer bottle back for another swig. "And if it's less than thirty seconds, what should you

do?" he quizzes.

"Take cover," I answer firmly.

"Good girl."

"Can I go play outside when it's over?" I beg.

"Sure. Monsoons don't got nothin' on Hurricane Remi," he teases.

Another flash of lightning pulls me from my memory, and I count.

"One Mississippi, two Mississ—" Thunder cracks through the sky not even three seconds later. God, I'm an idiot. I don't even have my phone on me. The tears are falling fast and hard now, mixing with the rain. I walk up to the keypad outside of the gate and stab random numbers in an attempt to get in. I try all the obvious number combinations to no avail. *Motherfucker.*

Finally, *thankfully*, a car comes around the corner. I step back behind the keypad as the car pulls up, and once they punch in the code, they're in too much of a hurry to realize or even care that I slip through the gate behind them. I rack my brain trying to remember where exactly Pierce's house is. It looks so different at night. When I pass the big "It's a Boy!" sign from earlier, I know I'm on the right track. Then, I see his house. Now would probably be the time to come up with something to say. An explanation as to why I'm here. Uninvited and in shambles. In the middle of a fucking monsoon. But etiquette has never been my strong suit.

I ring the doorbell and wait, suddenly afraid that he's not even home. His car isn't out front, but I assumed it was in the garage. Especially in this weather. But then he answers the door. All scruffy and sleepy-eyed perfection. He's shirtless, and his perfect V is showcased by low hanging gray sweatpants.

"Remington?" he asks, swinging the door open wider. The sleepiness in his eyes quickly morphs into concern. "What in the hell are you doing here? How did you get here?" He scans the street for my source of transportation before grabbing the hem of my shirt and yanking me inside. He slams the door and locks it for good measure. I don't answer his question. I don't even know what to say. All I do know is that I need him.

"Remington, say something. What happened?" His voice is hard but melting around the edges.

I should tell him all about my night with Ryan, with my dad—and I will—but right now, I don't want to talk about that. Pierce takes my face in both of his hands, searching my eyes. His thumbs brush across my cheeks while his fingers dig into the back of my neck, and the move is so symbolic of him. The perfect concoction of rough, yet sweet. Demanding, yet patient.

"Remington," he warns in that tone that never fails to send chills through my body.

"It's my birthday," I whisper.

Chapter Seventeen

Pierce

I was in my office, brooding over the fact that I didn't get to see Remington today while going over the new information I got on Ryan. I was debating how to tell her about my connection to him when I heard the doorbell ring. I couldn't believe my eyes when I opened the door to find my greatest temptation standing there, soaking wet with her clothes sticking to her body like a second skin. Her waterlogged hair dripping onto her signature white Converse. Her chest heaving and her nipples straining against her tank top. Her red-rimmed eyes. God, she's beautiful when she's sad. She made me want to slay all her dragons and then make her cry for me at the same time. My feelings for this girl never made sense. I've tried to fight this, to do the right thing, despite what my actions in my own classroom yesterday would have you think. But then she says the three words that change everything.

"It's my birthday," she finally whispers, green eyes looking up at me through thick, wet, dark lashes, and my resolve is gone.

The game has changed.

The curtain lifts.

The lawyer in me throws my body into gear.

My body gives the green light to my hands.

And then I'm on her, lifting her into my arms, wrapping her legs around my waist while she squeezes my shoulders. I slam her back against the wall by the front door, and she lets out a squeal. Her lips are parted, and I trace them with my tongue before sliding inside. I kiss her like I'm drowning and she's the air I breathe, and she kisses me like she's afraid I'll disappear at any moment. Like I'm going to come to my senses and stop her. If I were a smart man, I would.

I'm not going anywhere this time, Remi.

My lips find her neck, and I pump my hips into her wet jean shorts.

"Pierce. Yes," she says softly, breathlessly, urgently. And that's all the permission I need. I turn around and head for the stairs, holding her with one hand on the back of her neck and one on her ass. I take the steps two at a time while her hands grip my hair and her teeth bite their way down my neck. We're frantic and frenzied, both knowing what's about to happen. Neither one of us speaks, afraid it will break the spell.

I kick open the door to my room and lay her down on top of my bed. My hands wrap around the waistband of her still-soaked shorts and then I'm tugging them down—along with her underwear—while she rips her shirt off, exposing the most perfect pair of tits I've ever seen in my life. Full and porcelain with tight nipples in the softest shade of pink. I lean down to suck her nipple into my mouth when I see it. A tattoo underneath clear wrapping.

"When did you…"

"Today." She shrugs. My fingers graze her torso, skating up to the edge of the bandage, looking up at her for permission. She nods, holding her arms above her head. I peel it back, revealing two lines that give me an even deeper look into how Remi sees herself. Destructive. Crazy. And she is those things, but she forgot a few. Beautiful. Sensitive. Fierce. Strong. Loyal.

"You like?" she questions in a small voice.

"I love. You're incredible, Remington Stringer."

I step back to take a moment to brand this image into my brain.

She lies there, trembling, with her dark, wet hair spread across my stark white sheets wearing only her tennis shoes. Her tiny form looking even smaller in the middle of my king-sized bed. Her lips red and swollen. Her eyes begging me to follow through.

I've never been a religious man, but seeing Remington Stringer laid out on my bed like a sacrificial lamb makes me want to drop to my knees, bury my face between her thighs, and worship her. So that's what I do.

Never breaking eye contact, I kneel in front of her, running my hands up her thighs, stopping to lick the cut on her thigh, and trail my lips to the crease in her leg. My arms keep her legs pinned straight to the bed while I part her lips with my thumbs, exposing the pink inside. Fuck, she's gorgeous everywhere.

"Tell me you want me to taste you, Remi." My voice is strained, but I need to know she wants this.

"God, yes," she breathes, squirming below me. Her skin breaks in goose bumps before I even touch her.

Her eyes are still locked on mine, and I dip forward to take the first taste of what's mine. One shallow lick grazes her clit, and as soon as my tongue makes contact, Remi's hips buck toward my face on a gasp.

"Oh my God," she mumbles, clenching the sheets between closed fists. If I didn't know any better, I'd think this was new for her. That I'm the first man to sit between these creamy thighs and taste her on my tongue. That thought—regardless how off-base it may be—has me going back for more, and this time I'm not gentle. I suck and bite at her swollen clit, and then I split her slit with my tongue and eat her like my life depends on it. She brings her knees up, spreading herself, wanting more.

"Pierce," she whines. "It feels so—"

I put a hand on each knee, then pin them flat to the bed, exposing her to me completely.

"Fuck," I breathe. She's so smooth, wet, soft, and right now, she's mine. I flatten my tongue and lick her from her tight bundle of nerves down to her even tighter hole, and everything in between. When I fuck her with my tongue, she screams out, clenching around my tongue, and it has me rutting against the bed like a horny kid, desperately trying to relieve the ache in my cock. Her feet slide down my sides, working my sweatpants down.

When I can't stand not being inside her any longer, I kick my sweats off and crawl up her body. I palm her tits and suck one pointed tip into my mouth. Her back arches, and she grasps the back of my head, holding me to her chest. I move up to her lips and kiss her long and hard, letting her taste herself on my tongue, while I settle between her thighs. When my cock meets her slick center, I can't help the groan that comes from my mouth, or the way my hips thrust into her. I slide my dick in between her lips while Remington grinds against me.

"Shit. You're so goddamn wet, I could easily slip inside you," I rasp.

"So why don't you?" She's breathless, but bold as always. "I want this, Pierce. I want *you*," she insists, and before I know what she's doing, she wraps her legs around my back, angles her hips just right, and I freeze. The tip of my bare, engorged cock is just barely inside her.

Pure. Fucking heaven.

"Remington," I warn, squeezing my eyes shut. It's bad enough that I'm about to fuck my student. Fucking her raw is another thing entirely. Even I have limits.

"I need to feel you. Just a little bit," she begs seductively as she starts to move against me, working me inside her. Her eyebrows are pinched together, and she bites her bottom lip.

How can I resist when she begs so prettily?

I sit back on my knees and grip the base of my dick, jacking myself off with just the tip inside her.

When I can't take the teasing anymore, I pull out, ignoring her protesting whine and rub her clit with the head of my dick.

"Open yourself for me, Remi. Spread your pussy," I instruct as I lean forward and blindly reach into my nightstand drawer for a condom. She complies, her timid black painted fingertips dip inside while I rip the foil open with my teeth, then roll it on in three seconds flat and position myself back at her hot entrance.

"Stop me now if you don't want this." I brace my forearms on either side of her head, caging her in. Those big, green eyes look up at me pleadingly with so much trust, and I take that as my answer. I thrust into her with one sharp move, causing her to scream out, and Jesus, she's tight. So tight that it physically hurts.

"Let me in, Remington," I grit out through clenched teeth, working my cock inside of her. When our eyes meet, I'm surprised to find pain instead of pleasure painted on her face, and I pause.

"Don't you dare stop," she says, digging her fingernails into my shoulders.

"I couldn't stop now if I tried."

I stick two of my fingers into her mouth. "Suck," I command. And she does. Thoroughly.

I can't wait to feel that mouth on my cock.

I pull my fingers from her mouth, and she releases them with a *pop*, then I bring them down to where we're connected and rub her until she's writhing against me, begging for more, harder, faster. I sit back on my heels to watch myself driving in and out of her, and I could come from the sight alone. Her long, lean torso, the beauty mark below her right breast, her full tits bouncing as she meets me thrust for thrust, her head thrown back in ecstasy. This girl is lethal. Somehow, I know she'll be the end of me, but I can't bring myself to care. Because this right here? Would be worth a thousand deaths.

When her legs start to shake, I tuck one hand under the small of her back and cover her with my body again. I bury my face in her damp neck as I finally allow myself to let go. I fuck her punishingly. And maybe I am punishing her. For walking out on me yesterday. For not coming to class today. For making me want her.

"Come with me, Remi," I whisper into her ear before dragging the lobe between my teeth.

"Pierce, I'm coming! Fuck me, I'm coming," she chants into my ear as she clamps down on my cock. She milks the orgasm out of me, and I drive into her one more time, burying myself to the hilt as I spill inside of her.

"Fuuuuuuuck," I groan. Remington wraps her legs around my back, holding me inside of her. Our chests are heaving and sticking to each other, and my sheets are soaking from her wet clothes beneath her, but neither one of us makes a move to separate. I know that when we do, it will all hit me. The reality of what we did. What *I* did. The guilt. But I still won't regret it.

We lie wrapped up in each other, her nails tracing up and down my back while I bury my nose in her neck until the sheets turn cold and her teeth start to chatter.

"Shit, let's get you warm," I say apologetically.

"Mhm," she mumbles sleepily.

"Do you want to take a hot shower?"

"Uh-uh," she says, shaking her head, and I chuckle.

"Are you hungry?"

"I'm not anything. I don't ever want to move." She yawns and stretches, and I feel my cock start to harden again. I grind into her, and she winces from the move.

"Are you hurt?" I ask, pulling out.

"A little sore," she admits. "But it's a good kind of sore."

"Remington, this wasn't…" I clear my throat, unsure of how to ask.

"No," she says simply. "But not in a long time, and it was *nothing* like that."

"Like what?"

"Like *us*."

I kiss her hard, because I know what she means. I feel it, too.

Twenty minutes later, I lift her onto my bathroom counter, place her heels at the edge, and feast on her swollen pussy, then I go downstairs to fix her a BLT while she takes a shower.

She comes down with one of my plain white tees on. Long, bare legs padding down my stairs. Hips swaying. Wet hair dripping. Fresh, makeup-free face making her look so young and innocent. I notice the faint freckles across her nose for the first time, and I decide right here and now that I like this version of Remington best.

She eats, and I watch her.

She drinks one of my sodas, and I watch her.

She tells me to say something, but everything I have to say is either dirty as hell or scary as fuck.

I take her hand wordlessly and lead her back to my bedroom, feeling so much more myself—my real, pre-Gwen's death self—than I did when she first walked into my zone. Into my house. Into my domain.

She stops by my office and peeks through the slightly opened door.

"What?" I gruff out.

"I've always wanted to fuck on your desk." She shrugs with a grin.

"At school?"

She nods. "I want to feel my bare ass grinding against the papers from Mikaela and her stupid crew as you fuck me senseless."

I shouldn't be as hard as I am to hear it. That is for sure.

I kick the door open wider and cock my head to the side.

"Miss Stringer," I say. "On my desk."

She drops to her knees and crawls deeper into the room on all fours, her ass daring me somehow.

And I'm done for.

Officially and entirely hers.

Chapter Eighteen

Remi

I'm sitting in his office and telling him everything.

He is grading papers. He won't let me see what I got, but it doesn't matter. I already know I got an A. And not because I'm sleeping with my teacher, but because I'm damn good at debating, which I proved tonight when I convinced Pierce to fuck me for a third time.

The longing ache between my legs is replaced by a real one. I'm sore all over. I feel like he sliced me open and filled me with more than I can handle. My thighs are still shaking from the aftermath of every time we had sex.

Pierce is wearing his low-hanging gray sweatpants and a long white T-shirt. It's hot outside, but Pierce keeps his house like an igloo. He still looks expensive and rich, even in things Ryan usually wears. Pierce smells clean. Like soap and cologne and a little bit of me. And like sex. A lot like sex, actually.

"So your dad doesn't believe you?" he asks, running his hands through my hair. I am slouched under his desk, flipping through a stack of photos I recently had developed. Of our Sunday trip. Of Christian's new look. Then random ones, like my shoes on a cracked sidewalk. The single flower brave and strong enough to grow in our yard otherwise full of dirt and weeds. And of Pierce. So many pictures of Pierce. He has no idea. I have a hundred more waiting for me at home. Of him. Looking down to his papers behind his desk. Smirking at a student who answered his question. Looking at me with those eyes—that promise to give me pleasure and pain in spades.

"Nope." I blow a lock of hair from my face. "He believes Ryan. Even when I told him about Ryan wanting me…"

"I see." Pierce purses his lips together, and I know that he is pissed off. "So that's what made you run away?"

"I didn't run away. I just…*walked* away from a really screwed-up situation. Yes, that, and he didn't remember my birthday."

Pierce wheels his office chair sideways so that I'm placed between his legs, and I look up and see him staring at me hard.

"I want you to get your things and move away from there."

"I have nowhere to go, and before you suggest it, I can't live on the boathouse forever. It's too far away from school and civilization, and even though I hate how hot and cold you are toward me, even I admit that moving in together would be asking to get caught."

"What about Christian?" he asks. I shrug.

"His family is going through a rough time. I very much doubt they'd let some white trash chick live under their roof."

"You're not white trash," Pierce snaps through gritted teeth.

"That's not what the rest of the school thinks."

"The rest of the school can go fuck itself."

"Very mature." I laugh, but really, I feel a little better hearing that. He takes my hand and yanks me up to sit on his thigh. It feels so different, sitting on him instead of Ryan. I knot my arms behind his neck and stare into his too-deep blue eyes.

"I'll figure it out." I smooth his shirt for an excuse to touch more of him.

"No need. I will rent you a place near my house first thing tomorrow morning."

"You're insane."

"You're *eighteen*," he says. "You can live by yourself. All I ask is that we keep this quiet. For now."

"You know I will." And as I say it, I realize that I'm letting Pierce take care of me. I'm giving up something that's completely mine and placing my trust in him. I'm being taken care of for the first time in a long time, and I'm not sure how I feel about it.

"We'll get you your stuff from your place tomorrow after school." He smacks my ass a little and I wince because everything is still sore.

"I don't want to let go." My voice is below a whisper. Almost non-existing. Pierce knows exactly what I mean because he shakes his head.

"I don't want you to do this by yourself." He brushes

his thumb over my cheek. "You deserve so much more than this life."

"I know, but I want to find 'more' by myself. To earn it."

"You have earned it." His lips are now on mine, and his fingers are in my hair. "Now let me deserve *you*."

~

Pierce

The next day, I get a phone call from Ducky Woods, the PI I hired, and know that the Ryan Anderson case is bullet-proof. From a lawyer's point of view, I can tell you straight out that I can lock this guy in jail for a long time. Nevada doesn't take any bullshit when it comes to drug rings and weapons. And Ryan Anderson has been very busy with both. I hang up the call after arranging to meet at a coffee shop on the other side of town—as far away as possible from West Point—and even though he doesn't ask why, I know. I know why, and it's killing me.

It's time to tell her. Even after everything she's said to me about how her dad treated her, how Ryan shoved her into the fucking coffee table, I still know that she will be distraught. Guys like Ryan Anderson are not complete villains. I mean, who is? But when he doesn't try to shove his tongue down her throat and boss her around, he also takes care of her. Gives her money and rides and talks to her about how her day has been. I try to reason with myself. To tell myself that this is the best thing that could happen to Remi. And my sister, Gwen, deserves closure. She deserves the truth. But at the end of the day, even I can't take away one thing from Ryan Anderson that I'll never be able to offer Remington: *history*.

He was the one who kissed it better when she scraped her knee and bandaged her wrist when she fell off a tree and took her to see the Fourth of July fireworks when she was still oblivious to how pretty things that shine in the dark are.

I pass Mikaela Stephens down the hallway. She is wearing her cheerleading uniform—white and baby blue—and looks every inch of the drone she was raised to be. The fact that she is picking on my girlfriend, who already has so much bullshit to deal with in life, rubs me the wrong way.

Jesus Christ. Did I just call Remington Stringer my girlfriend? Even in my head, it seems…off. Off, but then oddly on. I try not to think about it too much.

I don't slow down as I pass her, leaning against her locker and clutching her books to her chest as she laughs with a couple of her friends, but when she sees me, she starts after me.

"What punishment did Remington get?" Mikaela keeps up my pace, and she's already out of breath.

"Remind me again how it's any of your business?"

"It's just that I didn't see her yesterday, and I was wondering if she got—"

"No," I say flatly. "Stop worrying about other people and start thinking about your own future."

"I got an acceptance letter from UCLA." Her voice is hopeful. Like she expects me to be proud of her. If anything, it reminds me that no one took Remington to look at colleges. No one guided Remington about where she should apply. No one even considered the idea that she will go to college. It's like her presence here, at West Point, is one big fucking joke. I make a mental note to help her with that too, even though I've spent the majority of my morning looking at apartments on Zillow so I can find her a place to stay. This girl is filling up every single blank moment in my life, and even though there were quite a few of those before she walked into my existence, I love how busy she makes me feel. How vital. How important.

"Good for you, Miss Stephens."

We stop by Charles' office. I knock twice. She flinches. I pay no attention.

"I wish you would hate me a little less, Mr. James," Mikaela whines, and I hate this nasally, teenager-y thing that she does. She leans a shoulder against the wall and circles the floor with her toe.

"I don't hate you."

"You don't like me either."

"I treat you like every single one of my students."

"Not like Remington. Remington seems to be getting a lot of one-on-one time with you." Her eyes dart to me, as if to say "busted". And I know that she is trying to blackmail me.

"Anything you wanna tell me, Miss Stephens?"

"There are rumors around campus." She smiles, a cunning, ugly smile, and even though she has a generically beautiful face, this peek to her personality makes her absolutely horrendous to look at.

"There are, I agree. They're called rumors for a reason. The consequences of spreading them and causing trouble for fellow students—and teachers—are heavier than you can ever imagine. You want to go to UCLA, right, Miss Stephens?" I lean toward her, just as I hear the headmaster shuffling in his office on his way to open the door for us.

Mikaela swallows. "Of course."

"Then I would advise against pissing me off. I promise you, Miss Stephens, I will not hesitate to write detailed letters to every single one of the schools you would like to attend and tell them what I think of you. And, of course, my colleagues will be happy to contribute to my personality assessment of you."

The headmaster opens the door, and we both erect our spines.

"Hello, Mr. James, Miss Stephens."

"Hello," I say, neutral as always, and Mikaela scurries away.

And I feel just a little more alive than I did when I first walked into school.

Chapter Nineteen

Remi

I see Benton in the hallway leaning against Mikaela's locker. She's French kissing him to oblivion and back, but he looks like he's barely holding back his lunch. When he sees Christian, though, he becomes ravenous. He snakes his hand into her skirt, and it rides up as he touches her sensitive skin where Pierce touched me yesterday, putting on a show. I look back at Christian across the hall, staring at them like they are everything that's wrong with the world. And to him, they are.

I rush over to him, slinging my backpack on both shoulders. Christian says I'm the only teenager he knows who actually still uses a backpack. I elbow him and pepper the gesture with a wink.

"Looking hot, mister."

"Yeah? Not hot enough for the guy I want, obviously."

I let my eyes drift to Benton and Mikaela's direction. I don't know what Christian sees in Herring, but whatever it is, I wish he could unsee it, because it makes my best friend seriously upset.

"Leave it alone." I tug on his uniform shirt, and he wiggles free from my touch and walks over to Benton. I grab his arm and pull him in the other direction, but Christian is a force to be reckoned with when he's mad. Apparently, anyway. He's bolting to Herring's direction, and the crowd slices open for him, like Moses parting the Red Sea, because everything about Christian's body language screams fight, and everyone is out for blood, especially when it's not theirs.

"The fuck!" I hear Benton's voice screaming before the thud of his back slamming against Mikaela's locker sends my heart somersaulting in my chest. I scurry toward Christian again, trying to pull him away from the scene, muttering, "he's not worth it" and "please stop" and hating the way this is unfolding before everyone's eyes, because Christian might be openly gay, but Benton isn't, and he seems like the type to recklessly do something horrible when things don't go his way.

"You're an asshole!" Christian screams in Benton's face, spit flying out of his mouth in the heat of the moment. People are circling the four of us. Some pull out their phones and take pictures while a lot of them whisper into each other's ears. Mikaela's eyes dart to mine, and her eyebrows furrow. She doesn't make a move to stop them from fighting, and for a flash second, I wonder if she knows her boyfriend is gay. She has to know he isn't interested in what she's packing.

"What the fuck are you talking about?" Benton laughs, but it's an unnatural, nervous laugh. Anyone can know that, I'm sure.

"You're a coward," Christian pushes his chest, "and a fraud." He proceeds. "You're a liar. You're a pawn. You're a fucking little pussy." Christian is on a roll now, and I want to throw myself between them, but selfishly know this would mean that I am going to be labeled "that girl" for the rest of the school year. Though I'm starting not to care.

"Are you high again? You look like a freak with that nose piercing."

"It's a septum, you trash, and your tongue was playing with it just a few days ago."

Holy. Shit.

Benton Herring's face contorts in anger and betray-al, and before I have the chance to stop him, he tackles Christian to the floor and slams his fists into his face while straddling him. I hook my arm around Herring's neck and try to pull him away, but he is too big and strong for me. He doesn't budge.

"Help! Jesus, what the fuck is wrong with you people?" I cry out as Herring mercilessly punches Christian like he's nothing but a ragdoll.

"Please," I say again, trying to drag Herring from above Christian. I can't see my friend's face. It's so bloodied I can't even distinguish his facial features anymore. I want to kill Benton. I want to yell my lungs out at Christian. Herring slows down, but I'm not sure why. The adrenaline in my body blinds me. Deafens me. People are shouting around me, and then they aren't. The commotion stops. I feel a firm, strong hand lifting me up to my feet, and it's Mr. James. Before I have the chance to react and fall into his arms and bawl my eyes out—wrong thing to do, Remi. Very wrong—he jerks Benton up by the collar of his shirt.

"Someone call an ambulance," he instructs, and my heart shatters on the floor right next to Christian when I take a good look at his face for the first time since he sort-of outed Benton.

"Jesus." I cup my mouth with both my hands. "Christ. Oh my God, Christian." I rush over to him and touch his head very gently. He looks dead. Legit ruined.

Herring must be taken away by someone else, because Pierce is right beside me a second later, peeling my hands off of Christian's face.

"Go to class, Miss Stringer," he orders, but his voice is oh-so-soft. Like velvet on my skin. I'm trying not to let it influence me, but there's no denying it anymore. I'm his, and every single piece of me belongs to this man to do whatever he wants with me. Me, Remington Stringer, who's been let down by every single man in her life. Every single man...but Mr. James.

"I'm so worried about him," I say, and as I do, I realize that I'm crying. My salt tears are in my mouth, and I shake my head, like this is somehow my fault.

"I'll keep you posted when I know more," he whispers to me, knowing it's wrong.

I nod. "Thank you."

I walk to class feeling like a total loser. In the hallway, people are still scattered around, and I hear them gossiping without even dropping their voice down.

"What was that all about?"

"Chambers basically outed Benton in front of the whole school."

"Like, whatever. Benton? No fucking way. Mikaela

Stephens is his girlfriend."

"Maybe she's just his beard."

"Do you believe the Herring rumors?"

"I dunno, man. If he wasn't gay, would he react this way?"

"Hey, did you hear Chambers and Stephens are bumping uglies?"

Remi

I take the bus home because Pierce has disappeared somewhere and is nowhere to be found. I'm not worried. It's something he does sometimes. I get the feeling it's got something to do with his sister, and even though I wish he would open up to me more, I know firsthand how bad it feels when you want to keep a secret from the world.

The bus ride is not really all that bad. It gives me time to think. I think of getting my fresh start, away from the toxic environment I call home. I think about how I'm going to go and fill my suitcase with only my most important belongings. I think about how I will mend my relationship with both my dad and Ryan—because I love them both despite of everything, or maybe even because of it—and how we're all going to laugh about it one, two, three years from now, when I'll be somewhere else. I imagine how it would feel to come visit them on vacation from time to time and to not feel trapped or controlled. To feel my family around me, to know that there are people who love me unconditionally, because even though I am madly in love with my teacher, what we have is different. What we have sweats and moans and thrusts and groans.

The bus stops around a mile away from my house, and I start walking, clutching my backpack straps in my hands. I sent Christian a few text messages earlier, so I check to see if he answered. He didn't. I stare at my texts to him.

Please tell me you're okay. Which hospital are you at?

I'm so worried about you. Why did you have to go and get yourself hurt?

Benton Herring is probably going to be expelled. It's senior year. His parents are pissed.

I open the gate to my house that doesn't really feel like my house anymore and walk in. Dad's not at home, but what else is new?

Walking over to my room feels final. The house is a mess again, but I guess Ryan is on another bender. My room looks torn apart, but all my shit is still here, albeit scattered. I pull out two big and old suitcases—one of them has a giant hole in the middle and the other doesn't zip all the way through, but they'll have to do—and start packing the very little possessions that actually belong to me. Clothes. A teddy bear Ryan got me when I was twelve, even though I was more into skateboards. Some books and pictures my dad bought for me along the years. Photos of my mom. Photos of Ryan and me and Dad. Just...things. Things that make me sad and nostalgic and hate what we all became.

I open my nightstand drawer and pause. My camera is not there. I blink. Close it. Open it again. It's stupid, I know, but there's just no way that it's not there. It was there yesterday. That's where I put it.

Only now it's gone.

I feel the panic grabbing my throat and squeezing hard. My camera. My mom's camera. The only thing I have left of her. This shit is not even worth that much money, so I know for a fact Ryan didn't try to sell it.

The photos.

Frantic, I flip over the mattress. I hide all of my photos underneath it. Everything I took pictures of. Because I'm the one who makes all the beds and changes all the sheets in the house. They're gone, too.

Fuck. Fuck. Fuck.

I turn the mattress upside down until it's on the floor. The photos are gone. Pierce's photos are gone. There's a hurricane in my stomach, and I practically fly over to Ryan's bedroom, even though I know he's not there. I throw the door open, and it's empty. There are needles on his nightstand and a gun on the messy bed. I want to cry. I want to kill him. I want to help him.

I'm out of the house in a second. I'm not even sure where he could be. As fucked up as our relationship may be, there's trust there, too. When he tells me he is going somewhere, I don't even ask why or where or when would he be home. I try the auto shop where he's supposed to be working, but the guy who owns the place looks at me like I've gone completely mad when I ask him if my brother has a shift and answers, "Who? Ryan? No, he's not here. Hasn't been in months."

I walk around in circles. I try the food mart down the road and a few of his friends' houses and even call Reed. Three hours pass. Four. Pierce is calling and texting me. I don't answer. *I need to sort this out first*, I tell myself. I need to make sure that Ryan keeps his mouth shut.

I go back home and see his bike parked in the middle

of the yellow dying grass, and I'm not sure what I'm more—relieved or scared. I run to the house and open the door.

"Ryan! Ryan!"

He is draped over the sofa like he's half-dead, and there's a girl straddling him. Correction: fucking him. She has long blonde hair. Dyed. And she is wearing a cheap school uniform. A uniform…not unlike mine. My stomach churns. I hold the handle to the front door, refusing to walk deeper into the living room. Danger is in the air. It's everywhere. It's in my bones.

"Get out of here," Ryan says, holding the girl's hips in his rough palms and driving her onto his dick, which I can see every time she pulls upwards, shining with her arousal.

"I need to talk to you."

"I'm busy."

"You have something of mine."

"What would that be? Can't be your virginity. You gave that shit away to the first horny kid to ask for it. You've been around the block, huh, Rem?"

"Fuck you, Ryan. I want my camera." I swallow hard. "And my pictures."

"Your camera is broken. I drove over it. It's in the backyard," he says, his voice flat and businesslike. "And I'm saving your teacher's pictures so I can show them to Dad. You seem to be keeping a lot from him lately. And me. I'm doing it for your own good, baby sister."

Then I do the unthinkable. I'm pulling at Ryan. I toss my phone onto the counter, then I jump on both of them, throwing the girl away from Ryan. She rolls on her back on our tattered sofa and screeches in annoyance. I grab Ryan by the collar and yell into his face, "Give me the pictures!"

"Not a chance on earth." He gets up, his dick still hard

and pointing right at me, grabs my wrists, and walks me over to the nearest wall. I try to wiggle free but can't.

"When are you going to see that it's you and me, Rem? It's always been us. Until he came along. He's ruining *everything*!" he yells, looking more than a little crazed.

"How can you really believe that after everything you've done? While your dick is still wet from someone else?" Does he not see how insane he sounds? His eyebrow lifts, amused, and I know I've said the wrong thing. He lets go of my wrists and takes a step back.

"You're jealous. Is that what this is?" he taunts.

"God! No! We could *never* be together," I say firmly, my throat thick with emotion. "Even if we could, do you really think I could ever want you now? Look at you. This isn't you. This isn't the Ryan that I love."

He inhales sharply and tugs at his hair. I see the change in his demeanor. His face morphs into something so menacing that I take a step back and discreetly reach for my phone on the counter. Keeping the phone behind my back, I swipe on the missed call notification so that it automatically returns the call. I don't want to set Ryan off, but I also know I need to get out of this situation.

"Where's Dad, Ry?" I ask, suddenly nervous to be alone with him. Well, almost alone. Movement out of the corner of my eye catches my attention, and I turn my head to see the girl righting her skirt and gathering her belongings.

"You two are fucking sick," she shrieks before walking to the door, shaking her ass harder than necessary. She pauses, waiting for a reaction, but Ryan doesn't even glance in her direction.

"Ugh!" she whines before finally leaving. Once she's gone, I try again, hoping Pierce has picked up by now and can put together where I am.

"Just give me the pictures, Ry. Please."

"I told you. Not a fucking chance. Did you really think you could fuck your teacher and get away with it?" He moves closer again.

"It's not like that." And it isn't. Maybe that's how it started, but now, it's…everything.

"I don't fucking care how it is. You're not seeing him anymore, except for class. You're lucky you even get that." Ryan brings his hand up to my face and strokes my jaw with his thumb. "And if I find out you've disobeyed me, sweet sister, not only will I tell your dad and the school," he brings his mouth close to my ear and tightens his grip on my face, "but I'll fucking kill him."

"Get off me," I grit out through clenched teeth. He's still completely naked and way too close. He doesn't budge. I hear my name being yelled by a familiar voice, and Ryan cocks his head at the sound.

"I said get off me!" I yell, wrapping an arm around his neck and pulling him in to knee him in the dick.

"Fuck! You little bitch!" Ryan roars, falling to his knees. I don't even think. I take off running.

"Remington! Remi!" I hear Pierce's frantic voice through the phone. Once I'm outside, I lift the phone to my ear.

"Pierce? I just left my house. Can you meet me somewhere?"

"I'm around the corner. I was already on my way to you when you called. Don't move." His voice sounds calm, but I know him well enough to know that below the surface he's anything but. I don't even make it to the end of my still-flooded street before I see his car barreling around the corner. He throws it in park and jumps out to meet me.

"Are you okay?" he asks, taking my face in his hands and bending his knees so he's eye level with me. I nod into his palms.

"C'mon." He opens the passenger door and helps me in, buckling my seatbelt for me. I love it when he does that. It's such a small, innocent gesture, and it should be the last thing on my mind, but it makes me feel…wanted. Treasured, cheesy as that may sound. My dad is indifferent toward me, Ryan wants to possess me, boys at school lust after me…but Pierce treats me like he needs me. And he hates that he does.

We pull up to my house, and I look at him, confused. "Pierce?"

"Stay in the car," he orders, opening his car door.

"No! Don't go in there. It's not worth it. Please, Pierce." I don't know who I'm more afraid for, Ryan or Pierce. All I know is that it's the last thing Pierce needs in his life.

"I said stay here. I'm just going to have a talk with him."

"Take me home." It's not a question. He knows I don't mean my house. He sighs, settling back in his seat after closing the door. He grabs a fist full of my hair, bringing my head to rest under his chin. He kisses my forehead three times before releasing me and turning the car back around.

Chapter Twenty

Pierce

I doubt Remington has eaten today, so I stop at an In-N-Out on the way back to my place. I look over to see her dipping a French fry into her chocolate shake, her heavy eyelids desperately trying to stay awake. This fucking girl. All in one day she's dealt with Mikaela, Christian and Benton, her dad, Ryan, and me. Yet she still sits there, eating a chocolate shake like all is okay in her world.

I, on the other hand, am about three seconds from exploding. I may appear calm, but I've done nothing but pummel him in my mind since I got the call.

"Food good?" I ask, gesturing toward her half-eaten burger.

"So good," she moans, leaning her head on the headrest. She drops her head to the side to look over at me.

"You take me to the nicest places."

"Brat." I know she's teasing, but it gets me wondering what it would be like if I wasn't her teacher, and I could take her on real dates. How we still have the whole school year ahead of us, and we're already in so deep. It would be selfish of me to let this continue. But I'm a selfish man when it comes to Remington Stringer.

"Have you heard anything about Christian?" I ask in attempt to distract myself from my current train of thought. I pull up to the gate and punch in the code.

"No. I tried to go to the hospital after school, but he didn't answer his texts to tell me where he was. Then when I called, his parents picked up and told me they didn't want any visitors." She clenches a fist on her lap, and I have to hold back a smirk. My girl is a little spitfire.

"He'll be okay," I assure her.

"I know." She nods. "God, I could punch Benton. All of this over a secret."

Remington hasn't explained their situation, but from what I overheard after the fight, I can fill in the blanks. When I pull into my driveway, she doesn't make a move to get out.

"Secrets ruin lives, Pierce." And I know she's not talking about Christian anymore. I don't have a response for that. I won't lie to her and tell her everything will work out, or that we'll both come out of this unscathed. Because one of us is bound to get burned. We both know that.

Finally, she unbuckles her seatbelt and hops out of the car. When we walk into my house, it's dark, tranquil, and deafeningly quiet. The complete opposite of the chaos that is Remington's life. She looks around, taking in her surroundings like it's the first time she's really seeing my house. I guess it kind of is, seeing as how the only other time she was here, I had her flat on her back in two seconds flat.

She heads straight for the stairs, tracing the bannister with one finger as she makes her way to my room. She looks back at me, her chin resting on her shoulder, her hair a tangled mess that spills down her back. The look in her eye is a stark contrast to the hardened one that usually resides there. She's dropping the shield, letting me see her vulnerable side, and begging me not to make her regret it.

"I need you. I don't want to think about Ryan or Kaela or my dad or any of them. In here—in your house—I feel like none of that can touch us. I want you to fuck me, Mr. James. Are you coming?" she asks simply, softly.

"Hopefully more than once."

I storm up the steps after her, and she giggles—fucking giggles—and runs for my room. I tackle her on my bed, her back to my front. Her ass to my cock. I grip both of her wrists above her head in one hand and smooth her hair out of her face with my other one. I grind myself into her backside, and she moans softly. I lick the shell of her ear before fisting her hair.

"I can't promise you forever, Remi girl. I can't even promise that one of us won't get hurt. But I can promise a few things," I whisper roughly into her ear. She arches back into me. "I promise to take care of you, even when you won't let me. I promise that while I'm with you, I won't so much as think of another woman, and I promise to fuck you good, and to love every minute of it." She wiggles against me again, her breathing turning ragged. I reach down and flip up her skirt. I palm her ass and squeeze before giving it a sharp slap, which earns me a yelp.

"Is that enough for you?"

"Yes," she whispers.

"Good. Because I'd like to fuck you now." I tug at her panties, sliding them down just far enough. I unzip my slacks and pull myself out. I slide the head of my cock through her slit, making sure she's wet enough—of course, she is; she's always ready for me—before shoving inside her in one hard thrust.

"Shit!" she yells on a gasp, lurching forward. I pull her back by her hips and hold her in place.

"Don't run from my dick, baby. Keep your ass up." She nods frantically, her face smothered in my sheets. I pull out at a leisurely pace before I dive back in. She moans, low and keening. I nudge her legs with mine until her knees are tucked up under her chest. Bracing my hands behind me on the bed, I lean back and watch myself slide in and out. She's on display for me, her uniform skirt bunched up around her hips. *Fuck.* The sight alone is enough to make me come. When she pushes herself up on her forearms and starts to fuck me back, I snap. I reach forward and fist her skirt, using it as leverage to fuck her harder.

"So good," she mumbles into the sheets.

"Everything is with you." She pulls away from me and my dick pops up, smacking into my stomach. Before I can ask what she's doing, she turns around, crawling back to me. She dips her head down and takes one long lick of my cock.

"I've been dying to taste you," she says before swirling her tongue around my tip, never breaking eye contact.

Jesus Christ.

When I think nothing can possibly be any better than Remington's tongue, she takes me into her mouth and closes her lips around me. My hips pump forward on their own accord, and she gags a little. I pull back slightly, running my hands through her hair.

"Suck me," I growl. And she does, with the perfect amount of pressure.

"Do you taste yourself on me?" She hums her answer and wraps one hand around my base, working my shaft while she sucks on my crown. I guide her movements, going a little deeper each time. When I hit the back of her throat, tears spring to her eyes, and it only makes me harder. She holds my hips and looks up at me, wide green eyes, black mascara running down her cheeks. *So damn beautiful.*

I lie on my back, pulling her on top of me in one swift movement.

"Condom," I say, gripping her thighs. I can't believe I nearly forgot. She leans forward and grabs one out of my side table before holding it out for me. I don't take it.

"Put it on me." She bites her lip and does as I say, tearing it open and then rolling it onto my cock that's still glistening from her mouth.

"Now, put me inside you," I instruct. There's no hesitation. She leans forward and reaches behind her, placing me at her entrance. She brings her hands on either side of my head before lowering herself onto me.

"Oh my God." She closes her eyes and throws her head back, circling her hips while I'm buried inside her. I unbutton her shirt, leaving it hanging off her, and pull her heavy breasts out of her black bra. I see a glimpse of her tattoo that I nearly forgot about before I lean forward, taking her nipple into my mouth and sucking. Hard. Her slow circles turn into rocking, and then she's riding me rough and fast.

She isn't putting on a show. She isn't screaming like a porn star. Her movements are uncoordinated and frantic, but she couldn't care less. She's taking her pleasure, and it's the sexiest thing I've ever seen in my life. She sits up, and the new angle has us both groaning.

"I feel so full. It's so deep."

"Lean back," I tell her gruffly. She does, ripping off her shirt and bra before resting her hands on my knees. I reach forward to rub on her clit with my thumb, trying desperately to resist the urge to come.

"Please don't stop," she begs, her eyes pinched shut. She grabs my wrist and holds the heel of my palm where she needs it.

"Come, baby. Come all over me," I grind out. I lift my hips, forcing myself impossibly deep, and I feel her pussy contract around me. She ceases her movements, so I sit up, wrap my arm around her lower back, and fuck her hard through her orgasm.

"I feel you coming, Remi. You're squeezing me so tight."

"Don't stop, don't stop, don't stop," she chants like a prayer. And I don't want to ever stop. I'll never get enough. Her mouth drops open in a silent scream, and I snake my tongue inside. The kiss is sloppy and desperate, and when she sucks on my tongue, I can't hold back. I grip her waist hard, holding her in place while I shove myself as deep as I can, coming like a geyser.

Remington drops her forehead to my shoulder, lazily rocking her hips as we both come down. I kiss her temple, tracing my fingertips up and down her spine.

"How'd I do, Mr. James?" she mumbles into my neck, and I chuckle.

"A+. Your best work to date, Miss Stringer." I lift her off me and lay her down before covering her with my comforter.

"Good to know." She yawns. "I should go to sleep. I have school in the morning, and my teacher is kind of a dick."

I laugh as I walk to the master bathroom to take care of the condom and clean myself up. By the time I'm out, Remington is curled up on her side, one hand under her cheek, and her lips parted ever so slightly. Quietly, I pad over to her and graze her flushed cheek with my knuckle. "What are you doing to me?" I muse aloud. I try to make sense of the overwhelming and foreign feelings that slam into me, but they all hit me at once, making it hard to grasp on to anything, save for one thing. *Mine.*

I take one last look at her before throwing my slacks back on and grabbing my keys. I know what I have to do.

Chapter Twenty-One

Pierce

When I was in law school, my lecturer showed up at my doorstep inside the dorms one day, unannounced. I remember clasping the door as he stood on the threshold, a seventy-something-year-old man with wafer-thin white hair and too many wrinkles to distinguish his facial features, and said, "You need to change courses."

"What?" I asked, laughing. I come from a family of lawyers, and this was the point where I still wanted to make my father proud. Or at least, the thought of disappointing my parents made me feel slightly uncomfortable. "Why would you say that?"

"You can't be a lawyer."

"Why?"

"Because you're no better than a thug."

"What makes you say that?"

"I see you, Mr. James. I watch you all the time, and when you don't like something, you snap. You don't have the self-control to become a lawyer. You're a hothead. You don't have the patience for it either. You'd make a horrible chess player."

"Thank you," I said, shutting the door in his face. I graduated with honors, but he was right.

I am hotheaded.

I *can* be ruthless.

Especially when something of mine is in danger.

Ryan is about to learn that we have something in common the hard way.

The minute after Remi fell asleep, I drove to her old house. I knew Ryan would be here. I didn't expect the big silver truck with the slogan, "National Pipes: We Create Careers, Not Jobs," to be parked right outside the house. Her dad is here, too. The slogan against this rotting, out-of-shape neighborhood is enough to make me chuckle. That is, if I still thought there was something to laugh about in this whole twisted situation.

I'm wearing my work clothes. Dress pants, crisp black dress shirt, and my brown Oxfords. I walk over to the door and knock once, twice, knowing they are here. The Harley Davidson is parked in its designated yellow-grassed spot, too.

The shuffling sound and indistinct chatter stir something in me. Not because I am worried about these two idiots, but because it kills me that this is the soundtrack of Remi's life.

Ryan opens the screen door, fiddling with the rusty lock. Everything rattles. I wait, still and composed, but mentally gearing up for a fight, wondering when the hell this asshole is going to look up and see that I'm not one of his drug-dealer friends.

"Yo, what's..." The door flings open, and he stands there in a dirty wifebeater, a six-day stubble, and that dazed look of a man who isn't sure what day or time it is. "What the fuck?" He blinks.

"The fuck is that you and I are going to have a long conversation tonight, whether you like it or not." I grab him by the throat and walk him back into the house. Ryan Anderson doesn't put up a fight. Not yet, anyway. My grip on his neck isn't as tight as I want it to be and I am taller and bigger. More menacing. Then there is my tone. My voice. I sound like a man you don't want to mess around with. Because I'm not.

I stop when he is next to his dining table and let go of his throat, throwing him into one of the eaten wooden chairs. Everything in the place reeks, him included. Ryan lolls his head from side to side and laughs manically.

"You're him," he says. My blood freezes in my veins. For a second there, I think he recognizes me from his time with Gwen. From the black hole that seems to have sucked me deeper into depression until Remington Stringer strode into my life with her long legs and pouty lips and gave me some of her light. "You're the motherfucking teacher, dude."

He's high. Wasted. Completely fucked up. He looks jaded, his eyes bloodshot, purple rings adorning his eye sockets. His skin is clammy all over. His arms and the sliver of flesh that peeks from his wifebeater. His chest. I grab a chair, spinning it around and plopping down, my arms embracing the back of it.

"Where's your deadbeat dad?"

"You mean Remi's dad?" He sniffs loudly and rolls his eyes, shaking his head. "Not giving you shit, man. Why would I even talk to you? Unless I get money out of it, of course."

"It's simple, Anderson. You will talk to me, because I'm the only person who can prevent you from being thrown into jail for a long time."

"You're full of shit," he spits to the floor. I stare at him like he is dirt.

"Dealing weapons and drugs? You're looking at fifteen years if you're lucky. But you aren't that lucky, are you? If you were, you'd be out of this shithole by now. So, let's try again. Where's Daddy Stringer?"

"He's fucking the neighbor next door. Her husband works with him at the same company, and he's gone on a long drive for the night. Want to go there and congratulate him on his pity fuck?"

Jesus, this guy is all class. I smile politely. "Guess it's just you and me then, pal. Do you know why I'm here, Ryan?"

He sits back and lights a cigarette, exhaling loudly. "Because you're a fucking pedo and you're looking for another piece of young ass from a neighborhood where girls don't have enough money to sue your fancy ass?"

"That's a lot of big words from a very simple man." I lean forward and tap his nose like he is adorable, and he swats my hand away and growls.

"It's a good thing you came here, *Teach*. I have a bone to pick with you, too."

"You do? How nice. We should do it more often," I say, but my heart is picking up speed, fast. My stomach lurches.

Maybe he is bullshitting, but I doubt it. Very much so.

"Yeah. I mean, I have pictures of you hanging out with my sister." Ryan tousles his blond hair with the same hand that holds his cigarette, slouching backwards and staring at nothing in particular, looking deep in thought. "Why would you fucking take her on your boat and out to eat? You're supposed to educate her, you feelin' me? Just give her *tools* for her future. You're giving her your tool, all right. But I don't think it's what they had in mind." He bursts out laughing.

I shake my head. "I don't think you understand. I have hard evidence against you, Anderson."

"You have a hard-on for teenage girls. That's what you have."

"I have photos of you running around and giving teenage kids Glocks wrapped around a towel. Selling a pregnant lady fucking coke."

"Who the fuck are you to lecture me!" Ryan flings his arms in the air, spitting as he yells, "Look at you and your own mess. You're fucking a teenage girl, for fuck's sake."

"I can put you in jail for a long time." I feel my voice rising along with the level of panic in my body.

"So can I."

"She's eighteen." What am I saying? What in the world am I admitting to?

"You're fucking done," Ryan spits.

"You killed my sister," I snap loudly. More clearly, as Ryan's face twists in confusion before recognition settles on it. "You killed Gwen. My sister. She's gone."

There is a beat of silence in which both of us take deep, huge breaths, and then before we know it, we are on the floor. I am punching him in the face, feeling his bones crack under my fist. He flails. I throw him across the room and launch at him again. This time he grabs my arm, ready for me, and twists it hard. I feel the pain but can't bring myself to care. The things that go through my head… They are more important than what I am feeling physically.

Gwen.

Remington.

The past.

The future.

My present. My present is a secret, but not for long, I decide. She craves normalcy. She *needs* stability. We'd never be normal, but the best things never are. I will be her constant. Her safety net. Someone she will learn to trust and not be afraid to depend on.

Ryan and I are a pile of limbs and blood before I hear my phone buzzing. It is the middle of the night, and there is only one person who could call me at this time.

I right myself, standing up and pushing my foot over his face, standing over him, stepping over his cheek.

"Hello?" I ask, breathing hard. "Remi? Hello? Are you there?"

I hear papers shuffling, the little sucks of air she takes in between. Then the phone goes dead.

Shit.

Remi

Even before I open my eyes, I know that I'm alone.

It's a feeling I've grown accustomed to in recent years. The chill of the sheets wrapping around me. I'm not even sure what wakes me up, but once my eyes blink open, I send a hand to the nightstand, feeling around for my phone, but coming up empty-handed.

I look to Pierce's alarm clock and check the time. Half past two a.m. The Jack and Jill bathroom light is off, the rest of the house dark and quiet. I wait for a while, willing myself to fall back asleep to no avail.

I sigh.

I check the time again. Three minutes past three.

Where the hell is he?

Walking over to his fruitwood walk-in closet, I borrow one of his white tees, inhaling the scent of his manhood, enjoying the soft fabric of the Balmain top caressing my body.

I decide to check his office. This wouldn't be the first time Pierce wandered down there at unspeakable hours. I walk down the steps and head toward the only other place, besides his kitchen, that I've been in this house. My knock is light, but it still makes the cracked door open wider. His brown leather executive chair is empty. The phone on his desk calls for me to use it. The same phone I studied religiously—it's a vintage rotary dial that probably costs a fortune—while I was bent over it, my face just an inch from the golden numbers that stared back at me.

I plop down in his chair and pick up the phone, dialing the number I memorized by heart long before I ever used it, and wait for him to pick up. I accidentally bump the mouse to his computer—who uses a mouse anymore?—and his monitor lights up, illuminating his desk. He doesn't answer. Fear gnaws at my gut, tugging an invisible string of panic. I'm about to hang up and recalculate my plan, but then I see something that makes me pause.

A manila envelope, not unlike the one I saw handed to him outside the café after school that day.

I hesitate. As much as I hate secrets—secrets are what threw my life into chaos and turmoil, what got Christian in the hospital—I recognize that it's not for me to read. At the same time, I think about all the things I'm not privy to. All the stuff Pierce James keeps away from me.

His family.

His sister.

His history.

His story.

To read or not to read—debate this, Mr. James.

My fingers find their way to the envelope. Slowly. Unsurely. They take their time, just like I do as I weigh the consequences. My father thinks I'm a liar. Ryan thinks I'm a slut. And Pierce…who knows what Pierce thinks. That I'm incapable of taking care of myself. Or maybe that I'm too young to fully understand whatever is going on around me.

But I understand it. Crystal clear. And I have a feeling things are only going to feel more real after I open this envelope, marked with the word *confidential* over it in bold, red letters.

I dump the contents of the envelope onto the desk with a soft thud and stare at it for a moment before I realize what I'm seeing. Before the names pop up. Before *my* name appears.

There are pictures.

There are testimonies.

There are unveiled secrets.

There is truth.

"Hello? Remi?" Pierce's gruff voice inquires on the

other line, startling me.

"Sweetheart." He sounds like he is out of breath. "Is everything okay?"

I let the phone slip from my fingers, and it hits the desk with a bang.

It was all a lie.

He never wanted me.

It was all a lie.

He used me.

It was all a lie.

We're nothing. Not even a secret. We're nothing but sin.

Pierce is still talking, but all I can hear is the sound of my own heart in my ears. The fact that it is still beating is almost reassuring, because it's hurting. Hurting so bad. Aching, breaking, slipping away. Suddenly, I'm weightless. Restless. I'm floating outside my body, and I look at everything that's happened to me in recent weeks—in recent months, really, ever since I started my senior year—and clarity washes over me like electric shock.

I drop the phone, clutching the papers in one of my hands.

My legs carry me to the front door, where I stop. My feet are bare, and I'm still wearing his clothes. How far can you run when the only thing that fuels you is anger, secrets, and deceit?

I'm about to find that out.

Chapter Twenty-Two

Remi

Tonight, I do something I never thought I'd do. Something I promised myself I wouldn't do, in fact.

Tonight, I sleep on the street. Okay, sleep is a little dramatic, but I'm feeling pretty melodramatic right about now. I mostly just wander around until the sun comes up.

It's not a conscious decision more than it is just the way things are. I cannot go back home—literally and figuratively. I need to let Ry calm down, I need to process all the information that I've just discovered, and the buses don't run from Pierce's neighborhood to mine in the middle of the night.

I kick little rocks and walk in what seems like circles for the longest time until I get to this gas station at an intersection in the middle of nowhere. I can see the city lights of Vegas twinkling in the distance. Gold, pink, purple, and green swirling around and around. It seems fitting that I was born in Sin City. I wonder what my mom would have said about all this. About what became of Dad and me. About Pierce.

I take out my phone that I found tangled up in the just-fucked blankets of Pierce's bed—it's not my camera, but it'll do—and capture the moment a homeless person walks out of the food mart next to the station with a sandwich in his hand and gives it to a homeless woman who is sitting on the side of the road.

The papers I found in Pierce's envelope made no room for misunderstanding. He sat on Ryan's information a long time and produced everything that could incriminate him. I was confused, upset, and frantic to leave. I barely made it back to Pierce's porch to put some shoes and pants on and grab the evidence against Ryan before I left. And now I'm wondering, was Ryan right all along?

He said Pierce was playing me.

He said Pierce had an agenda.

He said I was bound to get hurt.

All of those things happened. Pierce has hurt me more than anyone else ever did before, no matter how hard he pretended to want to protect me. My heart broke under his watch.

I walk over to the bus station the minute the clock hits six and get on the first bus back home. On the way there, I think about what I might find. Will Dad and Ry even forgive me? Is there anything to forgive, anyway? And do I tell Ryan everything—about Pierce's insane agenda against him, why on earth is Mr. James after my brother, anyway?—or simply keep it to myself and make do with the fact that Pierce doesn't have any access to all this evidence now.

When I get back home, everyone is gone. The living room is a mess. I feel lonelier than ever.

I walk over to my bed, bury my face in the pillow, and cry.

I cry until I fall asleep.

I cry until my hatred toward myself, and Pierce, and even Dad and Ryan turns into numbness.

I cry until there are no more tears left in me.

Pierce

I arrive at work in a particularly sour mood the next morning.

The fact that I'm sporting a shiner and a cut lip doesn't help matters either. I look like I've been in a dogfight. I feel like it, too. The way I left things with Ryan was bad—but getting back home and seeing my bed naked of her and my office desk naked of the evidence I gathered against him for months upon months is nothing short of tragic. My whole existence, everything I have and want and is worth living for, is suddenly out of reach, and I'm contemplating doing things I shouldn't even be thinking about.

To Ryan Anderson, mostly. But to the rest of this fucked-up place, too.

Because I won't delude myself. Remington Stringer was a troubled girl before she got here…but she is lost and gone now because of us, too.

The first class is a blur. I don't even bother to pretend like I care. I look ridiculous with my white dress shirt and slim black tie and those preppy blue dress pants that are supposed to make you look sophisticated. I'm anything *but* right now.

"What happened to your face, Mr. James?"

"I fell."

"It's on your arms, too."

"Fine, I got into a fistfight with a junkie."

"Ha-ha. Come on, what happened?"

Well, can't say I didn't tell the truth. First period passes, and then the second one is Remi's. She's not here, and I'm not surprised, but her empty chair is taunting me. I can't wait for the hours, minutes, seconds to pass so I can rush over to her house and smooth things over. Only I'm not sure I still can.

At lunch, Headmaster Charles catches me in the hallway. I'm breezing through students—through life—about to make an exit out the door and get myself some cigarettes and a Coke. I almost forgot about my vices. For a minute there, I stopped smoking. But then she left and I drowned right back into despair.

"Mr. James, a word?"

"Perhaps even a few, if that's what it takes to put your point across." I smile easily to him, clasping my leather courier bag under my arm. The headmaster falls into step with me, and we both stare ahead.

"Miss Stephens' parents called me this morning."

It takes me a second to remember because my mind is elsewhere. Mikaela Stephens. The girl who bullies Remi. I nod, wondering where this is heading.

"Her parents found text messages about a fight that

supposedly happened in your class with another student. Remington Stringer?"

No point in denying.

"Yes?"

"Were they disciplined?" I can hear the worry in his voice. The dread.

I stop by the door leading to the stairway to the street.

"They were both let off with a warning."

"Whose decision was this? The student board?" Headmaster Charles strokes his chin in my periphery. Oh, yes. That's the part where I should mention that in this fancy little school, people get judged by the student board. They're like the judge, jury, and executioner around here.

"I never brought it up to the student body," I say curtly.

"Why not?"

"Because I'm a grown-up capable of making my own decisions."

"That's not how things work around here."

"That's how things work for me." I turn around and leave him to stand there.

"They were also concerned that there may be something inappropriate transpiring with you and Miss Stringer. They said Miss Stephens confided in them about it this morning. I don't have to tell you how serious this allegation is, Pierce. Tell me now if there's any truth to it."

I'm sure their daughter fed them the only truth she knows. That Mr. James and Miss Remington have been known to stay in the classroom long after the bell has rung. Maybe she even knows that we locked the door a few times. I wasn't exactly careful the last few times.

"There's a little truth in every lie," I say. And that's the only information he's getting out of me.

I have no time for the Stephens. I have no time for Headmaster Charles. Quite frankly, I have no time for my students either. I decide on a whim that for the first time in a *long* time, I'm going to do something different. Something that isn't for anyone else but me.

I walk toward my car in the teachers' lot, start the engine, and drive to the bad side of Vegas.

To the only place where I want to be.

To *her*.

Chapter Twenty-Three

Remi

At noon, the door opens and slams. I'm still in bed, half-asleep, half-awake, and blinking at the ceiling. The papers I stole from Pierce are somewhere no one can find them—in an old textbook I saved from my old school. Maybe it's all the adrenaline that coursed through my veins last night, but today, I feel oddly lethargic.

"Anyone here?" I hear Ryan's voice, and the mere sound of him makes my whole body heave with uncontrollable sobs. I cry because I want to save him. I cry because I want to save *me*. I cry because once upon a time, he wasn't the man who tried to shove a hand down my skirt. He was the brother who taught me how to skateboard and got me photography accessories for my birthdays.

"Me," I barely whisper, still lying on my bed. "I'm here."

His footsteps become louder with every passing second. Fear stabs at my chest, mixed with an unexplainable longing. I can't wrap my head around everything that I'm feeling right now. There's too much pain in me to think clearly.

"What are you doing here?" he asks, his fingers hovering over my doorframe. He looks…like Ryan. Like a strong Viking. Like the man who helped raise me and tolerated my crush, then later danced on the line between appropriate and inappropriate. And even though he has lost a bit of weight recently, he is still beautiful.

I cup my mouth with my hand and shake my head, feeling the tears streaming down my cheeks. "Everything is so fucked up, Ry. I'm so mad at you. At him. At everything."

He is next to me in a second, sitting on my bed and pulling me into a hug. I bury my face in his shoulder. He smells of gasoline and cigarettes and home. Home that doesn't smell like flowers and cooked meals and a nice feminine perfume, but it is still *my home*.

"Oh, baby. Rem…" His voice disappears inside my hair, and he is stroking it, and I am breaking just a little bit more, nostalgia making my heart overflow. "What did the bastard do to you?"

"You're both magnificent bastards." I sniff in protest, wiggling away from him. "You. Pierce. Dad. You're all the worst. Dad believing your lies. You making my life hell. Pierce betraying me."

"I'm jealous." Ryan's voice is the softest it can be. "I'm fucking it up because I'm jealous of him. This was not supposed to happen this way. You became a different person since you started going to this fancy school, and it felt like you were leaving us." There is a pause. Ryan stares at the floor. Then, "He came here last night."

"He did?" I pull away so I can examine my stepbrother's face. He nods solemnly, pushing away a lock of my hair from my face. "Sure did, babe. Threatened me. That's how I got this pretty thing." He points at his cheek that's currently purple. I didn't even bother to notice that Ryan looks all kinds of banged up. I blink once, twice.

"Did you hurt him?" I don't know why I'm asking this. I certainly shouldn't care, but I do. He nods.

"He probably looks worse than I do today."

"Good," I say, straightening my spine. "Serves him right." But inside, my heart breaks for yet another reason.

"What'd he do?" Ryan demands, and there's a certain edge to his voice. The same violence that's soaring over us ever since he started mixing up with the wrong people.

And as much as I want to protect Ryan—the guy I grew up with, the guy who took care of me all those years, albeit in a weird, screwed-up way—I want to protect Pierce, too. They've both hurt me so bad. I shouldn't even want to entertain myself with the idea of helping either of them, but for now, I'm keeping Pierce's secret manila envelope for myself.

"Tell me, Ryan. What makes Pierce James hate you so much? What have you done to him?"

Ryan licks his lips and looks away.

Guilty, I think. *Guilty all the way.*

Pierce

I rap the door to her bathroom a few times, this time growling.

"Gwen, open up for God's sake. I don't have all day. I'm

on my lunch break. I need to teach third period in twenty minutes, and traffic is insane."

She doesn't answer. I feel full to the brim with discontent and annoyance. The whole Gwen situation grinds on my nerves. She is going to get help even if I have to drag her by the hair and throw her into the nearest rehab center with a room for a new tenant. Just a week ago, I spoke to Mother Dearest, who had agreed to shell out some money for a Santa Barbara resort where Gwen could get clean. We'd decided to split it halfway, me with my teacher salary and her with her indefinite amount of millions in the bank. I don't care. I just want Gwen to get better.

"Goddammit, Gwen, the water is leaking." I lift one foot upward and stare down at the water crawling from underneath her bathroom door. "I swear to God, if you don't open up right now I'm going in."

Nothing.

Up until now I didn't feel it. The fear that grips you by the throat and squeezes hard. I kick the locked door open and find her in the bathtub, naked, her head under the water. I run toward her, slipping a few times on the wet floor. Her whole body has sunk into the water.

And there are no bubbles.

No bubbles.

She isn't breathing.

"Gwen, Gwen, Gwen, sweetheart." My voice is foreign to my ears. I sound...frantic. "You're okay. Come on. Let's get you out of here. Come on." I grab her by the hair before dragging her out. I lay her on the floor and am actually stupid enough to worry about how cold it must feel against her skin before I dial 911. My fingers are shaking. I can't look at her. Not because she is naked. Because she is blue.

After I hang up on the girl from the emergency center, I roll my older sister to the side, trying to get her to throw up some of the water she's swallowed. Then I roll her back onto her back and try to administer CPR to her dead body. I don't cry. I'm not even all that sad at this point. I am mad. Fucking furious, to be honest.

"What the hell did you do that for? Fuck!" I roar.

"Shit, Gwen. You don't look hurt. You'll be okay."

"Gwen. Gwen. Gwen. Gwen."

The ambulance arrives a few minutes later. I watch from the corner of the living room as they zip her into a body bag. It dawns on me that I have no one to call. No one to share this with. I bet my parents won't be surprised if I call them.

"She looked...fine," I say to one of the paramedics.

Even to my own ears, this sounded crazy. My sister wasn't fine. My sister was a heroin addict. She was a junkie. She'd been looking gaunt, malnourished, and wild-eyed for a long time now. From about three months after she followed me to Sin City, to be exact.

"Looks like an overdose," the young, pimple-suffering man says, his voice apologetic. "I think she suffered from cardiac arrest, but you'll know more after they send you the report. I'm sorry for your loss."

"Yeah." I scrub my face with my palm. "Me too."

I go back home, get into my own bathtub, and stare at the tiles. I thought I had processed it, but I was wrong.

The penny drops two weeks later. I do well in those weeks. So well. Make all the necessary funeral arrangements, noti-fy my parents and our friends, have people come over—col-leagues, friends, ex-lovers—and help me set everything up.

It's two weeks later when I drive down the strip when it finally hits me.

The light is red. I look out the window of my car and see Ryan Anderson crossing the street with a random chick that looks like a typical drug addict. Smeared makeup, swollen eyes, and scrawny body wrapped in a mini skirt.

His arm is flung over her shoulder, and he is laughing and whispering something into her ear.

He did it.

He did it to Gwen, and now he is going to do it to this girl.

She is so out of it, she would let him get away with anything, I know.

The next morning, I hand my resignation to Headmaster Charles and decide to dedicate the upcoming months to making sure Ryan Anderson will never ruin another life again.

"Keep your resignation to yourself." Headmaster Charles *pushes the letter I wrote across his desk. "Let's talk about it next year. You might feel differently."*

"I will never feel differently. I can't work. I can't concentrate." I can't breathe. *My sister raised me, goddammit. And what have I done in return? Dragged her down a rabbit hole of drugs, alcohol, and bad choices.*

"You will, Mr. James." The left corner of Headmaster Charles' lip slides up in half a smirk. *"When you're ready, it'll happen. There's a lot to look forward to in life, even if it doesn't seem that way right now. Always remember that, hmm?"*

Pierce

The screen door whines as it swings back and forth, and how long has it been since this house has seen a handyman?

I want to get her out of here. I was goddamn close to doing that, too.

Pacing on her porch, I inwardly convince myself that I can reason with her. Remington is a smart girl. Surely, after I give her the whole truth, she will understand.

But then I remember that Remington is like a live wire. She's emotional and bold, and she doesn't do anything half-assed. She feels everything so much deeper than I—or most people, I suspect—and that's why she's so hurt. She's been badly burned by almost everyone in her life, and I'm no better.

I knock on the front door—it's locked, thank God— three times, lose my patience before the second is over, and ring the doorbell endless times. It's not working. Big surprise. I wait a few seconds, then knock again.

Nothing.

I know she's here. It's creepy as hell, but I can feel her. Like I know she's in a classroom even before I walk through the door.

"Remington!" I shout, not giving two shits about the fact that anyone can hear and see me. I'm way past killing my career. At this stage I'm pretty much dancing all over the corpse of it. "Open the door, sweetheart. Come on."

The worst part is that I can actually hear her sniffling. She is crying. I can peek and look at her through her window, but I'd like to think I have more dignity than that. "Remi," I say, now more softly.

Nothing.

"I have news on Christian. I know you want to know," I lie. Jesus Christ. I am a fucking douchebag, but I can't help it. After a few seconds, I hear her padding barefoot on the floor, and the door opens. She looks like hell. Pretty as spring, because it's still Remi, but still.

"How is he doing?" She hugs the door to her chest, like it can protect her from me. Like she needs to be protected. I shake my head.

"Sorry, I don't actually know. I just needed you to come here. I…"

As I start talking, she tries to slam the door in my face. I'm quick to sneak an arm and stop her—fuck, that hurts—and push the door open as I walk in without her permission. Technically, she can call the police. Logically, she should. But I'm taking some risks here in the name of whatever the hell it is that we have.

"You're a liar, a cheater, and an asshole," she spits in my face, pushing me away. Her eyes look sunken. Like she's been crying for hours. "I *trusted* you, Mr. James! It may not mean a lot to you, but to me? To me it was everything." She grabs an empty vase on her dining table and throws it across the room, and I feel a stab of pain, because I know that she's the only one here who would ever think to put flowers on the table. She wants everyone to think she's hardened and callous, but there's still a girl in there who, no matter how much life throws at her, still tries to make her dark world just a little bit brighter with some goddamn flowers. The vase misses me by an inch. I take a step toward her. She holds up a finger at me.

"Don't. You've lost your right to come anywhere near me. I will call the police right now if you don't leave. I don't even care enough to ask what fucked-up obsession you have with my stepbrother. I just want you out of my life. We have one more semester to tolerate each other. Don't come near me."

"You know that's not possible," I say coldly, taking

another step in her direction, knowing exactly what I'm doing and how dangerous it is, and still taking the risk. "I can't stay away from you."

"You can, and you will. From me. From my family. From everything I care about and you want to destroy."

"Remi, I did this for you."

"*Mr. James*," she enunciates, like we're not personal anymore. Like we never happened. Like I didn't study every single curve in her body and saw her bewildered expression as her body let go and combusted with pleasure in my hands. "I hope you don't believe the bullshit you're feeding me, because I sure as hell don't."

"Ryan is dangerous," I tell her. She is shaking all over and hugging her midriff. I want to make her pain go away, but I know that I can't, so I continue. "Ryan is the reason my sister died. She overdosed on the shit your brother gave her. He fucked her and he drugged her and ultimately he killed her." There is no emotion in my voice.

"Liar!" She lunges in my direction and pushes me away. "You're lying. Get out!"

"I was afraid he would do it to someone else." I stay rooted in place, staring at her dead in the eyes. "And then I met you, Remington, and that trickle of fear became paralyzing when I realized his next casualty may well be the woman I'm falling in love with."

No truer words were spoken, and yet, I don't find my truth particularly liberating or comfortable. I find it oddly infuriating. Maddening, even. Because this wasn't supposed to happen, and yet it did, despite my best efforts.

I fell in love with a girl who felt like a woman and made me feel like a man instead of a ghost.

I fell in love, at the beginning with an idea, in the

middle with her curves, and in the end, with the whole package.

I fell in love with my student, and now I am standing here, asking her to sin. Asking her to do the thing I would argue against and frown upon. Asking her to love me back.

Remi throws her head back and laughs before shaking it somberly.

"Get out."

"Remington..."

"No. Get the fuck out, Pierce." She stalks to the door and opens it wide. "Get out of my house, out of my life, out of my head. You've had enough time to tell me all of this about Ryan. You had the time to warn me. You had the time to explain yourself. You had every opportunity to make this right, or let me decide for myself if I wanted to be in a relationship with someone who relentlessly pursued the persecution of my brother. You're a lawyer, for fuck's sake. You know what he's facing. Don't tell me you don't recognize how bad you've hurt me."

"I know. And let me assure you..."

"No. You're done assuring me. Out," she says again, and this time I really have no choice. I can't force her to listen to me. "You're done here. Please don't make it awkward at school and make me do something that would jeopardize your career." She says that in the flattest voice I've ever heard her produce before adding, "And that goes for your plans to take Ryan down, too. I have leverage over you, Mr. James. I strongly suggest you leave my family alone and focus on your own. Go find another stupid girl to ruin."

Harsh words from a girl who knows what a harsh life feels like.

I give her one last look to see if there's room in her

heart to give me another chance. There isn't. Her face is hard, and her quivering lower lip is the only indication that maybe she once loved me, too.

"Out." The word falls from her lips more quietly now.

I leave, without the girl.

Without the evidence against Ryan Anderson.

And most importantly, without my soul.

Chapter Twenty-Four

Remi

Christian leaves the hospital two days later with a broken eye socket and a fractured nose. He looks like how I feel. A complete wreck. But as I dote on him in his room, I realize that it's not about me right now. I copied all the homework he missed out on from my notebooks and bought him his favorite quinoa and avocado salad from the bakery across the road from our school. I sit on the edge of his bed and tell him about all the latest gossip—leaving Benton out of it, of course—when he groans as he shifts in his place.

"Remi?"

"Yeah?"

"How do you think school is going to feel for me for the rest of the year?" His voice is small. He is referring to outing Benton—no matter what happened between them, I think he knows that he was wrong—and to the fact he is now the most hated person amongst the jocks. I want to tell him that it's going to be okay, but the truth is, he is probably the biggest outcast in our year other than me. Even though Benton Herring was quick to sweep the gay rumors about him under the carpet—he said Christian has had a weird fixation with him ever since he moved to Riverside High and that he had to turn him down a few times—I know that the story is far from over.

"Honestly? I think we should both invest in a good pepper spray." I sigh.

"At least we have each other." Christian brushes my dark hair, and I try to smile, but it is hard to look at him, with the purple and green rings around his eyes, the yellow of the fading bruises on his cheeks, without wanting to cry. I also want to cry simply because my heart is broken into a thousand different pieces, and I have no idea how to mend it back. I'm not even sure I want to. Part of me believes that I deserve all this pain. I did something wrong. I did my teacher. Maybe I *should* pay the price.

"You'll always have me." I take his hand and lace my fingers through his, reassuring him.

"So, what's up with Mr. James? Are you guys still seeing each other?" He perks up in his bed, scooting upwards to a sitting position. I smile through the pain, because that's what life has taught me.

"Not really."

"Why?"

"He wasn't who I thought he was."

"And why is that?"

"I thought, if anything, I'd be *his* downfall…" I say,

biting my lower lip and picking at my chipped, black nail polish. "Turns out he was mine."

⌐⟶

Remi

It's been two weeks since Pierce appeared at my door begging for me to listen to him. Begging for forgiveness. Two weeks, in which I tried to convince myself that in time, it would feel better. That it can't possibly hurt that bad. That life moves on. That he was just a teenage crush.

I see him walking down the hallway, and time stops. He walks in slow motion, at least in my eyes, but maybe it's because when it comes to him, everything else fades away.

He doesn't look at me. He doesn't talk to me. I'm trying to convince myself that he is giving me the space I demanded. The space I blackmailed him into giving me, threatening to tell the world about us. But the truth is, deep inside, I am scared and hurt and desperate. What if he got over me? What if he forgot all about me? What if I was nothing but a quick fuck?

I think about our time together more than I should— every waking moment, and then I dream about it in my sleep. And even though it's only been two weeks, every day, it's becoming a little harder to imagine exactly how his touch felt against my skin. How he smelled when we made love in his bed. How he tasted when we fucked on his office desk.

"Remington?" I hear a voice calling out my name and look up. It's Pierce. I swallow hard.

"Yes?" My back straightens at his voice. We're in the

hallway. He looks amazing in one of his sharp suits.

"Follow me." His voice is so distant and faraway. Like he is talking to me from the other side of the country. I hate it. I nod faintly and move in his direction, and he leads me to Headmaster Charles' office.

"Am I in trouble?" I ask behind his back as we walk past students, cheerleaders, and the commotion of lunch hour.

"Not at all." He takes a sharp right, exactly like I knew he would, and we're standing outside Headmaster Charles' office.

"What is going on?" My heart rate escalates, and I wonder if it can spontaneously burst from everything that's happening here. Has he told Headmaster Charles about us? Does he want me back? What is happening here?

"I've noticed that you haven't fill out any applications to colleges yet." He strangles the handle of the door leading to the office.

I shake away my disbelief and try to calm down. "Yeah. No. I didn't have time."

Riverside makes you log your history of applications and acceptance letters to their online system so they can send potential colleges all the necessary documents and reference letters. My file was blank, as I didn't have time or the right mindset to actually make any academic plans.

"Well, I took it upon myself to set you up with a few options." He knocks on the door softly, then opens it, and behind Headmaster Charles' desk is a woman I don't know. She is young, maybe mid-twenties, and she is wearing a suit and a sweet smile, her blonde hair in a tight bun.

"Hello there, Remington. I'm Holly Tate." She reaches with her arm for a handshake, but I don't make a move.

"I'm an external adviser. My job is to find students their best fits for college. Mr. James spoke very highly of you. I can't make any promises, but I can try to give you a few shortcuts to your colleges of interest once we look at your grades and electives."

I want to laugh and cry at the same time. He wants to look after me and secure my future after I threatened him and kicked him out of my house. Jesus. Only Pierce James would do something like this.

But I don't want his generosity. I don't want his help. I want to forget we've ever happened and move on.

"No, thank you," I hear myself say. Holly's smile melts on her face, and it gives me a little solace. "But I appreciate the offer."

I turn around and walk away. I hope he will follow me, but when he doesn't, I'm not surprised.

Everything is changing. We are changing. The only thing that's not changing is my family life. No. That stays put. Like a bad habit you can't seem to shake.

Dad is on the road again, with nothing but a quick text telling me that we'd work it out when he got back.

Ryan is back to disappearing and standing me up when he needs to be picking me up from school, sporadically giving me lunch and school money.

And the reality of my destiny is clear as the sky from Piece's boathouse on Lake Mead.

There's nothing to see here.

All the interesting, beautiful things are happening to other people.

Chapter Twenty-Five

Pierce

Gwen always used to say that hope is a contagious disease. If you're not careful, you can catch it. I used to laugh it off at the time. I didn't have hope because I didn't need it. I had her. I had friends. I had a glowing future ahead of me. I saw the world through rose-colored glasses. I thought I had it all.

Today, I have nothing.

I don't have any friends. I mean, I do. Of course, I do. But not real ones. I've pushed them all away.

I don't have a glowing future ahead of me. I have a mediocre job I hold onto because I don't want to leave this place.

I don't have Gwen.

And I don't have Remi.

That leaves me with spare time on my hands, so today I decide to do something productive with my life. I log on to my Amazon account and order what I wanted to order for her the day she showed up on my doorstep, soaking wet, telling me it was her birthday. Then, I drive to the nearest Safeway and buy Shelly her usual groceries fit for a kindergartener.

I'm trying to keep my world moving for no reason other than Remington Stringer. It occurs to me, as I walk down the aisles of the too-bright supermarket, that I have nothing to lose or to gain outside the game of winning her back.

After I'm done paying for everything, I drive over to Shelly's place. I know she'll be there, because unless she's scoring, she's at home. And last time I saw her, she was dope sick. Which means she hadn't used in a while. Hopefully, she was able to keep that up.

If she is home, no issues.

If she is scoring, I know exactly where she buys her drugs. On which street corners to look. And I know that even if I don't find her, she'll be back to her apartment as soon as she can to stick that needle into a vein.

When I get to her apartment building, it dawns on me that I haven't been here in the longest time. Since Remington and I got together. Revisiting Shelly was always about revisiting Gwen. And Remington provided the distraction I needed in protecting a woman I could actually save. I'm not sure Shelly can be saved. I doubt she even wants to be.

I knock on Shelly's door two times, the loaded paper bags at my feet. I hear music from the other side of the door. Breaking Benjamin is on full blast. She wouldn't be able to hear me even if I screamed to her from the other side.

Staring at this door takes me back to that time I looked at their bathroom door when I found Gwen. Everything looked so ordinary...until it wasn't.

I decide on a whim to walk in. She always locks her door even though she lives in a dumpster not even a homeless person would rob. I walk in and examine the living room. Empty. The music comes from the bedroom. I dump the paper bags onto her small to non-existing kitchen counter. It's already crammed with half-empty bottles of soda and torn chips bags. Then I proceed down the short, narrow hallway to knock on her door to make sure she's still alive and breathing.

The door is open.

I look in and see Shelly on top of Ryan fucking Anderson. He's sitting on her bed, his back against the headboard, as she fucking rides him with her shirt still on.

Ryan fucking Anderson who killed Gwen.

Ryan fucking Anderson who is killing Remi in an entirely different way.

Ryan fucking Anderson, who killed my hope, and when hope barged back into my life in the form of his sister, he made that go away, too.

Instead of thinking this through—which is admittedly what I should be doing—I act. I kick the door wide open and bolt in, fire in my eyes. My whole body is heaving with rage. I can finish this jerk in two minutes, I'm so furious right now.

"Shelly!" I scream, grabbing the stereo on the dresser by her closet and hurling it against the wall. The music stops. Shelly whips her head around and stares at me, her

mouth agape, from pleasure, shock, surprise, or all three—
I'm not sure. I don't even care. I point at Ryan, panting
hard, watching as his glazed-over eyes are trying to refocus and understand what's going on. He's wasted. She's
drugged up. Unbelievable.

"Get up right now," I grit out, "and leave Anderson and
me alone."

"Whoa, whoa." Anderson snaps out of whatever it is
he's on, pushes Shelly away so she rolls on the mattress,
and gets up on wobbly feet. He tucks his dick back into his
jeans, which he didn't bother to take off when he started
screwing my dead sister and his ex-girlfriend's roommate.
Class act. I cock an eyebrow, because more than it is infuriating, it is also pathetic. "What the fuck are you doing
here? Are you following me, Teach? Get the fuck outta
here."

"Shelly, out." I ignore him.

"Shelly, stay," he counters.

Shelly looks between us and decides to unglue her
ass from the mattress and leave after all. I'm much more
commanding than this idiot, and if she fears someone out
of the two of us, it's me. That leaves me alone with Ryan.
My head is a mess. I want to kill him—I *can* kill him, God
knows I'm capable of it—but at the same time I really need
to think this shit through for Remi's sake.

"She chose me," Ryan says nonchalantly, lighting a cigarette and puffing the smoke upwards. "Rem. She chose to
come back to me. Like I know she would. She is my destiny, Teach. I'm hers. You can't undo this. God wants us to be
together."

"Don't talk on God's behalf. You can barely form a
goddamn sentence."

"Tsk, tsk." Ryan laughs, shaking his head. "I see that you're still not over my future wife."

"I've literally just walked in on you having sex with another woman," I grit out. Ryan shrugs. My whole body is shaking. Fuck, I want to kill him.

"Remi knows the drill. But I'll always go back to her."

"You killed my sister," I tell Ryan. "You fucking killed Gwen. You gave her those drugs."

"*No*," Ryan drawls out slowly, and suddenly, he looks a lot more sober. He takes another drag of his cigarette, and even though I'm dying for one, I will never, ever ask this bastard for anything. I hear Shelly setting everything in the kitchen.

"Gwen did it to herself. I gave her drugs to sample, but she overdosed. She took three times what she usually did. I know because I measured every single fraction of a gram before I gave it to her. And she used everything. Gwen wanted to die. Her usual fix wouldn't have killed her. Put her in the hospital? Maybe. I'm not a killer. I didn't know this would happen."

"You're a fucking liar," I spit out. But Ryan's face contorts in pain, and he shakes his head some more.

"I'm not a killer, man. I cared about Gwen."

"You gave her drugs!"

"We *all* take drugs, motherfucker!" Ryan throws his arms in the air, exasperated. "What the fuck? I got her drugs like you'd get Remi dinner. This is our food. This is our lives. This is what we need to make it to the next fucking day."

"No." It's my turn to shake my head. Just…no.

"*Yes*," Ryan says. "Yes, I liked Gwen. But she was sad, man. She was sad all the fucking time. I was sad when she died. But I wasn't surprised. And I knew it wasn't an accident."

I shake my head, feeling the tears stabbing at my eyeballs. I want to get out of here. I want to stay and hear more. I want to fucking kill him. I want to ask him more about my sister. A sister I didn't know as well as I thought, but am starting to realize I have harbored resentment in quantities I'm not equipped to deal with.

"You'll drag Remington down the same path if you don't let her go, you know," I say instead of screaming and fighting and taunting him like I desperately want to. "You want her to stay so you can bask in her light. But she's going to end up a Shelly or even a Gwen if she doesn't get out of this town, and we both know it."

"No." Ryan stubs the cigarette into a wall to put it out. It's disgusting, but then again, this whole room is full of cigarette butts and smells of piss. "No, I'll get better."

"You won't, and we both know it."

"I will."

"You can't."

"She's mine."

"She's no one's," I admit. "But if she'll ever be anyone's, if you truly love her, you better hope like hell it's not you she'll belong to."

"Shut up!" he screams, tugging at his hair.

"You know it's true."

Ryan falls to his knees and cries. I want to do the same but stop myself. Instead, I take a step back. I watch him. I feel sorry for him. Life failed him the way it failed my sister. Or maybe they both just failed at life and didn't have the guts or strength to take another stab at the test.

"I don't want Rem to turn into Gwen," Ryan admits,

sniffing. He looks like a boy like this. Sitting on the floor, messing his blond hair with his fist.

"Then you know what to do about it," I say.

"Maybe," he answers.

Maybe is better than no.

Chapter Twenty-Six

Remi

The cafeteria looks smaller.

The hallways seem narrower.

Everything is closing in on me. I want to get away, but at the same time, I'm desperate to stay and see him. To feel him. To be around him.

Christian is trying to keep a low profile, something I'm not sure he is capable of doing. He is waiting for me by the door after each class, and we walk together—arms linked— to grab lunch or to our next period. I can almost smell his insecurity. Ever since he and Benton fought in the hallway, he's been trying not to draw attention to himself. But even in school uniform, everything about him is colorful. If he were a character in a book, he would jump out of the page. Like right now, we're walking toward the entrance, about to get out of school and hit the nearest mall, and he is telling me about his upcoming trip to New York—he is trying to get into NYU and is looking at the dorms—he flings his arms in the air and gets caught up in describing the big city to me before he takes it down a notch and lowers his voice.

"So, anyway, I need a new suitcase. And maybe a new tie. I want to look the part, you know? I really feel like I can reinvent myself there." We're both breezing through the doors, and my heart feels a little lighter to put West Point behind me. Leaving Pierce behind is another story.

Ryan has been okay in recent days. Mostly absent and very quiet, but not in the way he was when he was using. I don't know why, and I don't dare to ask. He's slowly turning into the old Ryan, and that's what's important.

"You don't need to reinvent yourself," I say absent-mindedly. "I like you just fine the way you are."

"Other people here don't."

"Other people here are stupid," I drawl.

"Because you're such a genius, aren't you?" I hear a familiar voice behind me and twist my head with a frown. Christian spins around, his whole body tilting to the voice. He reacts to it like I react to Pierce.

Addiction. Obsession. Attraction. Reaction.

"What do you want, Herring?" I feel my nostrils flare. I grab Christian's hand and squeeze it for assurance. "If you get anywhere near him, you'll get expelled." Benton should be expelled already, but Christian didn't want to press charges, and with both Mikaela's senator father and his own father, he never faced any real trouble. And he knows it.

"I just want to talk to him." Benton stares at Christian. Not at me. I can't read his expression, but surely it can't be good. Not after their last encounter together.

"Dream on," I snort out.

"Let's talk." Benton ignores me, taking a step toward Christian. "Alone," he says.

"No." I shake my head.

"Yes." I hear Christian say. I want to pull him toward me, but he is already walking over to Benton in the deserted hallway. I hear the echo of his steps. I watch his back. *This is love*, I think bitterly. *It pulls you in; it freaks you out. It outweighs whatever logical ideas and rational plans you make.*

"Be careful." My voice shakes. Benton says something into his ear. They're not too close, but they're close enough to look intimate. And even though no one is here but us, I know that something has changed in the jock. That this time, I don't need to be worried for Christian's physical safety. I need to be worried for his heart. "Hey, I can wait here for you? Maybe downstairs?" I try one last time. Christian turns around and shakes his head.

"You go. I'll call you after. Thanks, babe."

Reluctantly, I choke the straps of my backpack and hop down the stairs outside, taking them by the two's. I walk over to the bus station, feeling the sun on my skin. I try to think about any of the things that should occupy my thoughts: college applications, patching things up with Dad and Ryan, schoolwork. But nothing sticks. All I can think about is him.

I slouch on the plastic bench at the bus station and stare at the nothingness across the road. Buildings. Trees. People. My bare thighs are burning on the hot plastic, but I don't care enough to stand.

A vehicle I recognize stops in front of me, and the

passenger door flies open.

"Get in," Pierce tells me, leaning on his steering wheel.

"No," I say quietly.

"We need to talk."

I think about Benton and Christian. How Christian pretty much forgave Benton after he beat the shit out of him, or looked about willing to forgive him, and I shake my head. I can't afford to be blinded by love. Not after love kicked me in the ass and tried to take the only family that I have left.

"Not interested, Mr. James."

"Stop with the Mr. James. We're past that."

"A few weeks ago, you would have scolded me for calling you anything but," I say, and not softly, shifting on the bench. "Go away. Someone can see you. Don't want to tarnish that precious reputation of yours."

"Get in."

"No."

"Fine. I'll get out," he says, unbuckling his seatbelt and bolting out of his car in an instant. He is double-parked in the middle of the road, and I'm pretty sure he is breaking five hundred different rules at once.

I watch as he circles the car with something in his hand. It's a box. A big one. He drops it into my hands, and I can feel that it's heavy. It's wrapped in red, but it looks like a toddler wrapped it…before a car ran over it.

"This is for your birthday." He looks at me seriously. "I wrapped it myself." And it dawns on me that Pierce doesn't care much about anything. He could get caught, and he doesn't even give a rat's ass. He is standing here with his student, giving her a present. His stubble and bloodshot eyes also tell me that he is not feeling any better than I do.

"No gifts." I shake my head, shoving it back to his chest, still seated.

"Take it," he says. "You have to. I'll feel better if you do."

"Because I'm *so* concerned with your feelings right now."

"Listen." he sighs. "This is a mistake. All of this. It can't end like this."

"Who are you to say?" I laugh bitterly. "You were the one to fuck it up."

"I tried to protect you," he says, for the one-millionth time. "Get your head out of your ass, Remington. Your brother is dangerous. Your brother is dealing with very sketchy people, and I'm worried about your safety."

This time I can't help it. I stand up and toss the wrapped gift into the open passenger window of his car. "No, Mr. James. You wanted revenge. Forget about what we were. Forget about what we could have been. Remember how you used to say that you were worried you'd ruin me? That you'd break my heart? Well, congratulations. You did. Yours doesn't look to be in better shape than mine, though. So please, make it stop. *Just stop.* Let me lick my wounds in peace. I don't need you."

"It's a Polaroid camera." Pierce shoots me a pained look. A look I've never seen on his face. His throat bobs on a swallow. He looks down. "The gift for your birthday. To capture all the sad and beautiful things," he repeats my words from the second day of school, and my heart breaks a little more.

I start walking toward the next bus station, not looking back.

This is not a love story.

This is not even a hate story.
This is a cautionary tale.

Pierce

I drive after her.

I stop when I realize she's gone to another bus station.

I curse. A lot.

I make a U-turn.

I want to call her, my finger hovering over her name on my phone.

I don't.

I do.

I hang up.

Headmaster Charles is calling me. I don't answer.

Shelly is calling me. I hit ignore.

My mother is calling me. I pick up.

"You need to come for your father's birthday." Her voice throws me off-kilter. No *hello*. No *how are you?* No nothing.

"You need to delete my number and forget I ever existed," I retort.

"Maybe. Let's talk about it in person." This is so like my mother it's not even funny. I sigh. It's not like I have anything better to do.

"When?"

She gives me the time and the place. Says she'll text me her full Orange County address. I haven't visited since Gwen died.

"Is something wrong?" she asks after we're done. I'm

driving in circles. I'm *thinking* in circles. I shake my head, even though she can't see it.

"No. Not something." I laugh bitterly. "Everything. Everything is wrong."

Chapter Twenty-Seven

Remi

"I'm going out. Bus money is on the counter," Ryan shouts from the kitchen as I trying to mentally talk myself into getting out of bed. For the past couple of weeks, he's been leaving me money for lunch and the bus whenever Christian doesn't stay over and take me. "Figured you wouldn't want me or my bike anywhere near your school."

Not only has he been taking care of lunch and bus money, but he's even working on fixing the old Firebird up so I can have it. I don't think Ryan is doing better financially. In fact, he claims to have given up slanging drugs and guns—and pissed more than a few people off in the process—so he's probably hurting for cash. I think he gives up his own stuff to make sure I have everything I need. And it makes me feel even worse.

"Thanks, Ry," I call out, burying my face deeper into my pillow.

"Love you, Rem."

"Love you, too." And I do. Even though a big part of my heart is broken from Pierce, the other half that belongs to Ryan is starting to flicker back to life and fill with hope for the first time in a long time. Seeing him like this reminds me of one of my favorite memories of him.

"You ready, Rem?" Ry asks, grabbing his board out of the back of his Firebird. I grab mine, too, a hand-me-down from Ryan, and we walk toward the skate park.

"Why do you always gotta bring her? I thought we were going to pick up some skate park sluts," Ryan's friend, Ethan, complains from inside the chain-link fence. I roll my eyes and flip him off.

"Because I fucking want to. I'm teaching her how to ollie today. Ain't that right, Rem?" Ryan says with a wink in my direction, his blond hair shining in the sun.

"Yeah." I shrug, trying to play it cool, like I don't care either way. But I'm excited. I've been working on my ollie for weeks. And I love when Ryan lets me come to the skate park with him.

Ry grabs my hand and pulls me into the concrete park, past the half-pipe and the handrail, and leads me to a flat area to practice. I see a group of freshmen girls who went to my school last year sitting on the bleachers, snickering to each other when we pass, and a few boys from my school giving us curious glances. But, I don't care. No one will try anything with Ryan here.

"All right, Rem. Show me your stance."

I do.

"Lead with your right. You're goofy-footed, remember?

That can get tricky, but we're just doing stationary ollies for now."

I shift my feet.

"Like this?" I ask, tucking my long hair behind my ear.

"Good. Okay, now pop the tail back, then slide your front foot up the board and push forward."

I try, but I barely make it off the ground.

"Close. Try again. This time scoot your front foot away from the bolts a little so you have more room to slide. Pop, slide, push."

I try again, but this time I almost fall on my butt.

"Ugh!" I groan, frustrated.

"Here. Hold on to me. You're scared of falling, and that's half the problem," Ry says, grabbing both of my hands. "I won't let you fall, Rem. Try again."

I take a deep breath. Ryan's right, because this time, when I don't have to worry about falling, I land it. I don't get much, if any, air, but I freaking land it.

"Good job." Ryan smiles, and I squeal, throwing my arms around his neck.

"I wanna do it again. This time on my own."

"Let's see it." He smirks, his arms crossed over his chest.

I land it again.

"Fuck yeah, Rem!" He laughs proudly.

"Yo! Ryan!" Ethan yells from his place next to the freshmen girls, waving him over.

"Be right back. Keep practicing," he says, pointing a finger at me as he walks away.

I try a few more times and get a little better with each attempt. I'm feeling brave, like a badass, and I decide to try to ollie over the little rail a few feet away.

The first time, I bail because I don't have enough speed.

The second time, I bail because I don't have enough courage. The third time, I almost make it over the rail. The fourth time, I'm feeling good, and just when I'm about to slide my front foot, I feel something warm trickle down my leg. It distracts me, and I miss my jump. My board hits the rail and sends me flying forward. I land at the feet of one of the older boys I don't recognize.

"Sick!" he yells, nudging me away from him with his foot. "This is why we shouldn't let bitches in the skate park." His friends laugh, and I'm more confused than anything. They're all laughing and pointing now, and when I look down, I'm horrified to see blood between my legs. But I don't feel hurt. Not there, anyway.

A couple of the girls from my school make their way over to see what's going on, iced coffees in hand.

"Fucking gross, Remington! Plug that shit up," one of them says with a scrunched nose. I think her name is Sydney.

Sydney is an asshole.

My ankle is screaming in pain, and I'm trying to keep from crying, but my bottom lip starts to tremble, and my vision blurs with tears.

"Somebody come get their girl! She's bleeding all over the park," the guy from earlier yells. I reach for my board, embarrassed and in pain. I struggle to get up, and no one offers to help me. Suddenly, the boy in front of me looks terrified. Straight up, about to piss his pants afraid. And then I know why.

As usual, Ryan shoots first and asks questions later. He charges the kid, landing one solid punch to the face and he's out cold. He hits the pavement like a sack of potatoes, and everyone gasps.

"Rem! What the fuck happened? Are you okay?" he asks, frantic.

I nod shakily.

"Get the fuck out of here!" Ryan yells at the nosy assholes surrounding us. They're smart enough to listen.

"Can you help me up? I can't move my ankle, and I think I'm hurt," I say, gesturing toward the blood coating my legs.

Ryan sighs and scratches the back of his neck, uncomfortable.

"What?" I ask.

"You're not hurt, Rem. You, uh, started your period." He coughs.

"I'm eleven!" I screech. I feel blindsided. I mean, I guess I knew it was coming. But, I thought I had another year or two. I bet if I had a mom, I'd be more prepared. God knows my dad would rather hang himself than have this conversation with me. And now poor Ryan is stuck with the job.

"It is what it is." He shrugs. He stands and pulls off his black tee, his chest bare except for the cross tattoo on his right peck that one of his friends gave him at a party. He tugs the shirt on over my head, then lifts me into his arms like a baby. Ryan makes sure the shirt covers my backside and walks out of the skate park, just as the kid he knocked out starts to stir.

"Ethan! Grab our boards," he snaps. Ethan scrambles to do as he says.

Ryan takes me home, fills the bath for me, and then goes to the store. He comes back with two different boxes of tampons, three types of pads, panty liners, ibuprofen, a couple of DVDs, and chocolate. Lots of chocolate.

"What's all this?" Surely, I don't need all of these.

"The lady at the store said these ones," he picks up a box of tampons that look different from the others, "are easier *for beginners. I guess they don't have the applicator or some shit."* He shrugs.

"These ones are normal," he says, flipping another box over. *"And if you don't want to try those, you can just stick with pads. But don't ask me the difference, because fuck if I know."*

I can't help but crack a smile.

"And the rest?" I ask, amused.

"The ibuprofen is for the cramping. The chocolate, well, I'm not really sure," he says, itching his head. *"She just said it's a must. The movies are because there's not shit on TV, and I'm bored."*

"You're staying with me?" I ask, surprised. *"You can go back to the skate park, Ry. I'm fine here."*

"Nah. Rem and Ry for life, remember?" he says, bumping my fist with his and finishing the secret handshake we made up a few years back.

"Thank you. For everything."

"It's no big deal."

But it was to me. That's the real Ryan. Fiercely loyal and scary as hell. Ironically, a couple of weeks after that incident, I broke my ankle for real, and it wasn't anywhere near as traumatic.

I walk out of my room, trying to find an excuse not to go to school today. No one is going to stop me. I don't have any rules in this house. I kind of made up my own as I grew up, but I think I did a pretty good job because I'm not a drug addict, pregnant, or dead in a ditch. The house looks relatively okay. Not clean by any stretch of the imagination, but Ryan hasn't thrown a party in two weeks in here, and it shows. I text Christian.

Me: How did it go yesterday?

Christian: Fine, I think? I'll tell you all about it today.

Me: I'm not coming to school today.

Christian: Y?

Me: I don't know.

I do. Because I don't want to face Pierce. But I don't want to admit it either.

Christian: I'll come see you after school then.

Me: Please do.

He doesn't answer to that. I drop my phone onto the counter and look around me. I've never felt so alone.

⌒⤳

Remi

"Hey, what's up?"

"What's up is that I can't get anywhere near your street!" Christian sounds exasperated, huffing loudly. I hear honks from different cars, and Christian shouting, "Yeah, yeah, we know! We've been stuck here for twenty minutes now, assholes."

"Was there an accident?" I plop down on my couch and munch on the tip of my hair. It is legit the best thing to eat around here. I need to go to the supermarket before my dad arrives next week. Ryan is fine grabbing something from Wendy's at the end of every day, but when my dad comes back home from being on the road for weeks, I like to make sure he gets some home-cooked meals in.

"I don't know. Maybe? I mean, it looks a lot more serious than that. There are like five police cars here."

"Hmm." I roll my eyes. "Probably a burglary, knowing

my neighborhood."

"And three ambulances? And yellow tape. Never a dull moment in your hood. No wonder you're bored with our preppy school."

I lie on the sofa and start flipping through the very few channels that my TV has to offer.

"I'm bored right now," I whine. "Tell me what you see."

"Well." He sighs. "I see six...no, seven different police officers. At least one of them is hot."

"Yeah." My eyes become droopy and lazy. Perhaps because I haven't eaten anything all day. I kind of forget to function properly sometimes. Especially since everything with Pierce has happened. "And?"

"Caution. Ambulances. A motorcycle on the side of the road..."

My heart stops in my chest. "What?" I ask. "Repeat that, please."

"I said ambulances, a motorcycle..."

This time Christian doesn't even finish his sentence before I hang up. I'm putting on my white Chucks and flying out the door in a second. My heart is in my throat.

Ambulances. Motorcycle. Police. Ryan.

I run toward the main road. My legs are a separate entity from the rest of my body. I never knew I could be so fast. I arrive at the scene. It's already dark outside, and the red and blue lights are blinding me. I see the ambulances.

I don't see Ryan.

There's a cluster of people standing by, whispering and taking pictures. I slice through the crowd and run to one of the officers who is standing on the other side of the yellow tape, his arms folded over his chest. He looks somber and serious.

"What is this? What happened?" I ask him breathlessly. He barely even shakes his head to show me that he heard me. I'm not going to get shit from him, I know then and there. I look around. People are crying. Some women cup their mouths in disbelief. I'm not sure what's happening. I walk around trying to find a gap in the crowd, but there are too many people around the scene so I can't see what's actually going on in the road.

It's not until I get a text message from Christian that I remember I hung up on him.

Think we got disconnected. I'm gonna take off. Try again tomorrow?

I don't even respond.

"Remington?! Remington, is that you?" My neighbor, Janice, rushes toward me. She lives across the street and has like eighteen children from a bunch of different dads, and a little too nosy, but she is a good person. Hard working. She sometimes bakes stuff for Dad on his birthday. I don't even want to begin to think why they're tight or why she remembers his birthday.

"Hey." I try to smile, moving some of my hair from my face. "What's going on?"

"Did you see?" She jerks her thumb behind her shoulder, her eyes full of sadness. I shake my head.

"It's too crowded. I'm really worried. Ryan went to get us something to eat, and he isn't back…" I trail off. "I hope it's not an accident."

Her face melts in horror, and she grabs me and hugs me to her chest. She smells of cigarettes and vanilla. "It's not, honey. Not an accident."

I sigh in relief.

"He's been shot."

My veins fill with ice instantly, and I freeze.

"Ryan...someone shot your brother."

I tear myself away from her, and this time I don't try to sneak between the crowds. I shove people left and right, my eyes on the yellow tape. I kick, push, and deliberately step over other people's toes.

I only stop when I see Ryan's figure on the ground.

His eyes are still open. He is staring at the sky. He looks surprised more than anything else. More than scared. More than sad. More than anything.

He is lying on the road, and blood trickles from his white wifebeater. Wisps of his blond hair still dancing in the air. He can't be dead. Paramedics are rushing around him, but they don't try to save him.

"Why aren't you saving him?!" I scream, pushing my way through the horde of people in my way. I feel people pulling at my arms, trying to keep me back, but I can't be stopped.

"He's my brother! Let me go. He's my brother!" I manage to get to Ryan, and then I'm falling to my knees, lifting his head to my lap, and hugging him for dear life.

"Please no, please no, please no." It's all I can say, over and over. "Please don't let this be real. Please don't let this be real." I hear officers yelling about not touching "the body", and I want to fucking kill them for reducing him to just *the body*. He's my brother. My best friend.

"I love you, Ryan. And I'm proud of you. *So* proud. Rem and Ry forever." I sob into his hair. "I didn't even get to say goodbye!" It's not fair. It's not fucking fair.

I feel two strong arms lifting me away, so I kiss his face

one, two, three times. And then they're covering his body and taking him away while I stay frozen in place, oblivious of my surroundings.

Pierce

I watch the local news in the background as I make dinner. I'm chopping potatoes and onions when I raise my head to look at the dancing image on TV.

"The victim died of his injuries before arriving at St. John's Hospital. His family has been informed. Police are looking at the suspects as we speak."

"Drug connections."

"Dealing weapons."

"Four prior incidents."

"Rich criminal history."

This could describe most people in Las Vegas, but I don't need to see his mug shot on the screen to know that it's him. I just know. I grab my jacket and leave.

Remi

An hour later, the police show up at my doorstep. By then, I've already informed Dad, who cut his drive short and is coming back home immediately. By then, I've already packed a bag. I agreed with Christian to meet him on the corner of Main Street so he wouldn't have to wait in another traffic jam caused by the incident. We don't even know if his parents will let me stay.

"Yes?" I ask. Janice is holding me. She helped me into the house earlier.

The two police officers clutch their hats in their fists as they talk to me. I don't let a word seep into my brain. The words just kind of float around me in the air, almost visible.

Janice nods a lot.

Christian's car appears at the end of the street.

I walk over there after I'm done with the police, watching Pierce James standing on the other side of the street, saying so many things with one look.

I get into Christian's car and leave.

Chapter Twenty Eight

Remi

The first night, I cry in Ryan's bed until I pass out from sheer exhaustion. The second night, Christian's folks let me stay until my dad gets back in town, but they're not happy about it. I don't sleep a wink all night. All I can think about is how Ryan is dead and now I'm really alone.

Pierce

That night, I smoke.

I drink.

I visit Shelly.

She apologizes, saying she was fucked up on H and lonely.

I cry on her shoulder. *Fucking cry on her shoulder.*

I tell her everything.

She cries, too.

Shelly says something about how she'll make it better, but I know it's not true.

I crawl back home in the morning to find Headmaster Charles on my doorstep. Fuck. It's a school day, and I'm missing again.

"Am I fired?" I hiccup.

"Do you want to be?" He raises one eyebrow.

"Might as well." I shrug.

⌒

Remi

Christian goes to school, but I don't.

I stay in his room. It feels too weird to go out there and face his mom and aunt. The house is huge, but that's not necessarily a reassuring thing.

I spend the day surfing on Ryan's Facebook page, watching the condolence messages pouring in and crying.

⌒

Remi

Pierce is calling every half an hour.

I don't answer.

I don't eat.

I barely breathe.

I look at the screen, begging for Dad to call and tell me

that he is home. He doesn't.

~⇒

Pierce

I try her house.

I try school.

I try everyone in her neighborhood.

I know she's at Christian's. She must be.

So, I send her a few more texts before I flush my life down the toilet.

I need to see you. I'm so sorry, sweetheart.

I'm not giving you up. You do know that, right?

I will wait as long as I'll have to.

Actually, that's not true. I'm coming for you, whether you like it or not. Because you need me. Because I need you. Because this is how we both heal.

~⇒

Remi

Christian comes back home with Benton Herring. The latter looks sheepish and polite. They're holding hands. Maybe Christian's mom left, and that's why he is feeling so brave.

"I'm sorry," Benton says. I'm not sure if he means for how he treated me, how he treated Christian, or sorry about my brother. Maybe all of it. He doesn't even sound like himself.

I nod. "Me too."

Chapter Twenty-Nine

Remi

I meet Dad outside our door.

It's just too much to go inside the house without Ryan being there. I haven't been back since the first night. It's like admitting that he is actually gone, and I don't think I can do it. Not right now.

Dad is a wreck. His face is tired and pale. Stubble everywhere. His eyes are swollen and crusted with sleep in the corners.

I collapse into a hug. His arms feel good. Safe. Familiar.

The tears are slipping from the corners of my eyes before I can stop them. Janice and Christian are here, standing beside us, and they're not family, which makes me realize just how lonely we are. How lonely we've always been. Where are Ryan's friends? All of his entourage? I don't need anyone to answer this question. They all ran away or are currently being investigated or arrested. Ryan was bound to get caught. But not like that.

God, not like that.

Christian rubs my back in circles awkwardly. Janice sighs and looks away, tears in her eyes.

"You told me," Dad says, clutching me closer to his chest. "You told me, and I didn't listen."

"It's okay." I sniff.

Our world is broken, and nothing can fix it. The sun sets. The birds stop chirping.

And it finally hits me that Ryan is gone. Forever.

⌒

Remi

The next day is the funeral.

People from the neighborhood gather at the local cemetery, but not many of them. Not as much as I'd like to see, that's for sure. Some have work. Some don't have a ride. Some just don't care. I'm wearing a black long-sleeved dress, and Dad is swimming in a suit he borrowed from a neighbor who is three sizes bigger than him.

The event starts at church. An open casket event. Ryan is there, looking peaceful, beautiful, and more than all of that—he looks like himself. I know it's stupid, but it's truly difficult to comprehend someone is gone when they're physically next to you. When they look so alive. Just... asleep.

Then at the burial ceremony, I see Pierce. He doesn't even try to be discreet, even though none of the staff from school attended. Christian and Benton are here, side-by-side, and Mr. James is making his way to the front line of people, as if he knew Ryan, as if he cared for Ryan, and even though this is my golden opportunity to hate him again, to push him away once more, I don't have the energy to do so.

When the ceremony is over, I walk toward Christian and Benton. I hug my best friend. Herring taps my shoulder like he wants to tell me something.

"Mr. James is here," Benton says. I nod.

"He must've heard about my brother," I say dumbly.

"I think he's here for you." Christian's eyes are pleading. He wants me to give Pierce another chance. I think he'll feel better to know there's someone to take care of me while my dad is on the road. But being with someone just so you can depend on him is a horrible idea. That's how most women on my street ended up the way they did.

"Do I know you?" Dad approaches Pierce, who is wearing a sharp and expensive black suit.

"I'm a friend of your daughter's," he says softly, but also dryly. Not her teacher. Her friend. It doesn't escape me, and I hate that my heart flutters in my chest when I hear him owning up to what we are.

More than a student and a teacher.

More than words.

"You look a little old to be her friend."

"She's a little older than her years, sir."

I munch on my lower lip as I walk over to them. Pierce perks up, straightens his spine. The sun is unforgiveable. All of us are sweaty in our black attire, despite it being November. Welcome to Nevada.

"Remington," Pierce says.

"Pierce." I can't help but call him. Not Mr. James. Today, he is Pierce.

"Can I offer you my condolences?" he asks. I nod.

"*Alone*?" He stretches. I think I hear his heart skipping a beat as I follow him to an oak tree—a huge thing the size of my house, probably—in the corner of the cemetery. We both stand in the shadow. I fiddle with the hem of my dress. Now that we're alone, I drop my close-lipped smile and my soft eyes and become sharper around the edges. People are close enough to see what we are doing but far enough not to hear what we are saying. Pierce shoves his fists into his pockets and breathes in.

"I'm so sorry, Remi."

"Thank you," I say.

"You know it has nothing to do with me, right? I would never wish something like this upon my greatest enemy. And Ryan wasn't my enemy. Not anymore. He was…" I think Pierce is about to say "yours," but he stops himself if he does. Good. I don't want to hear it, and I definitely don't want to think about it. It's not even true.

"Before he died," I say, leaning my shoulder against the cool trunk of the dark brown tree, "he started acting different. Good different. Like the old Ryan. He was waiting on a call for a bed at an inpatient rehab center. He was trying. And then he was killed for it." My dad was told that they suspect someone was upset that he wasn't selling anymore. That, or he owed someone money.

Pierce nods. "We had a talk. I was hoping to get through to him. He really loved you, Remi."

"You did?" My heart shatters, but flickers back to life. I'm not sure why. Maybe because hearing something I didn't know about Ryan makes him feel more alive and the hole in my chest a little smaller. I'll shove everything into that hole inside my heart. Even Pierce's words, the most dangerous weapon of all.

"Yeah." He nods faintly. "I told him if he really loves you, he should take a step back. And he did," Pierce says. I swallow down my tears and shake my head.

"I can't live without him," I admit. It's true. He is—was—such a huge part of my life, I didn't even bother to check if he had a negative or positive effect on me.

"You can, and you will. I'll help you through it. Through everything."

"I don't want your help."

"I'm not asking." His voice is dry. "I quit my job."

My eyes fly up, and I blink. "You did what?"

"Quit."

"Why?"

"Because I decided to pursue you. And pursuing you while holding onto a job where I had so much more power over you wasn't fair. Or moral. Or right. I needed to refocus. You gave me what I needed. Now I'm going to give you what you need."

"And what is that?" I ask, leaning against him without meaning to.

"Peace."

Chapter Thirty

Pierce

I sit on Remi's bed, wondering if I did the right thing or the spectacularly wrong one.

That's what I loved the most about debate. There is no right or wrong in this world. No black and white. Remington and I live in the gray area. Logic is pointless. Gut feeling is dangerous. The only way to know whether you did the right or wrong thing is to ride it out and see it to the end.

Remi is in the living room talking to her dad. I make calls in the meantime. I call my mother to tell her I'll be coming to Dad's birthday with Remington—even though I haven't run it by her yet. I call Shelly, but she doesn't answer. Then I text Drew, my friend who's been begging for me to join his law firm since we first met when I moved here.

Me: I'm ready to go back to the dark side.

Drew: You mean practicing law?

Me: It's better than self-employment. Slightly.

Drew: You'll get a corner office if you decide to work with me.

Me: That's bad negotiation on your part. You don't even know what I'm offering.

Drew: You're offering yourself. Anyone would be a fool not to take that.

Tell that to my girlfriend.

Just then, Remi enters her room. She sees me smiling and pauses. She is still suspicious of me. I don't blame her.

"Everything okay?" she asks.

"Yes." I sit up straight on her bed, somehow still feeling like a perv for being here, even though her father is in the house too and we're completely clothed and not anywhere near each other. "What's happening?"

"Shelly is outside waiting for us."

"Us? Plural?" I get up. They don't know each other, but I've mentioned Shelly to Remi in passing a few times.

"She wants to tell us something. We're going to the diner down the road. Are you ready?"

I already have my jacket on. This should be interesting.

Remi

I order coffee, but don't drink it.

It's funny how this diner is just down the road from my house, but I've been here maybe three times in my entire life. I sit across from Shelly. Pierce sits by my side. We haven't spoken at all since we patched things up. Come to think about it, we haven't even officially patched things up.

Nothing makes sense in my world anymore, or at least that's how I feel. Not the part where Ryan died, and not the part where Pierce and I are okay somehow as a result. I now believe that he never meant to hurt me. I understand the 'whys' of it, and I know that he's who I'm supposed to be with. I know it with every bone in my body, and now I need to trust it. To trust *him*. But, something is still holding me back.

Shelly looks rough. She needs five hundred meals inside her, a good shower, a haircut, and a lot of TLC to look human again. Her whole appearance screams drug addict. The shit that's going on under her fingernails is probably toxic at this point. But all I see is Ryan, and I want to hug her. To help her.

"You don't know me." Shelly fiddles with a packet of sugar, but doesn't touch her coffee either. She has her bag next to her. Some designer knockoff. I blink, staring at her blankly. "But I know you. Well, kind of know you, really."

"Elaborate," Pierce orders dryly. Shelly shifts in her seat. We're sitting in a red classic booth of a diner. A waitress in a yellow uniform and white apron passes us by with a coffeepot and winks at Pierce as she pops her gum. I'm just about ready to explode.

"Well." Shelly drops the sugar and falls backwards to the headrest. "The thing is…okay, well, let's start from the beginning. Remington, Pierce's sister Gwen used to be my roommate. She also used to be Ryan's girlfriend."

I don't say a word. Just look at her. Ryan had a lot of girlfriends, so I'm not sure where this is going. She continues.

"Ryan used to talk about you. All the time. He was so proud of you. Said you and he were going to get out of this shithole together. He never used to use at first. Just sold. But once he started using, he became fixated on you. Obsessed, even. He turned violent. Manipulative. Deceitful. Before Gwen died…" Shelly chokes, and Pierce's eyebrows dive down, so I gather he has no idea where she's going with this either. Shelly starts crying, grabbing a few napkins, and blowing her nose loudly.

"Gwen knew she was going to die. She planned it. She was so tired of fighting." She takes a deep breath before continuing. "She decided to use whatever money her parents gave her for food and rent and…life, I guess, to pay for your tuition. She hadn't ever spoken to you, but she saw you around when she partied at your house with Ryan. Saw how he treated you. She said you reminded her of a tougher version of herself, and if she couldn't save her own life, then she might as well try to help yours. When she told me all of this, I didn't know she was planning to end her life, I swear," she cries, looking up at Pierce, her eyes begging for forgiveness.

I see it now. The guilt. The regret. She wears it like a second skin. And I know the feeling all too well. My hands fall to the table with a slap, and my mouth hangs open, tears springing to my eyes.

"Impossible," Pierce says, his voice quivering as he takes my hands in both of his.

"It's true." Shelly sniffs, producing something from her bag. A batch of wrinkled papers. Pierce takes them from her hand and frowns. I see my name there. I see Gwen's name. I see all the details. She went to my dad and offered him money. He was skeptical, but she insisted that she wanted to stay anonymous, so he made up the bullshit story about saving up. It all makes sense, yet none of it does.

He's lost his sister.

I've lost my brother.

And they were both connected with a tragic destiny.

Pierce lifts his eyes from the pages. "Gwen wanted me to meet Remi. She wanted me to take care of her."

Shelly smiles a sad smile through her tears. "I don't think *that's* what she had in mind." She gestures at our hands clasped together on top of the table.

Pierce shrugs and kisses my temple, like it's the most natural thing in the world. "I'll take whatever she'll give me."

Remi

When we get back to my house, Pierce throws random shit into a suitcase for me, while I sit on my bed in a daze. He looks so out of place in my tiny room with its peeling paint and ancient, hand-me-down furniture.

Pierce informs my dad that he'll be taking me back to his place, and not surprisingly, he doesn't put up a fight. I know we'll have to have a talk eventually, but now is not the time. Janice has been over non-stop, so I don't feel guilty leaving him. It's not like he's ever beaten himself up over leaving me.

The ride to Pierce's house is quiet, and the mood somber, but hopeful. I think we are both trying to work through what all of this means for us. I still can't believe Pierce quit his job. But, he said it was never what he truly wanted to do, anyway. He said everything has a season, and that season of his life is over. His hand is firmly wedged between my thighs, not probing or wandering, and he gives my leg a firm squeeze. I look over at him—all inky black hair, eyebrows furrowed in thought, hardened jaw, perfect fucking lips—and I wonder what I did to deserve someone like him. Someone who fights for me. Makes sacrifices for me. Believes in me. I don't know much about love, but if that's not it, I don't know what is.

"I love you," I confess. And I do. So much that it physically hurts.

His head swivels toward me, an eyebrow lifts in amusement.

"You just now figuring that out, sweetheart?" He laughs, the first real laugh I've heard from him in weeks, and I flip him off. "Because I've *been* loving you, Miss Stringer."

Now, we're pulling up to Pierce's driveway. Instead of getting out of the car, he slides his seat back and pats his lap. Wordlessly, I climb over the console, still in the dress I wore to Ryan's funeral. His *funeral.* It sounds so wrong. It *is* so wrong.

The second Pierce's strong arms wrap around me, I bury my face in his neck, basking in the comfort he's offering. His hands work up and down my back, soothing me.

"You get to be sad, Remi," he says gruffly, his lips touching my ear. "You get to be sad. You get to cry. You don't have to go back to school tomorrow, or even the next day, but after that..." he trails off, grabbing my chin in a silent command to look into his eyes. My glassy eyes lock onto his crystal blue ones.

"After that, you return to school."

I nod.

"You meet with Holly Tate again to discuss college options before the fall cut-off."

Another nod.

"You move in with me until further notice."

I nod—wait, *what?* Pierce shoots me a look, daring me to argue, and I roll my eyes and nod once more.

"And you're coming to dinner to meet my parents in a couple of weeks for my dad's birthday," he says as casually as he would when discussing the weather.

"Pierce—" I start, but he cuts me off.

"In Orange County."

"Jesus," I breathe, dropping my head to his shoulder.

"But right now," he rasps, lifting his hips and unbuckling his belt. "All you need to do is let me love you. Can you do that for me, Remi girl?"

"God, yes," I whisper.

"Good girl."

He unzips the back of my dress letting it pool at my waist, exposing my naked chest, before lifting my dress above my ass and sliding my panties aside. He leans forward, his hot mouth taking my right nipple into his mouth as I lift up and position his cock at my entrance.

I slide down onto his rock-hard warmth slowly, so slowly, welcoming every inch he feeds me. He looks into my eyes, searching, and it feels more intimate than him being inside me. Once he's fully seated inside me, I start to move on top of him. Pierce grabs the nape of my neck with one hand and grips my ass with the other, guiding my movements. What started as a slow and sensual dance quickly morphs into one of desperation, needing to be so enmeshed in each other so deeply that we're one entity.

I grind against him, hard but unhurried as our sweat mixes between us. Pierce's mouth comes down on mine, and his tongue sweeps past my lips. Oh, how I've missed the taste of him. Our tongues and bodies move in perfect harmony. *We were made for this.*

Suddenly, Pierce reaches down and pushes a lever causing his seat to recline and he lies back, crossing his hands behind his head. I grab the handle above his window and lift my hips before dropping back down. I do this until I'm practically bouncing on his lap, and I feel my orgasm building.

"Baby," he groans, and I know he's close, too. His hands move to my hips and smooth up the curves of my waist before palming my breasts. He squeezes them and then pinches my nipples, and I feel it straight down to my clit.

The pleasure coursing through me is too much to bear, and I collapse on top of him. One arm wraps around my back and the other one cradles my head to his chest as he takes over, thrusting inside me deeper than anyone's ever been, literally and figuratively.

This isn't just fucking.

This is passion.

This is love.

This is healing.

"I'm close," I moan, holding my ass in place while he

pumps into me punishingly.

"Come with me, pretty girl."

And I do. I come in never-ending waves until my legs are shaking. I'm boneless. Jelly. And still convulsing on top of him.

"Fuck, Remi," Pierces curses, shoving into me a few more times before lifting me off his cock so I straddle just his thighs instead. His hand comes around to fist his dick, and then I realize it's because we didn't use protection.

Pierce grips my hips and pulls me forward, his cock nestled between my lips. He holds me in place while he fucks me like that, his hard length slipping in my arousal but never penetrating, until his eyes close and his body jerks. Thick ropes of cum shoot onto his stomach that flexes with his climax. The sight, along with the friction against my clit, has me coming again.

"God, I love you," Pierce says, still catching his breath as he smooths my damp hair off my forehead.

"I love you, too, *Mr. James.*"

Epilogue

Graduation Day

Pierce

It's been seven months since I've last stepped foot into West Point, and even though I can't say I've missed it, I wouldn't miss this day for the world, either.

I sit in one of hundreds of chairs in the lush courtyard, tugging at my collar, ignoring the stifling heat and curious stares from parents, teachers, and underclassman. If they think I give two shits about what they think about me, they have another thing coming. Now that Remington is graduating, I don't have to worry about what they think of her either anymore. Shortly after Remington returned to West Point, Headmaster Charles called her in to question her about our relationship. Remington denied it, and since there wasn't any proof and I had already resigned, he dropped it.

I'm sitting next to Remington's father, Dan—which is essentially admitting to the world that I'm in a relationship with my former student—and ignore the way he nibbles on the dead skin around his thumb nervously. To say I'm not particularly fond of him would be the understatement of the century. He has treated Remi in a way I wouldn't even treat our future pet, let alone child. But for her, I play nice.

For her, I play games I never thought I would.

For her, I'm a changed man.

Dan and Remington are slowly building their relationship again. He apologized for being absent most of her life, and for not believing her when she warned him about Ryan. Remi accepted, but she's kept her distance. We've been living together, sharing a bed, and a kitchen, and things that are only ours—secrets no one else has access to—and even though sinners like me can only wish for heaven, my bastard ass has somehow managed to sneak through the door and step into this thing called paradise.

"The Land of Hope and Glory" assaults my ears from the speakers near the stage, and students are being called up to receive their diplomas. I scan the horde of pimply teenagers in royal blue gowns, looking for Remington in the sea of silk. I find her sitting next to Christian and Benton, even though their last names should have them completely spread out. She is squeezing Christian's palm in hers and whispering something into his ear, her leg rocking in place. Adorably nervous. Something flutters in my chest.

Christian has grown on me. He's at the house a few times a week, and he has zero interest in my girlfriend's soft, feminine curves and legs for days. That makes him tolerable—even if mildly—in my book. The other kid, Herring, well, the jury's still out on him. Christian and he are openly dating, but I still think the kid is an asshole. Guess Christian likes assholes. Literally.

Mikaela Stephens, surprisingly, wasn't too upset nor surprised when the truth about Benton came out. Turns out, little Mikaela was keeping secrets of her own, which came to light a couple months later when a screenshot of her kissing another student started circulating—a very *female* student. Everyone's got secrets. Ours just happened to have a happy ending.

Remington is wearing her blue robe over what I know is a very sexy, black tube dress. When she stands, I chuckle because she's sporting her signature white Converse. *Always such a rebel.* And I wouldn't have her any other way.

"Remington Nicole Stringer," Headmaster Charles calls through the microphone. He looks almost as proud as I am. It's hard not to root for a girl like Remington. People can't help but to be drawn to her. I know my sorry ass never stood a chance. I glance at Dan who bats angrily at his eyes, like he's mad at his tears for falling. I give him a firm shoulder pat, and that's about all I have in me.

Remi shakes Charles' hand, and he looks toward her shoes while saying something into her ear. Remi just beams her megawatt smile that's making an appearance a little bit more each day, gives him a thumbs-up, and mouths, "Working on it!" Charles shakes his head, but he can't hide his smile.

Dan and I stand and cheer, maybe a little too loudly, but ask me if I care. Remington busted her ass to get to this point, despite all the shit life threw at her, and was accepted into UCLA to boot. She's going to major in psychology, and I don't have to be a genius to figure out why. She is still hurting since losing Ryan, but more than that, she wants to understand the whys of it, and then maybe she can help others who suffer from the same afflictions. I couldn't be more proud of this woman.

I've been working at my friend Drew's firm, and we've decided to expand. I'll lead the L.A. office, and in just two more months, we'll both be moving to the Golden State. I try not to think about what would've happened if Gwen hadn't intervened. I know deep down that Remington would've crawled her way out of that neighborhood either way. She doesn't have one quitting bone in her body. But we wouldn't have met. I'd still be working my mediocre job, living my mediocre life, interacting only with Shelly. In reality, Gwen saved *me* by saving Remi.

Speaking of Shelly, I wish I could say she's recovered. She goes through bouts of sobriety, but it doesn't seem to stick. I even offered to send her to the best rehab center in the state, but she has to want it for herself. And unfortunately, she's simply not there yet.

When the ceremony ends, it's pure chaos. Everyone scrambles to their families. Hugging. Crying. Laughing. Celebrating. Taking pictures. I spot Remington, who's with Christian near the entrance, and I shove through the masses, making a beeline right for her. Before she even sees me coming, I lift her up and spin her around.

"Congratulations, sweetheart," I say, still holding her around the waist.

"Everyone is looking at us," she whispers with a smirk on her face.

"Then let's give them a show, Miss Stringer."

I grip the back of her head and kiss the shit out of her

for everyone to see. She opens for me immediately, and her hands come up to cup my face. We ignore the whispers, the hoots and hollers, the whistles. None of it matters. It's only us in this moment.

Sometimes secrets ruin lives. But sometimes they save them.

The End

Acknowledgments

First and foremost, thank you times a million to our readers! To our old readers for always being down to read whatever we decide to throw at them—whether it's sexy novellas, or full length NA—and to the new ones who took a chance on us. You have no idea how much all your teasers, comments, messages, and support mean to us. We hope you love Pierce and Remi as much as we loved writing them!

Thank you to our asshole husbands for keeping the kids alive and the house clean while we both try to balance our individual projects as well as Charleigh Rose.

To our kids, thanks for nothing. You're literally the worst and you tried your best to make sure this book wouldn't happen. You're lucky you're cute.

Thank you to Paige for busting your ass to get this baby edited on such short notice, and for always being so easy to work with. We've told you 2.5 million times, but you're the best.

Somer at Perfect Pear Creations, you're the bomb. Do people still say that? Whatever. Thank you for nailing this cover and being so patient with us every time we wanted something moved to the left a fraction of an inch. You're one talented mofo.

Thank you to Ella Fox for basically forcing us to write this, and then beta reading it. You've become one of our closest friends, and we love you. You're the realest bitch around. Thank you to Mary Elizabeth, BB Reid, BB Easton, K. Webster, and everyone else whose brain we've picked or vented to. You're all a bunch of weirdos, and it's probably why we get along so well.

Thank you to Stacey Blake at Champagne Formats for always fitting us in and doing beautiful work.

Thank you to Enticing Book Promotions for always being so thorough and making everything so simple. We love working with you guys.

To our IG girls, you rule. Per usual. Lastly, to our Facebook group, Charleigh's Angels. Quite frankly, you're a little perverted. But it's why we love you. We appreciate you more than you know. A big thank you to our admins: Serena, Amanda, Ofa, and Bex. Love you guys.

Stalk us! We like it.

Subscribe to our newsletter to get freebies and sale alerts, bonus material, and exclusive giveaways!
http://bit.ly/2bDdxZ6

Come hang out with us on social media! We love interacting and talking books with our readers.

Facebook page:
www.facebook.com/charleighroseprose

Facebook group:
www.facebook.com/groups/1120926904664447

Instagram: www.instagram.com/charleighrose